"I am quite capable of taking care of myself. I shall make do," replied Miss Butterberry primly.

"No, you will do as I say!" declared Peter. "Now ride to the front of the house, knock upon the door and go inside. Someday you will be thankful that your name was never linked with so vile a creature as myself. You will! I am—I am—a creature so despicable as to be beyond salvation."

"Ho! Beyond salvation? I am a clergyman's daughter and know very well that not the worst of the worst is beyond salvation."

"You are wrong, Mary. My soul is bound for fire and brimstone. Even your papa thinks so."

"My papa also thinks that you stole the money and the stickpin from the rectory, which proves how wrong my papa can be. Peter Winthrop," Miss Butterberry said in the veri-most composed voice, "if you do not take me with you, I *shall* go into Wicken Hall and I shall arouse the entire household, tell them I saw a thief ride off with a sack stuffed full of something even as I approached and send them after you at once."

"You would not."

"Yes, I would."

Other books by the author

Zebra Regency Romance by Judith A. Lansdowne

Novellas

LORD NIGHTINGALE'S TRIUMPH

JUDITH A. LANSDOWNE

ZEBRA BOOKS
Kensington Publishing Corp.
http://www.zebrabooks.com

To Molly Canary,
Thank you for your friendship and support
through the years.

INTRODUCTION

Welcome once again to the world of Lord Nightingale. *Lord Nightingale's Triumph* is book three of the Nightingale Trilogy. It was preceded by *Lord Nightingale's Debut* and *Lord Nightingale's Love Song* and is followed by *Lord Nightingale's Christmas*. Yes, I do know that that makes four and there are only three books in a trilogy—but then I explained all that in the introduction to book one.

If you have not read *Debut* or *Love Song* you may want to set this book aside until you do. On the other hand, you may not, in which case allow me to present a bit of background. In *Debut* Lord Nightingale brought together his singing teacher, Miss Serendipity Bedford, and his new master Nicholas Chastain, the Earl of Wickenshire. In *Love Song* Lord Nightingale teamed up with Delight, Serendipity's young sister, to unite the physically crippled Eugenia Chastain, Wickenshire's cousin, and the emotionally crippled Edward Finlay, Marquess of Bradford. Other key characters introduced in those two books were Wickenshire's mama, the Dowager Countess of Bradford; the nefarious Neil Spelling, Wickenshire's cousin on his mama's side, and the even more ignoble Henry Wiggins, Lord Upton, who is Serendipity's cousin. And let me not forget the lovely and stubbornly-determined Mary Butterberry, daughter of the local rector.

In *Lord Nightingale's Triumph,* Lord Nightingale once again displays his remarkable ability to create total chaos and out of it bring triumph, foiling another of nefarious Neil's plots and reuniting long-separated twin brothers. And oh yes, of course, he does play his own brand of Cupid as well.

ONE

The storm roared in from the Strait of Dover without the least warning and erupted over Wicken Hall late that September night. Lightning blazed and strobed and crackled against the sky beyond the Hall's windows. Thunder rumbled and crashed. Paintings jiggled upon walls; statuettes danced across mantelpieces; crystal pendants clinked lightly one against another as heavy chandeliers swayed from the vibrations that traveled through the Hall's ceilings and walls. On the second floor of the Earl of Wickenshire's main residence, however, not one person took note of the vile weather. After a day filled with arrivals and departures, hellos and goodbyes, kisses and tears and promises of delightful times to come, each and every member of the earl's household, including the earl himself, had fallen exhaustedly into bed and gained sleep without the least need to count even one woolly lamb.

Likewise, in the servants' quarters, not one toe wiggled, not one nose twitched at the uproar of the storm. And down the small hill at the rear of the Hall, in the loft that spread across the top of the stables, the coachman, the grooms and the stable boys snored heavily, unaware of the thunder, the lightning and the pounding rain. Only the horses and the mice shivered and shifted and gave voice to their annoyance at the foul weather.

Before the gate to the rose garden, whose high stone wall ran the entire length of the west side of Wicken Hall, a solitary figure sat his horse. A virtual river of rainwater poured from the brim of his hat as he lowered his head, then raised it again, attempting to divine by the brief and wild flickers of lightning the precise layout of the Hall and its grounds. He had debated long and hard the possibility of entering the Hall on the opposite side or at the rear, but in the end had decided upon the relative safety of the rose garden—no stable hands near to take note should his horse whinny, no fear of a hungry butler or the master of the house wandering into the kitchen for a snack at precisely the wrong moment, and not one window on the second floor that was not tightly shuttered against the storm.

The man in the scarlet cravat sighed softly to himself, swiped at the rain on his face with the back of a sleeve already soaked through and attempted to push the gate open with one booted foot. It did not move so much as an eighth of an inch. "Damnable thing is locked," he grumbled to himself. "Who the devil locks a rose garden?" With an exasperated sigh he dismounted, wrapped his horse's reins around the farthest gatepost, located the lock and set his very talented fingers to work upon it. In three flashes of lightning and an equal number of rumbles of thunder, the gate floated easily inward. He unwrapped the horse's reins and led the enormous gelding quietly inside, the sound of the horse's hooves on the narrow cobbled path that meandered among the bushes completely covered by the crashing and crackling of the storm.

Cautiously and with great consideration, the man in the scarlet cravat traversed the path from the front to the rear of the establishment and back again, halting from time to time to clear the rain drops from his eyelashes, or to pat the gelding's nose reassuringly, or to step in through the rose bushes nearer the wall of the building to peer more closely at a specific window. When at last he decided on the most likely one—a narrow casement of leaded glass near the front of the Hall—he led the gelding immediately beneath it, dropped the horse's reins straight down, muttered, "Like stone, Leprechaun," and stepped up into the stirrup. But instead of swinging onto the saddle, he gave the most agile of twists and rose to his knees and then to his feet upon the great beast's back. With considerable care, he reached out to feel for some safe purchase, and bracing his hands against each side of the deep indent in which the casement lay, he stepped up and onto the slippery sill where puddles of rain lay in the small hollows of stone that had worn away over the years. Pressed close against the glass, he slipped a small knife from the pocket of the hunting jacket he wore and began to poke and pry at the spot where the latch for the first of the casements ought logically to lie.

Miss Mary Butterberry came near to choking on her sobs as she urged her horse into the cattle barn that sat upon the northernmost boundary of the Earl of Wickenshire's estate. Dismounting, she hesitated, waiting for another crackle of lightning before she took a step away from her mount. She knew nothing of the inside of this place, and she had only viewed it once from the outside. Because she feared to move about blindly and so must wait for each flash of lightning to take another step, it was a spasmodic progress that she made to the lantern hanging beside the open barn door. But once she had the lantern in hand, it took her but five minutes to get the thing lighted. It would, of course, have taken her less time had she been able to cease sobbing, but that she could not do.

With the soft glow of the lantern to aid her, Miss Butterberry unsaddled Lulubelle and saw to the mare's comfort,
taking advantage of the straw and feed that the earl's men
had left behind them here at the beginning of the summer
when they had moved the cattle to the southern pastures.
She stepped out to catch a deal of rain in a bucket for the
horse to drink. Then, much overwrought, she sank down
onto a small pile of straw just outside the stall and began
to weep heartily, shuddering as she did because her riding
costume was soaked through and she had placed the only
blanket she could find over Lulubelle's broad and aging
back.

"It ought not to have stormed," Miss Butterberry said
with a sob and a hiccough. "Oh, Lulubelle, why did it come
on to storm? I am so very sorry that you got cold and wet
and that I cannot find a better place for us to hide than this
drafty old barn."

Lulubelle, who had been rubbed as dry as possible and
sported the old horse blanket, nickered with considerable
forgiveness.

"Yes, well, at least you have a blanket and so I do not
think that you shall get a congestion of the lungs. I would
hate myself so, if anything happened to you."

Lulubelle blew considerable air through her nostrils in
response to this observation, denigrating the very thought
that such a thing should ever happen to such a fine old
mare as she.

Miss Butterberry wriggled about in the straw, snuggling
into it as far as possible in the hope of finding some
warmth. She scolded herself roughly for crying and carrying on as though the entire world had fallen in about her
ears. "After all, it has not," she said aloud to no one. "The
world is only now opening itself up to me. Tomorrow morning this vile storm will be ended; the sun will rise; and I

will be warm again and on my way to London. He must
be in London," she added on a tiny breath. "Oh, surely, he
must be in London. Did not he mention the Tower in the
few lines that he wrote me? What other tower could he
mean, if not the Tower of London?"

Searching through the pockets of her riding costume,
Miss Butterberry produced the letter to which she referred,
held it beside the lantern and squinted at the wild hand-
writing that covered the page. It had come to her in a most
roundabout manner, this letter—by the hand of a little
Gypsy boy who had come knocking on the kitchen door of
her papa's rectory.

"Though how Peter could possibly be certain that that
particular Gypsy boy's caravan would pass through Wicken,
I cannot think," she murmured. "I am so very lucky that
cook or one of the girls did not answer that knock. Most
certainly they would have given this to Mama and she
would never have given it to me. She would think it perfectly sinful for Peter to be writing me letters without Papa's
permission.

The man in the scarlet cravat closed the window silently
behind him, fished the candle stub and his flints from the
inside of his left boot and hunkered down beneath the window sill to make himself a bit of light to see by. Next to
him upon the stone floor of the Great Hall lay the sack that
he had attempted to keep dry by carrying it against his
breast beneath shirt, waistcoat and jacket. It was not dry,
however, and he was sorry for it. He had wished to make
his prisoner as comfortable as possible. Now, that could not
be done.

Stuffing the top of the sack down into the waistband of
his breeches, he rose with the bit of flame cupped carefully

in his hands and made his way haltingly through the Great Hall in the direction of the front of the establishment. It seemed to take him forever, for though he had divested himself of his spurs beneath the casement, still his boot heels would clack against the stone floor. He paused long and often on his journey to the main staircase, waiting for the rumble of thunder to cover the sound of his progress. When at last he reached the stairwell, he gave thanks to see that the stairs were carpeted. He crept up them a step at a time, pressing close against the wall and keeping his feet as near as possible to the inside of each step. Even so, they squeaked a bit. And with each squeak, he paused and listened for some noise from above in response. None ever came, and after what seemed to him a veritable eternity, he reached the first floor landing.

He moved like a shadow down the corridor, cautiously entering each room and searching it, hampered by the small circle of light his candle stub provided, but determined to check into every corner, to gaze into every likely space. When he finally discovered the object of his search, he was amazed at the size of it and stared for a moment in true disbelief. By Jove, he thought, I hope the thing inside ain't as large as all that. I shall never be able to carry it off.

But then he told himself that of course the cage would be large because the parrot's keepers would wish to give the bird room in which to strut and hop and play. Silently, he lifted the edge of the covering and peered beneath it to discover one amber eye peering back at him. With a great deal of nervous energy, he set his candle stub on the nearest flat surface, took the sack from his waistband and laid it carefully upon a table so that he might easily open it with one free hand. Then he tossed the covering up to the top of the cage, opened the door and reached inside. He hoped to take the bird before it knew what he intended. He had been thoroughly warned that even with his gloves to protect him, the bird's intimidating beak could do considerable damage. He was thus surprised when, before he could attempt to grasp the bird, the bird hopped from its perch directly onto the back of his hand.

"Knollsmarmer," it said, blinking sleepily at the man. "Mornin' Knollsmarmer."

The man in the scarlet cravat was most taken aback. "Good morning," he whispered, his eyes wide.

"Mrrrrrr," replied the bird, sounding quite like a purring cat, and it sidled contentedly up the man's arm, ducked through the cage door and continued onward until it came to a halt on the man's shoulder, where it rubbed its red and white striped cheek against his own.

The man in the scarlet cravat was flabbergasted. This was not at all what he had been led to expect of the fowl. He reached up tentatively with his index finger and stroked the bird's head.

"Yo ho ho," mumbled the parrot at his touch.

"An old pirate, are you?" whispered the man. "Well, I expect I am as fond of old pirates as anyone, but that is neither here nor there, old man. I must put you into this sack, you see. It is the only way that I can think of to take you with me." He lifted the sack and jiggled it open with one hand.

The green-winged macaw stared down into it and ruffled his feathers and bobbed his head most knowingly.

Miss Butterberry woke with a start, sitting straight up and sending bits of straw slithering here and there. At first she stared about her in considerable confusion, wondering where she was and why the little bed she shared with her sister Clara had become so very hard and cold. But then she saw the flicker of the lantern and heard Lulubelle snuffling and remembered exactly where she was and how she had come to be there.

But what woke me? she wondered, glancing about the old barn. Was it a particularly loud clap of thunder? Well, it must have been, for there is no one about but myself and Lulubelle, and Lulubelle is fast asleep. She sighed and prepared to snuggle down once more amongst the straw, her damp riding costume clinging to her in the most aggravating manner. She shivered the slightest bit, because she *was* cold as she lay back down in the straw. And then she heard a sound distinctly different from the thunder and the beating of the rain against the barn, though muffled by it. Behind her, Lulubelle woke and whinnied.

"No, no, shhhh, Lulubelle," Miss Butterberry whispered, extricating herself from the straw and hurrying to the mare's head, where she began to stroke Lulubelle's brown-and-white nose comfortingly. "Hush, my darling. Listen."

Miss Butterberry's charmingly *retroussé* nose wrinkled the slightest bit in concentration as she attempted to hear again the sound that had seemed to her to be so clearly not a part of the storm. And hear it she did, a deal more loudly than at first. It sounded quite like the pounding of hooves and the whinnying of a horse who was definitely not Lulubelle.

"I am being absurd," sighed Miss Butterberry with a shake of her head. "I could not possibly hear the pounding of a horse's hooves in such weather as this, and the whinny is merely the wind playing about the eaves. Most certainly it is in my imagination, for who on earth would have need to ride about in such a storm as this at such an hour?"

It did occur to her that she had discovered a need to do precisely that, but she gave a shake of her head in exasperation at the thought. After all, she had not chosen to ride out into the storm. No sane person would. The storm had come upon her as a complete surprise and she had taken cover as quickly as she could. Certainly anyone else caught out in the storm would have done the same and have gone to ground long before this. No one would yet be riding about in search of shelter. And then one of the barn doors that she had pulled tightly closed squealed and flew open. Wind and rain gushed through it, and with the wind and the rain entered a shadowman on a shadowhorse.

Miss Butterberry ducked down behind the boards of the stall at once. Her heart thumped; sudden pricklings of perspiration popped out on her head. She held her breath and prayed silently that whoever the shadowman might be, he had not seen her abrupt movement, and that now she was as invisible to him as she could possibly be. Spectres of all the dastardly villains and visions of all the dastardly deeds that her mama and papa had ever warned her about flashed and fluttered and teased at the back of her mind. Truly, Miss Butterberry had all she could do to keep from shrieking and dashing out of the barn on the instant. She did, however, manage to avoid such a particularly stupid action, remaining, instead, where she was and peering through the stall's slats at the shadowman as he dismounted, leaned down and allowed the rainwater to pour from his hat brim onto the barn floor.

The man in the scarlet cravat had taken note of the lighted lantern and the old brown horse the moment he had entered the barn and had thought at once to turn Leprechaun about and ride away. The lantern had not been off its peg and lit when he had left the place shortly after the storm had broken, and most certainly there had been no horse in the barn but his own. As he dismounted, his spurs jangling, he leaned down and slipped the Italian dagger from the inside of his right boot. A perfect flood of rainwater poured from the brim of his hat when he did it, and puddled at his feet. Paying it not the least attention, he straightened and looked about him with great concentration, the carved ivory handle of the dagger turning over and over in his hand as he did so. "There is no need to make a game of it," he said quietly, turning first one way and then another. "I know you're here. If it is my blood you wish, come out and try for it."

Miss Butterberry's heart thwacked up into her throat.

"I know you're here," he said again, turning his back to her to stare up into the loft above him. "It is perfectly stupid to think that I do not. Your horse is standing here chewing hay right before my eyes. Attack at once if that is your intention. I have not the patience to be playing at cat and mouse. No, nor the will to do it, either. I have a friend with me who is likely near drowned and requires my assistance to recover, so let us get on with it."

Miss Butterberry, her hand to her breast, stood up at once and he spun to face her, dagger at the ready that very instant. The blade flashed briefly in the lantern light and then it tumbled with a dull clunk to the floorboards. He stared at her in the meager light and took a step forward and then another. His heart fluttered, rose into his throat and came near to choking him. Then it tumbled hastily downward, back into its rightful spot and began to pound like the surf on a winter's day, surging and ebbing and surging again. "Mary?" he whispered in disbelief. "Mary, is it you? No, it cannot be. I am seeing visions."

At those words, Miss Butterberry burst into tears and dashed from the stall directly into his arms. She clung to him as if he were a raft on a tumultuous sea. "Peter," she sobbed. "Oh, Peter, you have come back to me!"

"Mary?" he murmured again, his arms wrapping themselves about her without the least notion that they were doing so. "What in Jove's name are you doing in someone else's barn in the middle of the night? And soaked through with rain, too!" And then he hugged her so tightly that she could not possibly find the breath to answer him. He kissed her ear and her cheek and the loose, damp tendrils of her hair, and when she sighed within the shelter of his embrace, he kissed her sweet cherry lips as well.

Miss Butterberry kissed him back—a long, deep kiss that left her panting for breath. Then she rested her head against his broad and very wet chest and closed her eyes.

He held her within the circle of his arms as though he feared she would disappear the instant he released her. But after a time, he moved to take her by the shoulders and he forced her to step back from him so that he might see her face more clearly. "Mary," he growled, deep in his throat, "what *are* you doing here? Look at you, you are shivering with the damp. You will be ill."

"I am shivering," acknowledged Miss Butterberry, "but it is not with the damp, Peter. Oh, I cannot believe that you are here before me at this very moment. Surely it is Fate!"

"Yohoho," mumbled a muffled voice from behind them. "Avast me hearties. Wetwetwet."

"Oh!" Mary jumped at the words. "Who is it? Who is with you, Peter?" She stood on her toes to peer over his shoulder.

"By Jove, Mary, you have made me forget all about him. Yes, and Chaun too. They must be chilled through." So saying, Peter Winthrop released hold of Miss Butterberry and hurried to his horse. He untied a sack from his saddle bow and set it carefully on the floor.

"Wet," declared a voice from inside the sack.

"No, are you?" Winthrop responded, kneeling down and

beginning to untie the rope that fastened the top of the sack closed. "Fancy that."

"Wet," said the voice again.

"It is just as if he knows what he is saying," Winthrop commented as Miss Butterberry knelt down beside him. "Though he don't. At least, I do not think that he does. He is nothing but a bird, after all."

"A bird?"

"Yes."

"Knollsmarmer," declared the parrot confidently, galumphing his way toward the place at which Winthrop's fingers fumbled with the knotted rope.

"It is Lord Nightingale!" Miss Butterberry exclaimed.

"Lord Nightingale?"

"Lord Nightingale always says Knollsmarmer. It is his very own word. It must be him. Peter, that particular parrot is Lord Wickenshire's pet. Why is he here with you in the middle of the night, and in a sack of all things?"

Winthrop's lips parted, closed again.

"Peter?"

"I—I did never expect to meet with—Mary, my dearest Mary, I love you with all my heart."

"Well, I have never doubted that," declared Miss Butterberry confidently. "But that is not an answer to my question, Peter. Why have you got Lord Wickenshire's parrot in that sack?"

Winthrop nibbled at his lower lip. This little bit of skulduggery was not something of which he was at all proud. But he could not think of a thing to tell her but the truth. "I—I have stolen the confounded parrot from Wicken Hall, Mary, and if I do not get him out of this sack and dry him somehow, he will likely die of a congestion of the lungs before I can get him to London. He will be no good at all to me if he dies."

"You have stolen him? Peter Winthrop, you are not a thief!"

"I beg to differ with you, Mary, but apparently, I am."

Miss Butterberry stared at him in silence.

"You do not understand how things are with me, Mary. I have tried to explain it to you over and over again. I am in dire straits. I had to do something, Mary."

"Do something? Stealing is something? Peter, do you not remember how very bad you felt when everyone in Wicken thought that you had stolen the funds from the Ladies' Aid Society and my grandpapa's amber stickpin as well? You were desolate."

"Yes, well, but I did not steal *them*. I cannot think who did, but it was not me."

"So you said. And I believed you. But you *have* stolen something now, Peter. You admit it to me most brazenly. Oh, you poor little bird," she added as the knot came free and the green-winged macaw poked his head through the opening to gaze up at them. "Only see how wretched he looks, Peter. You have stolen him from his master. If you felt so very bad when you were merely accused of stealing, how will you feel about yourself now that you actually have stolen?"

"It is merely a stupid bird, Mary."

"It is thievery nonetheless."

Winthrop rubbed the back of his gloved hand across his brow as Lord Nightingale jumped wetly up on his knee and waddled higher onto his thigh. There the bird settled and began to pick at his bedraggled feathers.

"I had no choice, Mary," Winthrop stated flatly. "Out of necessity, I agreed to do the thing and I have done it. Now I am to deliver this bird to London, and I will do that too. I gave my word in the matter."

Mary glared angrily at him in the wavering lantern light.

Not one more word passed from between her lips. Outside the storm increased to a blustering gale. All around the two of them, thunder crashed and lightning crackled. A shrieking wind whipped the treetops to frenzy, and a mixture of rain and sleet rattled against the sides and the roof of the barn, but Winthrop took note of none of it, because at that moment, for the man in the scarlet cravat, all sound of the storm sank beneath Miss Butterberry's deafening silence.

TWO

"Wetwetwet," declared Lord Nightingale unhappily.

"You shall be dry soon and warm," Winthrop replied, rubbing at the bird with a piece of muslin he had discovered near one of the stanchions. Winthrop's gaze remained fixed on Miss Butterberry as she added bits of straw and wood to the small fire he had started for her in a silver epergne that he had discovered in the loft above. "You cannot intend to spend the night in this place, Mary," he began for what seemed to him the one-hundredth time. "Only let me finish drying this old peacock as best I can and I will saddle the horses and escort you safely home."

"No."

"But Mary—"

"No. I will not go. I have run away and I will not go back until I have done what I intended to do in the first place."

"You *have* done it," Winthrop replied. "You said that your intention was to go to London to find me. Well, you have found me, though you did not need to go to London to do it."

"But you refuse to return Lord Nightingale to Wicken Hall."

"I have explained that to you, Mary. I cannot return him."

"Then I cannot return home."

"I fail to see what one thing has to do with the other."

"Tempest fugit," offered Lord Nightingale, nibbling at the piece of muslin Winthrop brandished.

"My intention was not merely to *find* you, Peter Winthrop!" Miss Butterberry exclaimed. "My intention was to find you and then to *become your wife*."

"Mary!"

"Do you think me brazen? Well, I do not care a fig if you do. I have worn the willow for you for two entire years, Peter Winthrop. I thought I would die when you departed Wicken. But I did not die, I merely lingered on in the most abominable state. I have had quite enough of that state, let me tell you!"

"You cannot possibly wish to marry me, Mary. Have a thought to what you say."

"I *do* wish to marry you. And you wish to marry me, Peter Winthrop. You know it to be true."

Winthrop set the parrot flat on the floor and stood. Stuffing his hands into his breeches pockets, he stalked off to check on his horse and Mary's as well.

"Knollsmarmer," suggested Lord Nightingale, sidling a bit closer to Mary and the tiny fire.

"Yes, he is a Knollsmarmer, whatever that is," Miss Butterberry agreed with a most bewitching pout, though the pout was lost upon Lord Nightingale, who had not the least idea just how bewitching it was.

"Your reputation will be thoroughly sunk if you do not let me escort you back to the rectory at once," declared Winthrop from across a good deal of empty space.

"It is thoroughly sunk now," Miss Butterberry informed him. "We are alone together in the middle of the night in a barn, Peter. What woman's reputation could survive that?"

"Yes, well, but no one need know. You have sneaked in

and out of the rectory any number of times to see me, Mary. Clara will certainly not say a word. And who else is to know that you were gone this night if you are safely abed when the sun rises?"

"Everyone will know, for I will *not* be safely abed when the sun rises. I have left a note for Mama and Papa telling them not to worry, that I have gone off to search for you."

"Oh, my gawd, Mary, your papa despises me already. What will he think when he reads such a note as that?"

"He will think that I am doing a most foolish thing. But he will be wrong. I am not a foolish person and I do not do foolish things. Your brother, Peter, rented Squire Peabody's house for the summer. I do think you ought to know that. And I delivered him the letter you left with me. It was Lord Bradford for whom it was intended, was it not? 'Give it to the man whose shadow I am,' you said. I divined that you had meant your twin."

"Edward?" Winthrop ceased to fiddle with the horses and came immediately back to where she sat feeding the little fire. "You met Edward?" he asked, sitting crosslegged on the floor beside her. Lord Nightingale flew immediately to his shoulder and nibbled contentedly at one of his dark curls.

"Yes, and I know now that he is the Marquess of Bradford, that you are the sons of the Duke of Sotherland and that Lord Bradford's heart aches because he has been searching for you for years and cannot discover your whereabouts. He did think in August that he might find you at last, but you had departed Willowsweep before he ever reached it."

"Willowsweep?"

"Do not deny that you were at Willowsweep, Peter. Lord Wickenshire remembered you were hired to work on the house and told your brother as much."

"Edward is at Willowsweep now?"

"No. He has gone to Billowsgate to meet Eugenia's papa and to finalize the arrangements for their marriage."

"Eugenia? Marriage? Edward is to be married?"

"To my very good friend, Eugenia Chastain. She is Lord Wickenshire's cousin, and you will be certain to like her when the two of you finally meet."

"Mary, your friend and I are not going to meet. Not ever. If Edward's luck runs true, he will never see my face again."

Miss Butterberry placed one delicate finger on Winthrop's knee and began to draw nervous circles upon the damp kerseymere of his breeches. "Why?" she asked very quietly, blinking up at him from beneath long, dark lashes. "Why do you say that your brother will be lucky never to see your face again? He wishes to see you. He wishes to see you and to spend time with you and to—to love you. He wishes for those things almost as much as I."

Winthrop lifted her finger from his knee and placed it back in her own lap. "If you must do something with your hands, Mary, hold them to the fire. You are freezing."

"I am warm enough."

"Your teeth are chattering. I have an extra pair of breeches, a shirt and a jacket stowed away in a bag in the loft. There are more horse blankets up there as well. I will toss my extra clothes down to you and you will dry yourself and put them on while I make a bed for you up there in the straw."

"But—"

"Do not gainsay me in this, Mary. If you will not allow me to escort you home at once, then you must at least allow me to make you as comfortable as possible. Is it so much to ask that you not make yourself ill with the damp?"

"I know you, Peter Winthrop. You are hoping that I will

fall soundly asleep in that loft and when morning comes, you will sneak away and leave me behind."

"Balderdash. I willn't do no such thing."

"Ha!"

"All right. I will tell you what. I will think of some way to tether this handsome fellow up in the loft with you. You do not for one moment imagine that I will sneak away without the precise article that I came to fetch, do you?"

"No."

"Fine. Then I will toss you down my clothes and something for you to dry yourself with, too. And while you are dressing, I will make you a bed and discover some way to make the blasted bird stay up there with you," he muttered, standing and strolling toward the ladder that led to the loft.

"Yohoho," Lord Nightingale said, clinging to Winthrop's broad shoulder tightly with both feet. "Avast ye swabs! Knollsmarmer!"

Miss Mary Butterberry knew beyond a doubt that she had cast her reputation to the winds. Dry at last and warm in one of Winthrop's shirts, his jacket and a pair of his breeches, huddled beneath two horse blankets on a bed of straw, Mary rested her head upon Winthrop's saddlebag and listened to the sounds of the gentleman she loved below her—his light snoring, the soft rustle of the straw in which he lay, every now and again a muttered word. She wondered what it would be like to lie beside him, his strong arms wrapped gently around her as they slept, but she had no intention of finding that out at this precise moment. To cast her reputation to the winds was one thing; to cast her virtue to the winds was entirely another.

"Mama and Papa will likely think me lost to all common sense," she told herself quietly. "Well, but it does not matter a whit, because I know that I am not. It is merely that common sense is not at all useful when it comes to dealing with Peter."

"Not," echoed Lord Nightingale from inside a slatted wooden crate, peering out at her with one great amber eye.

"I am doing precisely what I must, Lord Nightingale," she whispered. "I must remain with Peter now no matter how he protests. He is the gentleman I intend to marry, you see. And if he stands in need of me now, before we take our vows, then I must stand by him now, before we take our vows. How else can he be certain that I will stand by him after we are married?"

It did never occur to Miss Butterberry that she and the gentleman she had come to know as Peter Winthrop might not be married. She had given her heart to him two entire years before, and not once since then had she thought to take her heart back into her own keeping.

Upon the floor of the barn below her, his clothing still damp with the rain, the second-born son of the Duke of Sotherland huddled in a pile of straw beneath a smelly horse blanket and dreamed the most incomprehensible dreams. At times he spoke—words meant to frighten off the ghosts that surrounded him. Once, very near dawn, he awoke struggling with the blanket, attempting to free himself from someone's grasp. He gazed about him then, realized where he was and why, and remembered that Miss Mary Butterberry slept in the loft above. That served to keep him awake for a goodly long time.

How can she have run away? he wondered. *Why* should she have run away?

But she had very plainly told him the why of it and the thought frightened him no end. "I cannot marry her. I am the foulest of villains and would only make her life a misery," he told himself quietly. "If she will not return to the rectory, I shall take her to Wicken Hall. She is a friend of Wickenshire's cousin, she says. Well, Wickenshire is a decent sort of fellow. He will know how to return her to her parents without sinking her reputation. Indeed, I will take her to Wicken Hall and force her to stay there like a good girl until I am well away from the place." But he rather doubted that he could do that. Miss Mary Butterberry was no ordinary young woman.

Winthrop grinned at the thought. No ordinary young woman, no. Mary was most extraordinary. "But that does not mean that she has the right to choose to compromise herself on my account," he grumbled. "I ought to have something to say in the matter. I shall trust in Wickenshire's honor, deposit Mary upon his doorstep and force her to remain there if I must beat her about the head with a milking stool to do it."

"Knollsmarmer," muttered Lord Nightingale sleepily from above. The unexpectedness of that voice caused Winthrop to reach for his dagger and leap to his feet.

"Knollsmarmer," Nightingale mumbled again. "Yohoho."

"It's the blasted bird," Winthrop sighed, tossing the dagger to the floor and lying back down. "Devil, but I thought Quinn's men had discovered me!"

What does that mean, Knollsmarmer? he wondered then. I never heard that word before in all my life until Trump was told to use it to identify himself to the bloke who hired us to do this little job. Well, but it ain't a *little* job. Someone is willing to lay down considerable blunt to be put in possession of that macaw. That they are, though I cannot think why.

Winthrop stood over Miss Butterberry's sleeping form drinking the very sight of her down, taking every feature upon that sweet face, every plane and curve of that delicious figure into the very heart of him. Did he never see her again for as long as he lived, he would never forget her. "Mary," he whispered after a time. "Mary, wake up. The storm has passed us by and the sun is rising. We must be on our way."

Mary murmured and turned on her side.

"Mary, darling, do wake up. We must leave soon."

"Peter?" Her sea-colored eyes came slowly open; long black lashes fluttered against soft white cheeks. "Oh! I thought you to be a dream!"

"No, I am not a dream, Mary. I have brought your riding costume up with me. It is not yet dry, but it is not so wet as it was last night. You had best don it. You cannot go riding about the countryside dressed as a gentleman. No, it would be most unseemly and devilish odd, too, to see someone in breeches riding sidesaddle. Hurry and dress, dearest. We must be off soon."

He deposited her riding costume, her stockings and boots upon the end of the pile of straw that had been her bed and knelt to free Lord Nightingale by the simple means of lifting the overturned crate and setting it aside. The parrot screeched and squawked at this, so very raucously that Miss Butterberry clasped her hands over her ears, though even that did not block out the horrendous sounds to which Lord Nightingale gave voice.

"Great heavens, I have not so much as touched you!" Winthrop exclaimed and Miss Butterberry giggled.

Quite happy to be set free from his makeshift cage, and continuing his ode to the morning, Lord Nightingale flapped his enormous wings once, twice, and then sailed from the loft to land on the top slat of Lulubelle's stall.

"I do believe Eugenia was not fibbing when she told me once that Lord Nightingale sounded like a murder being committed the very first thing every morning," Miss Butterberry called after Winthrop as he hurried down the ladder after the bird.

"Like several murders being committed at one and the same time," Winthrop shouted back. "Cease and desist, do, you wretched old peacock! My ears are ringing!"

When at last Miss Butterberry, in her puce velvet riding costume, cautiously descended the ladder, she discovered Winthrop waiting impatiently at the bottom. "I shall just go up and change into my dry things," he told her. "I have got an apple. I expect we shall have to share it, Mary. It is up in my bag."

"Yo ho ho," Lord Nightingale replied before Mary could. "Tempest fugit."

"No, it is tempus that fugits," declared Winthrop authoritatively, climbing the ladder rungs.

"Yes, but the tempest has fugitted as well, my Lord Nightingale," Mary smiled at the bird, "so you are not at all mistaken. Last night's tempest has most likely fugitted all the way to London by this time."

"Mornin' Genia! Mornin' Nightingale! Mornin' Nicky!" Lord Nightingale replied joyously. "Yo ho ho! Avast me-maties!"

When Winthrop returned, he fished the apple from his bag and used his dagger to peel the fruit and quarter it, placing two of the sections into Mary's hand. "I wish it were more, Mary, but I did not expect to feed anyone but myself. Now, I must only discover how to get that bird back into the sack and we shall be on our way. I wish the sack had dried more, but I expect it cannot be helped. I cannot think of any other way to carry him."

"I should think his lordship is hungry," observed Miss Butterberry, watching Lord Nightingale strut back and forth upon the top slat of Lulubelle's stall. "Perhaps you should offer him a bit of your apple, Peter."

Lord Nightingale was indeed hungry, and the apple Winthrop held up for his inspection brought the macaw traipsing along the slat to him. Nightingale inspected the fruit thoroughly, nibbled a bit of it, and then took the rest. "Good old bird," Winthrop murmured. "But now you must go back in your sack. Hold it open for me, willn't you, Mary?" he asked, putting both hands about the parrot and lifting him from his perch.

Lord Nightingale squawked and barked and mewed in protest, ruffling his feathers and pecking at Winthrop's knuckles.

"Oh, Peter, do put him down. You are frightening him by holding him so."

"I will put him down. Inside the sack. Hold the top open wide, Mary. Ouch! Devil of a bite, you old pigeon! Ow! Deuce take it! Mary, he has got away!"

Miss Butterberry grinned and set the sack upon the floor as Lord Nightingale soared about the barn. "He does not appreciate being forced into the sack, I think. Perhaps we can persuade him into it instead."

"Persuade him? How?" asked Winthrop, jumping to catch at the parrot as it flew low over his head.

"With the apple." Miss Butterberry took her remaining quarter of the fruit and placed it on the floor near the sack. Then she took the second of Winthrop's quarters, placed it inside the sack, and stood holding the sack open. In a matter of minutes, Lord Nightingale floated to the floor and gobbled the first bit. Then, with pigeon-toed steps, he waddled up to the open sack and peered inside. His head bobbed; his feathers ruffled; his tail cocked first one way and then the other; and finally he walked into the sack after the remainder of the apple. Winthrop went down upon his knees to peek inside. "He is just sitting there nibbling at it, Mary, as content as can be."

"Yes, but you had best tie the top closed, Peter, before the apple is gone."

"The apple is gone. He is merely peering back at me now. It cannot be very comfortable to be carried about on horseback in a sack, Mary. Especially a damp sack."

"Knollsmarmer," Lord Nightingale said, looking about him with some curiosity and deciding to peck at a loose string.

"I know!" exclaimed Winthrop, gaining his feet and going to dig about in his bag. He returned with the shirt that he had worn the night before, righted the sack and stuffed the shirt down into the bottom of it. "There, that will give him something solid to sit on while we are moving about. Look, he likes it. He is tromping around on it, making a nest."

Mary could not help but smile. Truly, Mr. Peter Winthrop was the sweetest of gentlemen. No matter how he attempted to disguise it, she knew that he was. Only look how excited it made him just to know that a bird was pleased.

"We must be off, Mary," Winthrop said then. "Already the sun is up. We cannot waste another moment."

Miss Butterberry was perfectly astounded to discover that the path they rode took them directly to Wicken Hall. "Peter, do you mean to return Lord Nightingale?" Her heart filled with hope. The gentleman she loved could not, after all, lower himself to thievery! "Oh, Peter, it is most certainly the correct thing to do, to return him. I am so very pleased that—"

"I am not returning the bird, Mary. I am returning you."

"Me?"

"Indeed. You are to knock upon the door and request Wickenshire to escort you home. He is honorable, is he not? And a friend? He will think of some way to protect your reputation, I assure you. Go around to the front, Mary, at once."

"I will not!"

"You must. It is early hours yet. You may say that you were riding and took shelter from the storm and now you wish to go home. No one will suspect that you were not alone in that barn, and Wickenshire will help you to put a good face on it. I remember him spoken of somewhat. He seemed a noble sort. Please, Mary. You will give my mind ease. No matter what happens to me, I will know that you, at least, will not suffer for my follies."

"I have been suffering, Peter, for two long years," declared Miss Butterberry with some vehemence, though she kept her voice low. "You cannot imagine how I have suffered—to know that I loved you with all my heart, yet *not* to know if I would ever see you again. I could not bear it another moment. And now that I have found you once more, I will never allow you to leave me again. I promise you that!"

"But, Mary—"

"It is my choice to make, Mr. Winthrop. It is my reputation, not yours; it is my life, not yours; and I will do with both what I wish to do with them."

"But, Mary—"

"No! If you do not come here to return Lord Nightingale," then you do not come here to return me either!"

"You have not so much as a change of clothes with you," protested Winthrop, at a loss to know how to convince her. "What will you wear in London? You cannot always be going about in a riding habit, and I have not enough blunt to be buying you things—not proper things, Mary."

"I am quite capable of taking care of myself. I shall make do," replied Miss Butterberry primly.

"No, you willn't! You will do as I say! Now ride to the front of the house, knock on the door and go inside. Someday you will be thankful that your name was never linked with so vile a creature as myself. You will! I am—I am—a creature so despicable as to be beyond salvation."

"Ho! Beyond salvation? I am a clergyman's daughter and know very well that not the worst of the worst is beyond salvation."

"You are wrong, Mary. My soul is bound for fire and brimstone. Even your papa thinks so."

"My papa also thinks that you stole the money and the stickpin from the rectory, which proves how wrong my papa can be. Peter Winthrop," Miss Butterberry said in the verimost composed voice, "if you do not take me with you, I *shall* go into Wicken Hall and I shall arouse the entire household, tell them I saw a thief ride off with a sack stuffed full of something even as I approached and send them after you at once."

"You would not."

"Yes I would. In the blink of an eye. And then where will you be, sir?" It was the most audacious bluff. Mary's changeable sea-colored eyes met his cold blue ones deadon; her hands held firmly to the reins without the least trembling and she did not blink, not once. He must believe me, she warned herself as his gaze probed hers, or there will be nothing left for me to do but wear the willow until I wither away and die.

Peter Winthrop opened his mouth to speak, closed it again. He shook his head and stared down at the ground.

"Tempest fugit," muttered a muffled Lord Nightingale into the expanding silence.

"Come, then," muttered Winthrop in a tone so low that

Mary doubted at first she had heard him correctly. "I am a murderer and now a thief, why should I quibble at ruining a young lady's reputation, eh?" He turned his horse around and set off at a gallop toward the main road.

Mary, taking one long look at Wicken Hall, turned Lulubelle and set off after him. What had he said? she mused, nibbling at her lower lip. Had he called himself a murderer? Oh, surely not! He did have such a tendency toward melodrama! Whatever it was that drove him to hide from his father and brother, to wander from village to village pretending to be nothing more than an itinerant laborer, whatever it was that rankled at him and made him declare himself unfit to be her husband, certainly it could be nothing so dastardly as murder!

THREE

Mrs. Emily Butterberry screamed the most unholy scream. The Reverend Mr. Butterberry tossed the three books he was carrying into the air at the very sound of it. He attempted to catch all three, caught none of them, watched them thump to the carpet of his study and then dashed off in the direction of the kitchen.

"Emily, what is it?" he called. "What has happened?" A vision of his dear wife's blood flowing like claret overwhelmed his mind. This, however, was rapidly replaced by the spectre of one of his girls lying senseless upon the kitchen floor. And then again, he imagined Lucy, the cook, covered in steaming water from an exploding cookpot. "Emily! Emily! I am coming, my dear!"

He spun around the newel post, pounded down the corridor, leaped into the kitchen and slid halfway across it, coming to a stop by clunking into the edge of the kitchen table behind which Mrs. Butterberry sat screaming and crying and pounding upon something which lay flat on the table top. Beside her and behind her stood five of their six daughters and Lucy, but not one drop of blood was to be seen, or one senseless body lying upon the floor, or even one drop of water dripping from the cook. "Emily, what is it?" panted the Reverend Mr. Butterberry. "Girls, what has happened to your mother?"

"Oh, Papa, it is the most frightful news," Miss Clara Butterberry said, patting her mama's shoulder with one delicate hand. "It is Mary."

"What is Mary? Where is Mary?" asked Mr. Butterberry, noting that the eldest of his daughters was indeed the only young woman not present in the kitchen. "Move aside, girls. Move aside," he ordered, stepping around the table, scattering the young ladies and drawing his wife up into the safety of his arms. "That's better, m'dear. No need to scream. I am here now and there is nothing will harm you."

Mrs. Emily Butterberry rested her head against her husband's firm, familiar chest and hiccoughed. She swiped at her eyes with the back of one hand, slicking her tears across one very pink cheek. She took a very deep breath, shuddered, then looked up at Mr. Butterberry from beneath long, wet, thick lashes.

Mr. Butterberry's heartbeat noticeably increased when she did this, for Mrs. Butterberry had always been a most alluring woman and was even more so when she cried. Unlike most of the female population, including her daughters, Mrs. Butterberry's eyes never became red and puffy when the tears came. Her face never appeared scrunched up, wrinkled or abominably blotchy. No, not Mrs. Emily Butterberry. When Mrs. Emily Butterberry cried, her cheeks blushed a lovely pink, her tears sat like spangles upon them, glittering and gleaming, and her beautiful brown eyes became deep pools of melted chocolate into which any gentleman with the least bit of sensibilities would wish to plunge without a moment's thought as to what might lie at the bottom of them. Mr. Butterberry's arms tightened around Mrs. Butterberry. He had all he could do not to kiss each and every tear away on the instant. But, as much as he wished to do that, it would prove most unseemly with five of his daughters and a cook gathered around him.

"Emily, you must tell me what has happened," he said, instead of kissing her tears from her cheeks. "What made you scream so, and why were you pounding on the kitchen table?"

"I w-was not p-pounding upon the t-table, Henry. I was p-pounding on Mary's note."

"Mary's note? Why should Mary write you a note? Where is Mary?" he asked, looking about the kitchen for his eldest girl.

"That is just it, Henry! She is gone!"

"Gone? Gone where?"

"Gone! Run off!"

"Mary?"

"Only read the note, Papa," suggested Clara, the second eldest of his girls. "It explains all."

"It explains nothing!" exclaimed Mrs. Butterberry. "How could she? Oh, Henry, how could she? Our Mary has not only placed herself beyond the pale, but in the gravest danger and all because of that horrid Peter Winthrop fellow!"

"He is not that horrid Peter Winthrop fellow, Mama," Clara corrected. "Do you not remember? He is Lord Bradford's twin, the second son of the Duke of Sotherland and he is actually called Lord Peter Winthrop *Finlay*."

"I do not care if he is called His Royal Majesty," declared Mrs. Butterberry, resting her head against Mr. Butterberry's chest. "He has caused your sister to do the most perilous thing, Clara, and I shall never, never forgive him for it!"

The Earl of Wickenshire stood stock-still before the empty cage, his forest green eyes wide in disbelief. "Have you searched everywhere, Jenkins?" he asked at last. "Are you certain?"

"Everywhere," murmured the earl's butler, the paleness

of his countenance betraying the fact that he was most distraught—more distraught than he had been in ages, in fact. "I fear that Lord Nightingale has not merely escaped his cage, my lord. He has been stolen again."

"No, how could that be? And why? Aunt Winifred's will has been settled. Neil can gain nothing by possession of Nightingale now. And who else would want the old pirate? Nightingale knows how to open his cage door, Jenkins. You know that he does."

"Yes, but he does not know how to toss his coverlet up, upon the top of his cage, my lord."

"It may have caught on one of his nails and he pulled it up that far."

Jenkins sighed and shook his head sadly. "At first I thought that as well, my lord. I sent the entire staff—all except cook, of course—to search the house for him, but he is nowhere to be found. And the lock on one of the windows in the Great Hall has been broken, my lord."

"Broken?"

"The lock on the garden gate as well."

"Well, I'll be deviled," muttered Wickenshire, rubbing at the back of his neck with one large hand. "The lock on the garden gate? Who in Hades would break into a gentleman's rose garden? Did he bring a ladder with him, do you think, Jenkins?"

"A ladder, my lord?"

"Indeed, you did not any of you discover a ladder lying about the grounds?"

"No, my lord. I did not think to tell the staff to look for a ladder, but they would have told me had they discovered one."

"Well, there must be one, Jenkins, or our burglar is at least eight feet tall. He must be to have reached one of the windows in the Great Hall."

"That did never occur to me, my lord. Eight feet tall. Great heavens! Only think of a burglar who is eight feet tall!"

"Eight feet tall or carrying a ladder about with him as he travels. Such a fellow certainly cannot go unnoticed upon the road, eh, Jenkins? I expect he must be terribly damp as well, for he will have made his entrance during the storm last night, after we were all asleep. Someone would have heard the ruckus else."

"Do you think there was a ruckus, my lord?"

"Well, there would have been, Jenkins. You do not think for one moment that old spit and feathers would have gone *quietly* off into the night?"

"N-no, my lord. Certainly not. The only person with whom he goes anywhere quietly is Miss Delight, my lord, and yourself, of course. Oh, and Lord Bradford."

"Bradford? He goes about with Bradford?"

"Oh, yes, my lord. Very fond of Lord Bradford, Lord Nightingale became while you were gone. Because the two of you are similar in build and coloring, I should think. But that is not to say that Lord Bradford came and stole the bird."

"Of course not. For one thing, Bradford has gone off to Billowsgate with Eugenia to meet Uncle Robert and formally request her hand. And for another, there is no reason for him to steal Nightingale."

"Oh, no," said a voice from behind the two. Wickenshire turned to discover his countess poised upon the threshold, staring at the empty cage. "It is true then, Nicholas. Lord Nightingale is missing."

"Not merely missing, Sera, but abducted."

"No!"

"Yes. From what Jenkins tells me, most certainly abducted."

"Well, but who on earth would wish to abduct Lord Nightingale?" asked Serendipity, Lady Wickenshire, crossing to her husband and tucking her arm through his. "And why?"

"That is precisely the question, Sera. Why? He is rowdy and undisciplined—a perfect terror on his best days. And he is worth perhaps fifty pounds—if a fellow could find a person foolish enough to be duped into purchasing the old pirate."

"Nicholas, for shame. You love Lord Nightingale."

"Yes, but that does not make him worth anything at all to anyone else, Sera. Oh. No, it could not be."

"What, Nicholas?"

"You do not think, Sera, that perhaps our thief intends to sell Lord Nightingale back to *me?*"

Wickenshire was just setting out on horseback to see what he could see. He had noted hoofprints at the garden gate and more beneath the window of the Great Hall through which the burglar had supposedly gained entrance. He had caught sight of them again crossing the verge. And just to the south of the stable, where rainwater still puddled on the lower ground, he had seen them plainly. He had just stepped up into the saddle and turned Gracie's head in the direction of the south meadow when he heard a vehicle come racing up the front drive at the most preposterous pace and, within moments of that, a furious pounding on the front door. "Devil it, but something's wrong there," he murmured, dismounting again and tossing Gracie's reins back to Bobby Tripp. "Hold her for me, Bobby. I shall return in a moment or two. Something going on that I ought to know about, I expect."

"Yes sir," nodded the groom.

Wickenshire's long legs carried him swiftly around to the front of the house, where he discovered the front door standing wide and a gentleman shouting wildly at Jenkins and apparently shoving the ancient retainer back into the Great Hall.

"What the deuce is going on here?" Wickenshire bellowed, breaking into a lope, bounding up the front step and striding purposefully across the threshold. "See here, my dear fellow," he roared, hoping to be heard over the man's own shouts. "You may not come here and assault my butler, no matter what you think I may have—Reverend Mr. Butterberry?"

"Oh, praise be! You have not ridden out as yet! Jenkins was attempting to convince me that you were not at home."

"Yes, well, I would not have been at home had you come a moment later—or had you arrived a bit more quietly."

"Yes, yes, I know I am not quiet! I drove poor Jimbo up the drive as though the devil himself were after me, and now I am shouting at Jenkins, and at you as well, which I have not the least cause to do, but I cannot help myself! My lord, I stand in dire need of your assistance—and at once!"

"My assistance?" asked Wickenshire, waving Jenkins off to his other duties. "In what, Butterberry? Come upstairs with me and sit for moment. You are as pale as tripe and breathing like a gentleman who has run the entire length of the hedgerows."

"No! There is no time for sitting. We must be off at once."

"Off? Off to where?"

"To London!"

"To London? Now? Right this minute?"

"Yes, yes, right this minute. If you will not accompany me, then I must go alone, though I doubt I will find her do I go alone. I am an old man and not up to the new tricks."

"New tricks? What new tricks? Butterberry, you are not making a bit of sense. You will come upstairs with me," Wickenshire declared, taking the parson's arm and escorting him, with some force, up the staircase. "Mama," he called as he caught sight of the dowager countess exiting the morning room. "Mama, the Reverend Mr. Butterberry requires some strong tea at once."

"He does?" asked the dowager, peering at Mr. Butterberry with concern. "Take him into the breakfast room then, Nicky. I am quite certain the pot is still warm in there."

They rode slowly in deference to both Lulubelle's age and Lord Nightingale's comfort, though how comfortable the poor bird could be tied into a bag that swung from his saddle bow by a rope, Peter could not imagine. "At least the sun is strong and the bag has dried," he observed. "Your riding costume is dry as well, is it not, Mary?"

"Yes. Are you certain this is the way to London? Why do we not take the main road?"

"Because I expect the gentleman to whom this bird belongs will be looking for me," Winthrop explained. "And you wrote to your papa that you were going to London, so he will be looking for you on that very road as well."

"No, he will not. Papa will not come after me at all. I have taken Lulubelle, which leaves only Jimbo, who is not broken to the saddle. And the gig has a broken axle which leaves only the cart. Papa does not drive the cart well at all. Besides, I told Mama and Papa both not to worry about me."

"And so you think they will *not* worry about you?" Winthrop gave a sad shake of his head. "Mary, ofttimes you are a perfect gudgeon. Have you no idea what could happen to a young lady alone upon the road to London? Your papa cannot know that we are together. He certainly does not know that I will protect you with my life. His heart must be in his throat, and he will drive a chariot hitched to a goat if he must to come after you."

"No, I am certain you mistake the matter. My sister, Clara—you do remember Clara—is to be married in two months, and there are any number of things that Mama and Papa must do to prepare. Besides, everyone knows that I am perfectly capable of taking care of myself. I have taken care of myself and five sisters for ever so long. No one will bother about me."

"Come after you directly, even if it means that Clara *never* marries the fellow," Winthrop observed. "Come after you riding crosslegged on a tortoise, your papa will, if he must, and keep on until doomsday to discover your whereabouts."

"Whatsay?" asked a muffled voice.

"I said that her papa will never cease seeking her, you old pirate," replied Winthrop, giving the lump inside the bag a soft pat. "We are very near a place called Pippintern, Mary. I have been here before. It is just to the southwest of Sittingbourne. Are you hungry? Well, of course you are. You have had naught but a bit of apple to eat this day, and that at dawn," Winthrop answered his own question with a scowl.

"I am positively famished," Mary confessed. "Perhaps there is an inn or a public room in Pippintern where we may—oh, I did not think."

"Did not think what?"

"Have you money, Peter? I have got one pound, six shillings in my pocket. I did not plan to be purchasing meals and the like for two of us, you see."

Winthrop gazed at her through eyes as blue and seductive as a summer sky and thought how ingenuous she truly was. Oh, she might imagine herself to be the most competent, knowledgeable young woman in all the world, but it was only because there were so very many things that she did not know. Obviously she had not the least conception of the cost of things. "Not to worry about money, Mary. I can afford to feed both myself and you, but—"

"But what?"

"Nothing. It is nothing. Even if they have discovered by now that I have left London, Quinn's men will not think to look for me in such a small place as Pippintern. It will not matter a bit if I am seen by everyone in that entire village."

"Quinn's men? It will not matter if you are *seen?"*

"I did attempt to make things clear to you, Mary," Winthrop began, halting his horse and gazing straight into her changeable sea-colored eyes, which at that precise moment seemed to him to have become a bewildering mixture of emerald and blue. "If you will remember, I did try to explain things clearly the very moment I realized that we— loved one another. And I tried again to make everything clear the day that I noticed one of Quinn's men standing outside the blacksmith shop speaking with the smithy. And that very same night when I told you goodbye, I thought I had said everything there was to say. I attempted to explain to you again last night, too, but you do never listen to me. Will you listen to me now, Mary? Will you pay attention?"

Mary nodded and sat very quietly upon Lulubelle's back as the old mare lowered her head to munch at the grass.

"I am a villain, Mary. A foul, dastardly villain. I have murdered a man without the least cause—a gentleman by the name of Tobias Quinn—a gentleman to whom I owed allegiance and loyalty and my very life. Damnation, Mary, but I am the vilest human being ever to walk the earth. To

this very day Quinn's men dog my heels. Over and over I
elude them, but they do never cease to search for me. They
will see me hanged if they can, and I cannot but think them
right in their craving for it."

"Balderdash! You are not a murderer."

"Yes, I am."

"No, you are not. And if this Mr. Quinn's men are forever
chasing after you, it is merely because they do not understand the true circumstances of their master's death."

"The true circumstances are . . ." Winthrop replied, sitting up straighter in his saddle and pushing his hat farther
back upon his head so that a riot of dark curls tumbled
across his brow. "The true circumstances are that Tobias
Quinn gave my mother and me a home. He put food in our
stomachs and a roof over our heads. He saw that I was
tutored and brought up a gentleman, and he looked to provide for Mama's every need every hour of every day. And
regardless of these things, without one thought for the ex-
penditures of time and money and—yes—love, without one
thought to any of it, I stood before him one afternoon and
in a matter of a moment sent his soul reeling into the un-
derworld."

"You are always so melodramatic," observed Mary with
a disbelieving cock of one adorable eyebrow.

"No, I am not!"

"Then tell me the truth of it. What happened precisely?"

"Very well. I will tell you what happened precisely. My
mama had been ill for the longest time, but she would not
have a physician to attend her. She had always been frightened of physicians. She and Quinn would fight over the
matter time and time again. Well, one afternoon I heard
Quinn bellowing like a mad bull as I entered the house.
'Ye will do as I say, or I shall wash my hands of ye and
the lad both!' he bellowed. 'I will not argue about it no

more! I have sent a man for Dr. Harley and he will look
to you the moment he enters this house!'

"Well, I heard Mama burst into the most ragged cries. I
dashed up the stairs and into her room, to send Quinn away,
you know, and console her. But just as I reached her side,
she sat straight up in her bed and screamed the most terrible
scream."

"And?" asked Mary when he did not continue, but
looked away from her, back over his shoulder, and swiped
surreptitiously at his eyes. "Peter, you said that she
screamed the most terrible scream and then what happened?"

"She died," muttered Winthrop, turning back to her, his
blue eyes filled with unshed tears, the lips she adored
straight and pale and trembling. "Just like that. In an instant.
Dead."

"Oh, Peter!"

"Yes, well, I was not thinking of nothing, Mary, but my
mama and how she fell back and lay so still on the bedstead.
She had left me. She promised never to leave me, but she
had left me, just as my papa and Edward had left me,
though they, at least, were *not* dead. But Mama was gone
beyond restoration. And without the least consideration of
the matter, I put the blame for it directly upon Tobias Quinn.
I was so furious with him, Mary, that when he bent down
over my mama to see did she still breathe, I grasped him
by the shoulders and sent him spinning away from her,
across the room and out the door. I followed him out into
the corridor, so filled with anger that I wished only to put
my hands around his neck and squeeze the very life out of
him. He spoke to me. I remember that he spoke to me. He
said something over and over as I came after him, but I did
not understand a word of it because—because—well, I do
not know why, but I cannot recollect a word of what he

said to this very day. At any rate, I did not put my hands around his throat and strangle the man. Instead I let my hands ball into fists and I landed Quinn the most severe facer."

Mary, Lulubelle moving only the slightest bit beneath her, waited patiently to hear the rest of the tale, but he did not continue. He only sat his mount and stared down at the ground, blinking back tears that he did not wish her to see.

"You landed him a facer. That means that you punched him in the face with your fist, does it not, Peter?"

"Yes."

"And then?"

"What?"

"What did you do next?"

"Nothing."

"Peter Winthrop, do you expect me to believe that you killed this Mr. Tobias Quinn simply by punching him in the face?"

"Oh. No. The thing is, Mary," he said in a raspy voice, still refusing to look at her. "The thing is that I landed Quinn a facer at the top of the staircase and knocked him all the way to the stone floor at the bottom. I expect that he broke his head or his neck."

"You expect he did? Do not you know?"

"No, I do not. Donovan and Kelsey came running in and began shouting that the master was dead, that I had murdered the master at last. Well, I turned about and ran to the back stairs and escaped out the kitchen door and I have been running ever since. And they have been chasing after me ever since. No matter where I go, Mary, one or another of Quinn's men eventually turns up there. But I do not stay and face them and offer myself up in retribution for the horrendous thing that I did. I do not. I cannot. I am not only a murderer, Mary, I am a coward as well."

Miss Mary Butterberry could not think of precisely the right thing to say. She nibbled at her lower lip. She raised one hand and brushed at the mere wisps of black curls that had come loose from their pins and blew about her face. She studied Winthrop, glanced away, stared back at him again.

"Now do you wish to return home, Mary?" he asked quietly, his fingers toying with the sack tied to his saddle bow. "Now that you have finally listened to me and heard and understood? I will take you back directly."

"No. I will not go home. You are not a murderer, Peter Winthrop. You did never intend to kill that gentleman. Your mama died right before your eyes. The two of them had been fighting and she died. You must have been mad with grief, and he the person you—"

"I have thought about all that, Mary. I have picked it all apart over and over again in my mind. And I have decided that if I could, I would take everything I said and did that afternoon back. I would not so much as whisper a word of denigration at Quinn or lay a finger upon him in anger. He was always most considerate of Mama and unfailingly kind to me despite my foul temper. But I cannot take any of it back. Quinn is dead and gone. It is my fault that he is. I murdered him, and despite all the prayers that I pray over and over again in my heart, I will not ever see him resurrected. Not Quinn, and not Mama either."

"How old were you, Peter, when all this happened?"

"Eighteen."

"Oh, Peter, just a boy! And you did not attend your mama to her resting place?"

"I could not. I dared not be seen lest I was taken up at once and carried to the gaol. I hid myself away amongst the seacaves and on the night before her funeral, I made myself a place where I might lie flat and unnoticed amongst the thorn bushes to bid her farewell. I could not believe what I saw, Mary. Mama was buried as befits a queen. I cannot think who it was saw to the thing. Who expended such monies as must have been required. She was carried to the graveyard in a shining black hearse pulled by four black horses with black feathers on their heads. Before the horses walked a tall man in top hat and tails with an enormous staff, and with him, three children with baskets of flower blossoms. And the hearse was followed by thirty carriages. Thirty! I should never have believed such a thing. And each of the women in the carriages wore black and each of the gentlemen had been provided black hatbands and black scarves for their sleeves. And as they came so very slowly along the road, the church bells tolled. Oh, how solemnly they tolled, Mary. I shall never forget the sound of those church bells—not until the day that I die myself."

FOUR

Delight knelt on the window seat and stared out across the sun-dappled park. Her pale blue eyes overflowed with tears. From time to time she wiped her nose with her sleeve and sniffed in the most unladylike manner. Beside her, neglected, lay remnants of cloth and stiff silver paper and any number of threads and pieces of yarn.

"Delight, dearest, you are crying," observed Serendipity as she peeked in at her sister. "Oh, my dear, you must not cry," she said, stepping into the tiny chamber that Lord Wickenshire had proclaimed with great ceremony to be Delight's very own sewing room. With quick steps she crossed the carpeting to stand behind the child and placed her hands comfortingly upon Delight's shoulders, bestowing a kiss on the soft blond curls.

"I cannot help it, Sera. Lord Nightingale is gone. He has been stoled an' we willn't never see him ever again."

"Oh, that is not true at all."

"Yes, it is," insisted the little girl, breaking into loud sobs. "Lord Nightingale is stoled an' Nicky does not care one bit. I thought Nicky and Lord Nightingale were friends."

"They are, Delight. Nicholas loves Lord Nightingale."

"Then why did he go off with the Reverend Mr. Butterberry without even looking for Lord Nightingale?" Delight rubbed at her eyes with both fists as her hot little tears slithered down her flushed cheeks. "No one has gone to look for Lord Nightingale, not even Mr. Tripp. An' Lord Nightingale has been goned all night, Mr. Jenkins says."

Serendipity did not quite know how to respond. She took her sister into her arms and hugged her mightily. Then she settled herself on the window seat and pulled Delight onto her lap. "Do you know what stolen means, Delight? It is not at all the same as if Lord Nightingale has gotten himself lost. To be stolen is a very different sort of thing."

"It means someone has taked him away."

"Just so."

"Then why does not Nicky go an' take him back again? I would go an' take him back again if I knowed where to go."

"Well, and that is just the thing. Nicholas does not know where to go either. He has not the least idea who has taken our Lord Nightingale."

"But Nicky did not even *try* to find him. He jus' yelled at Mr. Tripp to hitch up the curr'cle an' off he rode with the Reverend Mr. Butterberry."

"Yes, that is quite true. But he did not do that because he does not care about Lord Nightingale. He did that because Miss Mary Butterberry has run away and her papa cannot find her without Nicholas's help."

"I cannot find Lord Nightingale without Nicky's help."

"But a young lady alone, upon the road to London, is a deal more important than a parrot, Delight."

"Miss Butterberry is not stoled."

"No, but—"

"Lord Nightingale is stoled! It is a diremost thing to be stoled, much more dire than to be runned away. I know. I have been runned away an' it was not hardly anything at all. No one even noticed it 'cept me."

"When did you run away?"

"Once when I was only little. I runned away from Papa. All the way to the pump house. An' no one did not even notice. Papa an' you an ever'one would have noticed if I had been stoled!"

They rode together slowly toward Pippintern, Miss Butterberry and Mr. Winthrop, both of them silent, both deep in their own thoughts. Only Lord Nightingale mumbled and muttered inside his sack. "Howdedo," he muttered and "Mornin' Genia," and "Mornin' Nightingale." He twiddled about in the comparative darkness of his cloth cage tugging at bits of fiber and stomping upon Winthrop's shirt, adjusting to the swinging of the sack as he did to the swing that Wickenshire had hung for him in his cage.

I am the most despicable gentleman upon the face of the earth, Winthrop thought, reaching down to give the parrot a soft pat. How could I agree to Mary's accompanying me? How could I? Have I gone completely mad? Have I not a shred of honor or nobility left in my bones? No, not a shred, he decided, gazing at the young woman who rode determinedly beside him, nibbling at her lower lip. I have not a shred of honor or nobility. Not a shred of decency either. It is bad enough that I have ruined my own life, but here I am, ruining Mary's life as well. And why? Because I love the gel? His eyes, as they turned from Mary to gaze at the path ahead, grew cold as ice. If I truly loved the gel, he thought, I would see that she got safely home as soon as possible without word of this adventure reaching anyone else's ears. Yes, I would. And I will too, he decided on the spot. I must have been mad not to force her to remain at Wicken Hall this morning. But I will rectify that bit of ill judgement as soon as we reach the Red Cock Inn. See if I do not.

Miss Butterberry gazed at Winthrop out of the corner of her eye. The sight of his chin just then tilting upward, as if in defiance, tugged at her very soul. Surely there was something she could do to help him. Oh, most certainly there was. He is *not* a murderer! she told herself. If these men who press him, who force him constantly to run and hide, believe him to be a murderer, then they must have it pointed out to them that they are wrong.

And I am just the one to do it, she thought. The very next time that Peter sees these men, I will simply go up to them and force them to see the truth of the matter. He did never intend to kill that gentleman. It was an accident. And accidents *do* happen. And once I have pointed out as much to them, I will point it out to Peter as well, because it will not do at all for him to continue thinking of himself as a murderer. "You ought not despise yourself so," she said quietly.

"What, Mary?"

"I merely said that you ought not despise yourself as you do. I cannot see that any of it was your fault, Peter. Not truly."

"Then you are blind."

"No, I am not. And I am not deaf, either. I heard every word that you said and I have considered all that you related to me, and I find that you are as innocent as a newborn lamb."

Winthrop shook his head in frustration.

"It was an accident, Peter."

"My hitting him was not an accident. I intended to land him a facer and I did."

"Well, I will not argue with you about it. Not at the moment. But it was an accident, and you have berated yourself quite enough over something that you did never intend. And if these men do not cease hounding you, you ought to set the constables upon them."

Winthrop groaned. "I am the one forced to avoid the constables, Mary, not they!"

"Balderdash!" cried Lord Nightingale raucously, startling them both. "Balderdash!"

"Just so," Mary smiled gently. "You see, even Lord Nightingale agrees with me."

"He is the dangedest bird, ain't he, Mary?" asked Winthrop, his thoughts of himself momentarily turned aside. "Do you know, there are times when I believe he truly knows what he's saying."

"Do you?"

"Yes, though it must be quite impossible. I wish I knew why the man wants him. I hope he does not intend the old bird any harm."

"Who?"

"The gentleman to whom Trump spoke in London. Some gentleman has offered to pay an enormous sum for this parrot, Mary. Fifteen hundred pounds, in fact."

"Fifteen hundred pounds?" Mary fairly gasped. "Someone is willing to pay fifteen hundred pounds simply to be placed in possession of Lord Nightingale? Who?"

"I have no idea."

"But Peter, surely you spoke to someone and—"

"No, it was a fellow named Trump made the bargain on my behalf. Attempting to help me gain enough money to buy passage to India, Trump was. A good fellow, despite his calling. It is a deal more expensive than I thought, Mary, to sail on an Indiaman—especially when you do not wish the captain or the crew to take note of your face or to have your proper name placed upon the manifest."

"Despite his calling? This Mr. Trump is a good fellow despite his calling?"

"Indeed. I should never have thought that a resurrection man could turn out to be such a thoroughly good fellow."

Miss Butterberry brought Lulubelle to a complete halt and stared at Winthrop with the most amazed look on her lovely face. Her heart positively thumped against her ribs with terror and pity. Oh, how very near Hades he has been made to dwell, she thought, aghast. And all alone, with no one to support him, to give him solace. "A resurrection man? Peter, do you mean to tell me that a resurrection man made this bargain for you? That you have been on speaking terms with a graverobber?"

"Not have been, Mary. I *am* on speaking terms with a graverobber and with his partners as well. That is the Red Cock Inn before us. We shall say that we are brother and sister visiting in the area and have come to inspect the village, eh? That will do it."

"Do what?"

"Explain why we are riding about together without so much as a groom to play chaperon. We look enough like brother and sister, I think, that no one will tip to the fact that we are not."

Miss Butterberry had never considered that particular matter at all, but as they halted before the inn, she had to admit that with his dark curls and her tresses black as midnight, perfect strangers might believe them to be related. Their noses were both small and tilted a bit upward and they possessed similarly long, dark eyelashes, though his eyes were a most disconcerting blue that could chill a person to the bone on an instant, and hers were forever changing between green and blue and gray and a blue-green color that reminded one of the precise spot where the seawater returning from the shore met the waves moving inward.

Winthrop stepped down and strode across the wood planking into the inn, his spurs jangling. "I should like to bespeak a nuncheon for my sister and myself," he said, addressing a rather rotund man behind a long, high mahogany counter. "Have you a private parlor where a gentlewoman might dine undisturbed?"

"None."

"None?"

"We have got the public room an' the porch, but there bean't anybody in the public room nor on the porch, so I reckon as how she wouldn't not be disturbed either place."

"I see. The porch is at the rear of the establishment?"

"Aye."

"I expect that will prove private enough. We will dine on your porch then, sir. Have you some fruit you can give us along with our meal?"

"I have got apples."

"Apples will do quite well. We will have three apples and whatever is available from the kitchen, and I must ask you for a pen and a piece of paper as well."

"A pen an' a piece of paper?"

"Yes. I will pay you for them," Winthrop added, fishing about in his waistcoat pocket and producing a shilling. "I should like to leave a message with you for someone, you see."

"For who?"

"For our father. He is a clergyman."

"A clergyman?"

"Precisely. The Reverend Mr. Butterberry he is called. I am not certain he will drive this way, but the Red Cock is not far from the London Turnpike, is it?"

"Not but a hop an' a skip."

"Yes, so I thought. Well then, I should like to write him a note on the odd chance that he may appear at this establishment. You willn't mind?" Winthrop fished another shilling from his pocket and followed that with a half-crown.

"Not at all. Not at all," agreed the innkeeper, one large palm closing about the coins. "But how will I be a recognizin' of this here parson?"

"Well, I am expecting him to ask after us, you see. At the very least, he will ask after my sister, for he does not yet know that I have arrived. It is a Miss Mary Butterberry whom he will mention. Perhaps he will merely describe her to you. She is rather a small young woman with black hair and—that is to say, she looks a great deal like me—well, but you will see her when you bring our nuncheon. At any rate, if an older gentleman should ask after her, you must simply give him the letter which I will leave in your care."

They sat on benches at a large wooden table and looked out over a tiny flower garden. Just beyond the garden, Leprechaun and Lulubelle stood and nibbled at blades of long, sweet grass.

"What is it you are doing?" Mary asked, washing down the last bit of a meatpie with a sip from a tankard of thick, sweet bock. "Who is it that you are writing to?"

Winthrop looked up and smiled at her in the most boyish manner. It was a smile designed to set her immediately off-guard and it did exactly that.

"A note to Trump. The innkeeper has promised to send it on to London with the rest of the mail. It is just to assure him that I have the bird and am on my way."

"Oh. Will it reach London before we do?"

"By early this evening. Which we will not, because I have no intention of traveling at any greater rate than we have so far, Mary. I cannot think but that Lord Nightingale would suffer some injury should we attempt to travel at a gallop. We will take our time and put up at an inn once the sun is low in the sky. Then we will ride slowly into

London in the morning. Here," he added, tugging the fine little Italian dagger from his boot. "Cut up one of the apples for Lord Nightingale, will you not? I expect he is as sharp-set as were we."

As soon as he had finished his writing, Winthrop left her for a moment, stepping back inside the inn. When he emerged, he strolled out to where the horses stood, lifted the sack from his saddle bow and carried it back to the porch. "I cannot think it is at all right to be carrying the poor fellow about in a sack," he murmured, untying the rope. "But I cannot have him flying off, either. Hey, my good fellow," he added, opening the top and staring down into the sack. "Like a bit to eat, would you?"

"Yohoho. Knollsmarmer," Lord Nightingale sang out contentedly, peering up at him. "Sack."

"Sack? Did you hear him, Mary? He said 'sack.' Do you think he knows he is in one?"

"Peter, what are you doing?"

"I am fishing him out, Mary."

"But he will fly away."

"No, I don't think so. Not before he has eaten, at any rate. I will just let him perch here on the end of the table and we will feed him the apple and then put him back in the sack. You willn't fly off, will you, Nightingale?"

"Knollsmarmer," declared the macaw as Winthrop lifted him from the sack and set him on the table. The macaw fluffed his feathers and preened himself a bit, shuffled pigeon-toed across the table to the place where Mary sat, peered down into her tankard and drank a bit of the bock, then pecked at a quarter-piece of the apple.

Winthrop stood over him, his hands ready to catch the bird should it show the least sign of taking to the sky, but it did not. Nightingale merely bobbed his head up and down

at them both, pecked at the apple, rolled it about on the
table, nibbled first at one side and then the other.

"I do not care if we mus' walk all the way to China,"
mumbled Delight as she reached the end of the meadow
and made her way into the woods. "We will find Lord
Nightingale an' bring him straight back home with us."

"Rrrowf!" agreed Stanley Blithe, dodging about her
heels, his pink tongue lolling with happiness.

"Sweetpea wished to come as well," Delight informed
the enormous puppy, "but she is merely a cat and cannot
be depended upon to keep up with us."

"Rrrr-ow," agreed Stanley Blithe. "Rrrrr-woof."

"Just so. She is always going off upon her own, an' we
cannot take time to wait for her. Not today, we cannot. Lord
Nightingale has been stoled, Stanley Blithe. Do you know
what it means to be stoled?"

"Grrrrr-ow."

"It is the most direful thing to be stoled. It so very
direful that we cannot wait anymore longer for Nicky to
come home. He willn't probably come home until it is
night, Sera says, an' then it will be too late to look for
Lord Nightingale. An' Lord Nightingale will be terribly
frighted. Uh-huh. Yes, he will, because he has not never
been outside at night before. An' he will screech an'
screech an' screech, because he will want Mr. Jenkins to
put him to bed, you know."

"Rrrrrrr," Stanley Blithe observed and dashed in a wide
circle around her, dodging in and out among the trees.

Delight giggled and then dodged in and out among the
trees after him. She was not at all a very large sort of girl.
Eight years old, with hair as lightly golden as a single shaft
of sunlight and eyes as pale blue as a faded watercolor sky,

she stood only as high as Lord Wickenshire's waist and weighed considerably less than a sack of potatoes. But she was a very determined little sack of potatoes, and she had thought the matter over very carefully for the longest time. "I am quite certain that me an' you can do it," she called to Stanley Blithe with confidence. "An' just think how happy Nicky will be when he gets home an' finds Lord Nightingale is already rescued."

The path through the woods led to Squire Peabody's pasture, which the two passed through quite unnoticed. They continued on until they reached the far end of Squire Peabody's drive, and that they followed until they reached the high road.

"Now," Delight declared, catching Stanley Blithe by the scruff of the neck and demanding his attention. "You mus' just sniff this an' then find which way Lord Nightingale went." She presented him with one of Lord Nightingale's cherry red feathers, which she had discovered upon the bottom of the macaw's cage. She dangled it hopefully under Stanley Blithe's huge black nose and crossed her fingers. "You mus' sniff it, Stanley Blithe," she told him again, when the puppy stuck out its tongue to lick the feather thoughtfully instead. "I read in a book how it is done, an' it is done by sniffing. See?" Delight sniffed at the feather herself and then lowered it once again to Stanley Blithe, who obligingly inhaled and sneezed.

"Good boy," Delight said excitely. "Now you mus' only find his trail by sniffing for him."

Stanley Blithe stuck his wet, black nose up into the air. Then he stuffed his wet, black nose deep into the weeds beside the road. Then he barked wildly and dashed off across the nearest field. Believing with all her heart that the dog was indeed following Lord Nightingale's trail, Delight dashed happily and hopefully after him.

It was not until her feet were growing very tired inside her stout little boots, her pretty blue bonnet with its wide poke brim was hanging only by its riband around her neck, and her stomach began to feel very empty, that Delight ceased to keep her eyes on Stanley Blithe and the trail he followed and stopped to gaze upward at the sky. It was not at all as bright a sky as it had been, and she could see the sun far across it in the west turning the clouds to pinks and oranges and bright, bright reds. "Stanley Blithe," she called, gazing about her. "Stanley Blithe, come to me, do."

"Rowwof?" asked the dog, galumphing up to her and sitting quite properly at her feet. "Grrrrrf?"

"Are you quite certain that Lord Nightingale and his stealer went this way?" she asked, for the first time doubting that the puppy knew exactly what he was to do. "I only ask, Stanley Blithe, because I have not seen the tiniest sign of it. Not even one feather."

Stanley Blithe blinked up at her with the most innocent gaze. Then he licked her hand and wiggled his bottom about upon the grass. Then he jumped up and loped off in the direction of the setting sun, and Delight, not knowing what else to do, for she had no idea where, exactly, the two of them were, ran as fast as she could manage after him.

The Reverend Mr. Butterberry, his hat planted firmly on his head, his lower lip caught determinedly between his teeth and a terrible passion blazing in his eyes, urged Wickenshire's horses forward at a spanking pace, so spanking a pace, in fact, that Lord Wickenshire, mounted upon Gracie, was hard put just to keep up with him. The clergyman drove with grim and silent fervor along the most expedient route to the city of London. Whenever he came upon a dray or a hay wagon, or a cart returning from one of the village markets, he hailed its driver to ask if the man had seen a young gentlewoman on an elderly brown mare. He stopped the team as well to question each and every pedestrian he spied beside the road and asked the same of them. And when, with a shake of a head or a muttered breath or a "No, sir, not a sight have I had of a young woman in a puce riding costume," they disappointed him, the Reverend Mr. Butterberry merely urged the horses back onto the road and set them to their paces again with a mighty vengeance.

Wickenshire was amazed at him. It had long been the considered opinion of every man and boy in and around Wicken, his lordship included, that the Reverend Mr. Butterberry was so ham-handed as to be unable to drive his way from one end of his drive to the other without overturning his vehicle and tangling the horses in their traces. Obviously, thought Wickenshire, every man and boy of us has been thoroughly deceived on that account. "You will pardon me, Mr. Butterberry," he said, just after the reverend had stopped to inquire of a milkmaid and just before he gave the horses the office to start again. "You will pardon me, sir, but when did you learn to drive like a regular Jehu?"

"Years ago, my lord, when I was a young gentleman without a wife and six daughters to support. Then I had the most likely little red gig. You will not remember it. It was before you were born, I believe."

"A little red gig, Mr. Butterberry?"

"Indeed. A gentleman may drive a little red gig, just as he may drive a finely made curricle like this one. What a gentleman cannot possibly drive are carts and gigs that are continually breaking down. Carts are impossible things. Uncontrollable. I cannot think why they are allowed on the road. And ancient gigs that have been put back together time and time again no longer drive as they should. They go one way and another depending upon which axle is newer or tighter or—but when a gentleman has a wife and six daughters at home a cart, and a gig that is forever being repaired, is ofttimes all he can afford."

"I see," nodded Wickenshire, who knew to the cost of a single cravat what it was like to be respectable but impoverished. "But perhaps soon you may—well, there will be more in the tithes this year, you know. Wicken Hall has come about at last, Mr. Butterberry, and is showing a profit."

"So! Wonderful! And my Clara is to marry Mr. Arnsworth," smiled the reverend. "That gentleman's fortune is not to be scoffed at. He will wish to bestow some gratuity upon the church in which he is married."

"Not to mention wishing to impress his bride's father," grinned Wickenshire, hoping to make the reverend smile just a bit. "You may have a spanking new little red gig again, Mr. Butterberry, and sooner than you think."

"I care nothing for a gig," sighed Mr. Butterberry, "if I lose my Mary."

"No, of course you do not. There is an inn up ahead, just off the main road at Pippintern. We will stop there, inquire after Mary and have some dinner, eh? You have had nothing but tea this morning at Wicken Hall and the sun is about to set."

"I am not in the least hungry."

"No, but my horses are tired, sir, and will not go much farther. I keep a team at the Red Cock. We will have a bite while the horses are being changed, eh?"

"Yes, while the horses are being changed, but then we must be off again. We must catch up with that girl before she reaches London, my lord, or there is no telling what may happen to her."

Wickenshire knew this to be true. While the danger for

a young woman riding alone along the road to London was considerable, it was not near as great as what could happen to a young woman alone and friendless in the streets of London Town.

FIVE

As evening approached, Miss Butterberry sat on Lulubelle's back and gazed about her with considerable astonishment. "Are there always so many people choose to stay at this place, Peter?"

Winthrop shook his head. "No. It is most odd, Mary. The Queen's Ten is generally patronized only by a few elderly ladies of Quality. Never have I seen the yard so filled with vehicles. We are merely a few hours from London. Most travelers stop here to change horses. They do not generally choose to spend the night. Something is afoot. I will go and see."

"Do be careful, Peter," Miss Butterberry adjured him as he stepped down from his horse.

"Be careful of what?"

"Well, we are very close to London, and you did say that you last saw Mr. Tobias Quinn's men in London. And—"

"I will be on guard," Winthrop replied. "Never fear, Mary." With a frown on his face, Winthrop strolled across the rough-planked porch of the Queen's Ten Inn, turned in through the open door and stared about him. The house was bursting at the seams with gentlemen of Quality.

"What the devil's going on?" he hissed to himself.

"Be a mill in Gadshill termorrow," a young woman with a tray of drinks in her hand answered him as she passed him by. "I don't be approvin' o' mills, but Pa does like 'em. They be excellent fer business."

"Wot kin I do fer ye, sir?" asked a giant of a man from behind an enormous oak bar.

"I am seeking lodging for the night for my sister and myself," Winthrop replied.

"Are ye now?" The innkeeper looked him up and down with some consideration. "Well, an' ye have come ta the wrong place this day, m'fine fella. Ain't a room ta be 'ad wifin leagues o' Gadshill. Not this evening nor termorrow. All filled up. The gen'lemen o' Quality has done descended."

"Yes, so I perceive. Like a swarm of flies, eh?"

" 'Zactly like a swarm o' flies," laughed the innkeeper. "All a buzzin' an' a soarin' about. 'Zactly like flies. 'Course, some is soarin' an' buzzin' more 'n others, mind ye. If'n there were a room, I'd not be so much as thinkin' ta trust me own sister in this place ternight."

Winthrop stood with his boots planted firmly apart and rubbed at the back of his neck with one gloved hand. Truly, he had not expected this. This put a distinct crinkle in his hastily devised plan. He could not possibly abandon Mary at an inn filled to the brim with Corinthians, though he had promised himself to do precisely that. The Queen's Ten Inn had always been a perfectly acceptable hostlery and he had told himself that Mary would be quite comfortable and well looked after here until her papa came for her. And her papa was already coming for her. He had no doubt of that. So, he had left the name and direction of this inn at the Red Cock and had urged the reverend to continue on as rapidly as possible to the Queen's Ten Inn where his daughter would be waiting. But this—he could not abandon her to this inn filled with raucous and rowdy gentlemen even were a room to be had. "We shall be forced to continue on to London,

I expect," Winthrop sighed. "Might I leave a message with you for our father, sir? He will be expecting to meet us here this evening and will be most disturbed—"

"Roth," came a cry from the among the Corinthians, interrupting Winthrop's words. "Roth, do my eyes deceive me or has an angel truly descended into our midst?"

"By Jupiter, Charles, the gods have chosen to smile upon us tonight. 'Tis an angel indeed! Come, sweet angel, and use your wings to cool my feverish brow."

Winthrop, scowling, turned just as Miss Butterberry, with the sack containing Lord Nightingale clutched tightly in one hand, grasped at his sleeve, her cheeks flaming.

"Mary, I told you to remain outside."

"I—I grew worried about you, Peter."

"Yohoho!" mumbled Nightingale, stomping about in the bottom of his sack. "Keelhaul the lubbers!"

"Yes, I should certainly like to do that," muttered Winthrop, taking the sack from Mary, grasping her by the elbow and turning her back toward the open doorway. "Come, Mary. There is not a room to be had here."

"The angel may have my room," called one of the gentlemen loudly. "More than pleased to let her have it."

"Stubble it," Lord Nightingale growled loudly. "Beaunasty. Stubble it!"

"I say," pointed out another of the Corinthians, "the fellow with the angel has called you a beau-nasty, Roth."

"Perhaps he would care to proclaim me such directly to my face?" replied Viscount Roth, rising from a chair before the hearth and strolling nonchalantly toward Winthrop and Miss Butterberry. *"Would* you care to proclaim me a beaunasty directly to my face?" he asked coolly, coming to a halt between them and the door to the inn yard.

"No," Winthrop said. "I merely wish to escort my sister from this place."

"Your sister? The angel is your sister, you say? Ah, now that puts a different light on everything. I do apologize for myself and my friends, Miss—Miss—?"

"Butterberry," supplied Winthrop quietly, his grip upon Mary's elbow growing tighter, warning her to maintain their facade. "Our father is the Reverend Mr. Butterberry of Wicken. You will pardon us, but we must be on our way."

Roth bowed graciously. "Viscount Roth at your service, Miss Butterberry, and yours as well, Mr. Butterberry." And he invited them with a wave of his hand to step past him and exit the establishment.

"Maggoty scoundrel!" declared Lord Nightingale as Miss Butterberry and Winthrop began to walk toward the doorway.

"What?" cried Roth.

"Seascum!" Nightingale replied, jiggling about in his sack, making it swing back and forth in Winthrop's grip.

"I do beg your pardon," Roth said coolly, stopping Winthrop's progress by placing one hand on his shoulder. "I hope that I misheard you, Mr. Butterberry. I sincerely hope that I did. For I warn you, sir, if I did not, and if one more word of that ilk passes your lips, I shall not be held accountable—"

"How dare you to threaten my brother!" exclaimed Miss Butterberry, removing the viscount's hand from Winthrop's shoulder by plucking it up between index finger and thumb and allowing it to drop with a great show of distaste. "You are decidedly foxed, sir, and hearing things. My brother's lips have not so much as twitched, and yet you accuse him of ill-mannered speech. I should take myself off to my chamber, if I were you. You are doubtless quite ill, my lord."

"But he called me seascum," Roth muttered, his gaze snapping from Winthrop to Miss Butterberry. "Such words are—"

"I called you nothing of the sort," interrupted Winthrop. "I have not said one thing since I told you our names. If you will step aside, my lord, my sister and I must be on our way."

Again Roth stepped aside, his cool gaze remaining on them as they passed. But no sooner had they got by him than Lord Nightingale began a raucous, rowdy rendition of the most nefarious words he had ever learned. "Thatchgallows!" he cried loudly, dancing about inside his sack. "Beau-nasty! Chicken nabob! Villain! Son-of-a-seawitch!"

"Do be quiet, you old pirate, and settle down," Winthrop whispered, coming close to losing hold of the sack entirely. "You are going to get me into the most enormous brawl if you do not."

"Heytheremister, I saw Hiram kiss yersister," Nightingale sang out in the most jolly tone. "Knollsmarmer, Knollsmarmerditcomepon themthere!"

"What the devil?" murmured Roth, staring down at the sack, his eyebrows rising in wonder. "What the devil?"

The shiny black traveling coach, with a crest upon its door and its box, fairly soared over the road as evening closed around it. The young postilion mounted upon the inside wheeler was growing drowsy from the length of the ride. The coachman on the box had long since ceased to pay any great attention to the four matched blacks under his command. There was no traffic anywhere about and had not been for the entire afternoon. Up behind the splendid vehicle two footmen in livery of blue and silver clung to their perches with increasing awareness of the length and boredom of this final stretch.

Inside the coach a gentleman of considerable years scowled out the window, surveying this portion of the hinterlands with great distaste. His dark hair, liberally tinged with silver, curled about his ears and down the back of his neck in a most reckless manner. His huge gnarled hands rested on the silver head of an ebony walking stick, long fingers clasped and unclasped the figure of the unicorn into which the silver had been formed.

"See Edward into the ground before he marries some Miss Nobody from nowhere," the Duke of Sotherland grumbled as he watched the land in the final glow of the setting sun flow past his window. "Doing it to spite me. Choose himself a bride without so much as a by your leave, will he? Send me notice not to appear at his wedding, will he? I will box that boy's ears so hard that he will hear no one's words but mine ringing in his head for the rest of his days. He will pay dearly for this rebellion."

Overcome with boredom, the duke set his walking stick aside and rummaged around beneath the facing seat until he came upon the silver flask he kept there. He opened the flask, tipped a portion of the Irish whiskey into the cap and spilled it all over his pantaloons as the coach lurched to the side of the road. With angrily shaking hands, he filled the cap again and spilled half of that down the front of his ruffled shirt as the coach lurched again and again and slowed to a stop. "What the devil is going on!" he shouted, grabbing up his walking stick and jabbing at the hatch with it. "John, why do we stop? Open up, you ignorant peasant and explain yourself!"

The coachman would have answered immediately if he had still been sitting on the box, but he had leaped to the ground the moment the horses had ceased to move forward. "Are ye all right?" he cried, rushing to the side of the road. "By Jove, I didn't see ye there, not either of ye! What is it with ye, Dick, be ye blind?" he called over his shoulder to the little postilion whose face had gone instantly pale. "Was ye not watching atall?"

Receiving not the least answer to his pounding on the hatch, but hearing, when he ceased to pound, a decidedly infuriated barking, the duke lowered the isinglass window and peered out. "What the deuce?" he mumbled, and scowling at the unexpected interruption of his journey, he opened his own door and let down his own steps, which he had never before been known to do and which thoroughly appalled his footmen, who were still clinging to their perches behind the vehicle. He then stepped down onto the road, where he was immediately accosted by a great, hairy dog with a long pink tongue. "Down. Sit. Sit down, sir!" he demanded, and Stanley Blithe, recognizing at once the voice of authority, did as he was told. "Now, what is all this about, John?" the duke grumbled, standing beside his coachman and peering down. "Good gawd, a child? You ran down some farmer's child, John?"

"No, he didn't not," Delight responded as the coachman helped her to her feet. "I jumped out of the way before he could."

"You did, did you? Well, that's a bright child. That's a smart girl. Why are you crying if you have not been run down?"

"Sure an' she has hurt herself ajumpin' into the ditch," murmured the coachman.

"I am not speaking to you," declared the duke. "You may return to the box, John. I will speak to you when we have reached our destination and not before. Now," he continued as the coachman hurriedly departed for his box, "why are you crying, child? Have you twisted your ankle or some such? I expect if you have we must carry you home in the coach."

"You must?" asked Delight, swiping at her eyes with the

back of her hand. "Must you carry Stanley Blithe home as well?"

"Stanley Blithe? Who the devil is Stanley Blithe?"

"Rarrf," answered the dog.

"He is," answered Delight, pointing.

"Oh. Well, he may run alongside of us."

"No, he may not," Delight corrected the gentleman. "Stanley Blithe has run an' run all afternoon an' he is too tired to run anymore. An' we are lost," she added tentatively. "If I have not twisted my ankle, but I am lost, will you still take me home?"

"No," declared the duke.

"Then I *have* twisted my ankle an' it hurts dreadful," Delight responded.

Sotherland shook his head. "A bright girl, a sharp girl! A girl of which any father might be proud!" he said. "Where do you live, child?"

"At Wicken Hall."

"Wicken Hall? Is that not the residence of the Earl of Wickenshire?"

"Yes," Delight nodded. "Do you know where it is? I am Nicky's very own sister-in-law."

"Imagine that," murmured the gentleman, and Delight noticed at once how the gentleman's eyebrows wiggled and how impressed he appeared to be by the relationship, and so she attempted to impress him again on Stanley Blithe's behalf. "An' Stanley Blithe is Nicky's very own dog-in-law," she declared, looking up at the duke, her blue eyes bright with hope.

For the first time in more years than he could remember, the Duke of Sotherland felt the urge to smile. He fought it down at once and frowned quite competently around it. "Frederick, come and lift this child into the coach," he growled at one of the trembling footmen. "It seems she has twisted her ankle. Charles," he ordered the other, "put that furry beast inside as well."

"The dawg, Your Grace?"

"Indeed, the dog. And be quick about it. I have every intention of arriving at our destination before dark, though we must make a side trip to deliver this young lady to her brother-in-law first. John," he called up to the coachman, "stop at the first hovel you come upon and obtain directions to Wicken Hall."

The innkeeper at the Red Cock Inn welcomed them heartily. "Not many travelers along this road of late," he commented, escorting them to the public room where the table was already laid and a quiet blaze danced cheerfully upon the hearth. "Not the time for a large fire, of course, but a small fire is a comfortable, cheering thing when a man has been journeying about the country."

"Just so," Wickenshire agreed.

"Whatever it is you have prepared for dinner, just send it to us quickly, will you not?" ventured Mr. Butterberry. "Our time is precious. We cannot linger."

The innkeeper nodded. "I understand perfectly, sir."

"A young woman has not, perchance, stopped by this establishment earlier today, eh?" Mr. Butterberry asked at an encouraging look from Wickenshire. "Fine-looking young woman. Black hair. Puce riding costume."

"The Reverend Mr. Butterberry hopes to meet with—" Wickenshire began the story that the two of them had concocted to safeguard Mary's reputation.

"You are the Reverend Mr. Butterberry!" exclaimed the innkeeper. "So I began to think! Your children resemble you, sir. Fine children, too. Said you would be asking after them."

"My *children?*" whispered the Reverend Mr. Butterberry.

"Well, and he did say that you would not be expecting *him,*" nodded the landlord sagely. "He did say that, but your son has left this letter for you, Reverend Butterberry." The landlord took a folded piece of paper from beneath the smudged apron that stretched tightly across his broad stomach and presented it into Mr. Butterberry's hand. "He said as I was to expect you this very afternoon and to be certain that you received his letter from my own hand. Now, if there be nothing else ye wish, gentlemen, I will just be pouring you a bit of wine, and m'girls will bring your dinner shortly."

"Thank you," Wickenshire replied, waiting impatiently for the man to depart. "Your son has written you a letter and left it in the care of the innkeeper, Mr. Butterberry?" he asked in astonishment, once they were alone. "Your son?"

The Reverend Mr. Butterberry studied first one side of the folded paper and then the other. "Must be some mistake," he muttered. "But it has got my name upon it all right."

"Perhaps you ought to unfold it and see what it says."

"But I do not have a son. Why would some fellow claim to be my son and leave a letter for me at the Red Cock Inn? How would the man even know to expect me? Until you told me ten minutes ago that we would change teams here, I did not so much as realize that the Red Cock Inn existed. I am not generally a traveling gentleman. I have not traveled more than a league from Wicken in the past twenty years."

"Nevertheless, someone has guessed that you would be on the road this day, Mr. Butterberry, and has chosen to represent himself as your son. Most likely someone who has come upon Mary. May I suggest that you unfold the thing and read it?"

Mr. Butterberry, his hands trembling with fear that it was, indeed, a letter from some fellow who had come upon his eldest daughter, taken her captive and intended to hold her for ransom—which is a purely stupid idea, he told himself, because everyone knows that Wicken is the poorest parish in England—Mr. Butterberry unfolded the letter and read the lines scrawled wildly across the inside. Then he held the note closer to the candles that adorned the dining table and read it again. "Winthrop?" he muttered. "Winthrop? That thatchgallows?"

"Peter Winthrop?" asked Wickenshire, his heart abruptly beating a bit faster. "Do you say the note is from Bradford's brother, Mr. Butterberry? And he yet signs himself Winthrop?"

"Aye, so it seems. My Mary is safe, he says. She will be awaiting me at a place called the Queen's Ten Inn near Gadshill. I must come as swiftly as I can, he says, for if I do not arrive soon enough, Mary may discover that he has gone on without her and follow him into London before I can stop her. That villain! That dastard! That scoundrel! I know that you have been hoping to help Lord Bradford find his brother, my lord, but I cannot think it at all a good idea. Born for the gallows, that rascal. I will comb his hair with a carving knife, I will, the very next time I come upon him for this! Ruin my Mary and then abandon her? I will order up his liver with my tea!"

"He will not have ruined Mary, Mr. Butterberry. He is a gentleman. We ought to be relieved to know that he is with her—not only to keep her safe along the road, but to see that her plans are foiled and she is returned to you safely. That must be his intent. Why else would he label himself your son? Because he rides with Mary and has labeled himself her brother, I should say. Attempting to safe-guard her and her reputation. She will *not* be ruined," added Wickenshire hastily as he watched an impressive shade of red creep over the Reverend Mr. Butterberry's neck and up into his ears.

"I do appreciate your pointing that out, my lord," managed Mr. Butterberry, his embarrassment catching in his throat. "I should never have believed that my Mary could—"

"Well, but only your family and mine, sir, know of this . . . jaunt Mary has taken," offered Wickenshire calmly. "We shall collect her at the Queens Ten Inn as the note says and you will drive her home in the curricle with myself riding beside you. When we reach Wicken, no one in the village will think anything but that I invited you and Mary to spend a night or two at Wicken Hall to help us prepare for Eugenia's wedding."

"Yes," nodded Mr. Butterberry. "And when we reach home, I shall lock the girl in her room and feed her on bread and water until she regains her senses."

"No, you will not. I do not believe that for a minute, Mr. Butterberry. It is an odd thing, though, that note from Bradford's brother."

"Odd? That he should know I would follow after Mary, do you mean? The lad knows me, my lord. He knows me well enough to know that I would not sit back and do noth-ing when one of my daughters has placed herself in such danger."

"Of course. Anyone who knows you, knows that. But I thought Mary wrote that she had run off to London to *find* Peter Winthrop, and yet here they are together before ever she has reached London at all," Wickenshire mused, tugging at an earlobe.

As their dinner came through the door on the arms of two of the innkeeper's daughters, Mr. Butterberry stood and strolled to the window, fishing through his pockets in the most surreptitious manner. He did not return to the table until the girls had departed, whereupon he settled back into his chair and unfolded a much-folded sheet of paper. "It says here, my lord, that Mary is bound for London to discover the whereabouts of the gentleman she loves. That will be Peter Winthrop, though she does not mention him by name. Her mama is certain she means Peter Winthrop, and Clara is certain as well."

"Yes, I thought as much. That she was going to London to seek him out, I mean. She does not say that she is traveling to London with him. There is something havey-cavey going on, Mr. Butterberry. I did not mention it to you earlier, because Mary's fate is much more important a thing, but last evening Lord Nightingale was stolen."

"What? Your parrot? Stolen?"

"Wicken Hall broken into in the most brazen manner and Lord Nightingale taken off. This was not the work of any ordinary burglar, Mr. Butterberry."

"I should think not! To break into Wicken Hall!"

"Yes, that too, but what I mean to say is that this burglar did not take one other thing. Not a ring or a snuff box or a piece of silver. Nothing but Lord Nightingale. And now a gentleman who disappeared from Wicken two years ago has somehow met with your daughter along the road *from* Wicken to London. He did not travel to the village to see your Mary, Mr. Butterberry, or she would have written you a very different sort of note. I wonder, could Winthrop have entered Wicken Hall and snatched Lord Nightingale from hearth and home? And if he did, why? What earthly reason could he have had to do so?"

"If we eat in haste and drive like the devil," suggested Mr. Butterberry in a most unclergymanlike fashion, "we may reach the Queen's Ten Inn before that thatchgallows

Winthrop departs it. Then you shall ask him that question direct, my lord, right after I have blackened both the scoundrel's daylights for him."

SIX

As twilight stretched inexorably toward dark, the Duke of Sotherland sat stiffly upright on the front-facing seat of his traveling coach, his mind boiling with bitterness until it seemed to him that he could taste the acrid thoughts upon his tongue. His cold blue eyes stared, unseeing, out the window and his hands fastened on the head of his cane as though it would flee from him if so much as one finger eased free of it.

"I shall beat Edward senseless with my own fists," he muttered at the darkening sky, "and then I shall lock him away at Northridge and feed him on nothing but bread and water for the rest of his life!"

"Ooooh!" responded a tiny voice filled with awe.

The duke started at the sound of it and blinked himself out of his thoughts and into the immediate present. "Great heavens, I had forgotten you were there. Pay me no heed, child. My words were not meant for your ears."

"I should dread to be Edward," Delight replied, huddled cozily in the corner opposite Sotherland. "Who is Edward? Did he do something very bad?"

"Yes."

"What?"

"It is not your business."

"But it is the very first thing that you have said to me

in ever so long. Why did you say it, if it isn't not my business?"

"I was speaking to myself."

"Well, you ought to speak to me," Delight pointed out with complacent righteousness. "Sera says that one must always speak to one's guests, even when one does not like them. An' Stanley Blithe an' I am your guests because you asked us into your coach. You did, you know."

"Who is Sera?"

"My sister."

"Ah, that will make her the Countess of Wickenshire?"

" 'Zactly so. An' she knows all about proproperty, an' she is teaching it to me."

"Propriety," corrected the duke, scowling at the back of the seat above Delight's head.

"All right," Delight agreed. "I 'spect you have got it correcter than I have. When I am nine, I shall be able to remember it 'zactly, Nicky says."

"Remember what?"

"That word. Propripety. You are susposed to look at me when we are speaking. That is one of the rules, too."

"Indeed." The duke ceased to stare past the child and fastened his gaze fully upon Delight. "Does it not frighten you to have me scowling down at you then? I thought to have me glaring at you would frighten the devil out of you."

"Uh-uh."

"Good heavens, child, what happened to your face? Did that maggoty driver hit you with the coach after all?" The duke leaned forward and touched the birthmark on Delight's cheek, which he had failed to note until then because his mind had not been on the girl at all since the footman had lifted her into the coach.

"I told you before he did not hit me. I jumped out of the way. I am the verimost best of jumpers. I can jump from anything, even from Gracie's back when she is falling."

"Gracie?"

"She is Nicky's mare and she is always stumbling. That is why Nicky taught me to jump so good, so that I can ride Gracie and jump off before she falls down and he willn't need to worry about me at all."

"I see. But that tells me nothing about the mark on your cheek, my child. Where did it come from?"

"It comed when I was kissed by Glorianna, the Queen of the Faeries. It means that I am special. Do you know about faeries?"

"Of course I know about faeries. They are peasant dreams woven for the entertainment of unwashed babes."

"They are what?"

"You heard me, I think."

"Wrroof!" exclaimed Stanley Blithe, pulling his shaggy head back in through the open window, bestowing a wet lick upon Delight's winestained cheek and then staring most belligerently at the duke. "Grrrrrwrroof!"

"That was bad of you to say," explained Delight to the frowning duke. "Even Stanley Blithe thinks so."

"What? What was bad of me to say?"

"What you said about faeries. Stanley Blithe did not like to hear it one bit."

"Oh, he did not? Well, he need not hear anything else. I can stop the coach right now and put him out," the duke grumbled.

"No, you cannot. That would be cruel an' you are not cruel."

"Me? Not cruel? A mistaken assumption, my gel. I am a veritable Turk. A proper tyrant. And a villain as well."

Delight giggled. "I like you. You are verimost funny."

"Funny?" bellowed the duke. "Me?"

Delight covered her mouth with one hand and nodded.

"Grrarf," Stanley Blithe agreed, tongue lolling. Then he placed his two front paws upon the opposite seat, stretched across and licked the duke flat on the face.

Sotherland swatted at the dog with the back of his hand but missed by a considerable bit as the puppy dodged back into its place beside Delight, then turned and once again stuck its head out the window. "Audacious dog!"

"He knows that you did not mean it about the faeries, or about putting him out," Delight said as the duke swabbed at his face with a handkerchief. "An' I knows it, too. You are verimost good at pretending. Almost as good as me an' Nicky."

"I meant every word that I said, young lady."

"Uh-uh. No you did not. Everyone knows that faeries are not pheasant's dreams about unwashed babies. Do you know any stories about faeries? Nicky knows lots an' lots."

"No."

"Not one?" asked Delight, her eyes sparkling up into his.

"No."

"Not even a teensy-tiny story about a teensy-tiny faerie?"

"No."

"Oh. That is verimost sad. Everyone should know at least one story about faeries. I do. I know a verimost splendid story about Glorianna. Shall I tell it to you?"

"No," replied Sotherland emphatically.

"It will make you feel so much better to hear it."

"I feel perfectly well, thank you."

"But you are still frowning. People who feel perfeckly well do not frown. They always smile." Without the least invitation from his grace but with all the confidence of one who knew her kindness must be welcomed, Delight stood, placed her hand on Sotherland's knee so as not to fall, and changed seats. She squiggled up next to him like the weary child she was and leaned her head comfortably against his arm. "This is the story about Glorianna an' the blind weaver an' the weaver's mice," she began, giving the duke's forearm a supportive pat. "It is verimost splendid. Once upon a time . . ."

The Duke of Sotherland sat staring off into nowhere. His hands remained firmly clasped on the head of his cane as he allowed her sweet, childish voice to paint him a landscape overflowing with faeries and gnomes and animals that apparently spoke as clearly and precisely as men and women did. He heard Delight exclaim and declare and denounce and hurrah as the tale unwound. He felt her shiver at the fearsome parts and bounce a bit on the seat at the most exciting parts, and snuggle closer against him at the loveliest, most comforting parts, and deep inside of him something that he had long ago forbidden to rise from where he had buried it, something that he had covered over and hidden away in an attempt to forget that it even existed, something that he had long ago forgotten about as completely as a gentleman could, began to ache.

Every gentleman in the public room who was not too fuddled to gain his feet and stumble in their direction converged on Miss Butterberry and Winthrop and their talking-singing sack.

"I do apologize, Miss Butterberry," Roth said with a bit of a bow, "but what the deuce? Who said that? You cannot have a person imprisoned in there?"

"It is Lord Nightingale," replied Miss Butterberry to Winthrop's chagrin.

Wonderful, thought Winthrop. She has announced it to

practically the entire world. Now when Wickenshire comes looking for the thief who stole his pet, each and every one of these gentlemen will be able to give him a perfect description of me. Of course, they will say that I am the Reverend Mr. Butterberry's son, but since he knows Mr. Butterberry and is perfectly aware that Mr. Butterberry has only six daughters, Wickenshire will know immediately that I am not who I told them I was.

"Lor' Night'gale?" mumbled Mr. Charles Stickley, kneeling unsteadily to poke at the sack with his finger. The sack poked him back immediately, which caused him to giggle.

"D'you mean to say that you have got some teeny-tiny lord imprisoned in a sack?" asked Lord Mitchum drunkenly, bending to peer down over Stickley's shoulder. "Imagine that! I will give you t-ten guineas—w-wait," he said, pausing to investigate the contents of the pouch in his coat pocket. " 'Zactly so. I will give you t-ten guineas to see him, Butterberry."

"Twenty guineas," called a voice from the rear of the group.

"Thir-thirty!"

"Fifty guineas!"

"Say yes, Miss Butterberry," urged Roth before Mary could so much as part her lips on the subject. "That last was Fortescue. And when Fortescue offers fifty guineas just to peer inside a sack, a person is bound to take him up on it. Not one to go about offering such sums, Fortescue. Clutchfisted. And then, after you have accepted Fortescue's fifty," he added thoughtfully, "you very well ought to accept Darling's thirty, and Harry's twenty and then Mitchum's ten."

Fifty guineas, thirty guineas, twenty guineas, ten guineas, why it was practically a fortune! Miss Butterberry glanced at Mr. Winthrop, saw his frown, but chose at once to ignore it. She was not at all certain how much his intended voyage to India might cost, especially since she was now to accompany him upon it, which would, by all means, add to his original estimation, but she was quite certain that almost one hundred guineas would be a more than welcome addition to their coffers. And if it was not all needed to purchase their passage, why, there might well be enough left over to procure a special license which would allow them to be married anywhere at any time without the least interference. Perhaps they might even be wed in a small chapel near the docks before they boarded the Indiaman. Yes, that would be perfect, for then she might lie safely and honorably in Peter's arms every night of the voyage and be welcomed upon Indian shores quite properly as Mrs. Winthrop.

"I—that is to say—my brother and I," Mary began softly.

"You did say that your father is the Reverend Mr. Butterberry of Wicken?" Roth interrupted her, thinking her opposed to showing them what the sack held. "I have been to Wicken once or twice and, no insult intended, Miss Butterberry, but a few extra guineas would not go amiss in your father's hands—for the parish, my dear," he added hopefully.

"I dare say it would not," murmured Mary as she stepped to the outside door and drew it closed. "Do set him free, Peter. It is cruel to keep him confined when he has such a fine opportunity as this to take the air. I doubt not but Lord Nightingale has quite exhausted all of his imagination in finding things to do inside a sack and has grown most bored. He will be pleased to step out and meet these gentlemen."

Winthrop's cool blue eyes watched with considerable thought as Roth tipped the last drop of ale down his throat and then passed his empty tankard among the other gentlemen. Another tankard was added, and another. Golden guineas clinked into those pewter cups as steadily as had raindrops into certain portions of the barn the evening before. When at last they all returned to Roth, the viscount added twenty guineas of his own, then placed the tankard into Mary's hands. "There. An offering for your father's parish," he said. "Now we beg the privilege of having Lord Nightingale made known to us."

Oh, what the devil, thought Winthrop as Mary's glance fell pleadingly upon him. So what if Wickenshire learns my description? Quinn's men already know exactly what I look like. It will just be someone else chasing after me and asking questions about me. I expect Twelvestring Jack does not go around worrying about how many people have seen his face. Hundreds have.

With a shrug and a sigh, Winthrop undid the knot, opened the sack and peered down into it. "Good evening, Nightingale," he said. "Would you care to come out and meet some gentlemen?" Then he knelt down upon the floor, and held the top of the sack open. Lord Nightingale waddled cheerily out into the public room. "Yo ho ho!" he cried as he emerged. "Howdedo."

"Well, I'll be buggered!" exclaimed Charles Stickley. "Will you look at that, Roth. It's a parrot, ain't it?"

"Mornin' Nightingale," proclaimed Lord Nightingale, peering up at the gathering of gentlemen, first through one amber eye and then the other. "Mornin' Genia! Yo ho ho!" With a ruffling of his chest feathers, a cock of his tail and an absolutely ear-piercing shriek, he flapped his green-tipped wings and soared up and over them all to land upon the top of one of the tables at the rear of the room. "Wet," he muttered to himself, sidling about. He nibbled at a few peas left on one of the plates, dipped his broad beak into one of the wineglasses and took a prodigious large sip, tugged a slice of orange from a bowl of rum punch, held it in his claws and ate every bit of it, and looking up to discover Winthrop laughing at him from across the room, flew once more and landed upon Winthrop's shoulder. "Knollsmarmer," he stated with great goodwill. "Yoho-hoKnoooollsmarmer!"

The befuddled and the not-so-fuddled Corinthians were pleased with Lord Nightingale beyond measure. They rushed about the public room collecting everything they thought the bird might eat and carried peas and potatoes, broccoli and beans, bits of cherries, strawberries and rum-soaked orange slices back to Lord Nightingale on eager, open palms. "It is the best thing since Brownlea's ferret," observed Mr. Stickley most enthusiastically. "I have never seen anything quite like it. Not close up, I have not. I wish it would sit on my shoulder."

"Perhaps it will," Roth observed. "What does your parrot like to eat best, Miss Butterberry?"

"He is most fond of apples, my lord," Mary responded. "And I should think he would like some water as well. He has not had a drink of water since we stopped for nuncheon."

"No, but he has just had a goodly sip of port," murmured Winthrop, rubbing at Nightingale's breast feathers with one knuckle. "And every bite of orange he takes has a drop or two of rum in it. He will be chirping merry in a moment."

"All of which reminds me what inconsiderate beasts we are. You and your brother, Miss Butterberry, have not yet dined," Roth observed, "yet here we are, preventing you from doing that very thing. Wadsworth! Wadsworth! Something substantial for Miss and Mr. Butterberry, eh? At once! You shall put it on my bill. And an apple and a bowl of water for their bird."

"No, we cannot," protested Winthrop, perplexed that the

offer should rankle him so, for it was made with a good
deal of thoughtfulness. "Father will have my head do I allow my sister to dine amongst a throng of Corinthians. I
ought not to have allowed her to enter this place at all."

"The private parlor then," suggested Stickley. "Fortescue, will you give up the private parlor for Miss Butterberry,
eh? Eat out here with the bird? Deal more interesting, I
should think."

"Will not eat at all," replied Fortescue. "Welcome to
m'parlor and m'dinner, Miss Butterberry. Only beg to be
allowed to coax that fellow upon m'shoulder."

"That will satisfy propriety, will it not, Mr. Butterberry?"
Roth asked hopefully. "And if you will consent to dine here
with us, then we may continue to watch this fine fellow
and inconvenience no one."

Winthrop nodded. He took his watch from his waistcoat
pocket and stared down at it. He wondered, not for the first
time, just how far behind them Mr. Butterberry might be.
Mayhap, if they lingered long enough, the old gentleman
would catch them up. Not that he had the least wish to be
present when Mr. Butterberry arrived, nor did he want the
old parson to know that it was he who had stolen Wickenshire's bird, but it seemed likely that, having done his best
to slow their progress by riding cross-country and traveling
in circles—sometimes covering the same ground three times
without Mary's noticing—it seemed likely that Mr. Butterberry must come up with them soon.

Even if Mr. Butterberry did not depart Wicken until
noon, Winthrop thought, he must be within an hour or two
of us by now. If we wait for a bit, and then proceed slowly
he will be able to catch us up just beyond this place, long
before we reach London. "Do you know, London is not so
very far, Mary," he murmured. "We will reach it soon
enough. And we must eat something somewhere. I do not

see why you should not dine comfortably in the private parlor while I have a bite to eat out here and allow these gentlemen to give Nightingale a bit of exercise."

"Are you certain, Peter?"

"Yes."

Lord Nightingale tilted his head and stared at the time-piece in Winthrop's hand with one amber eye. He danced back and forth upon Winthrop's shoulder and bobbed his head up and down. Then he clutched the cloth of Winthrop's coat tightly with both feet, leaned cautiously downward, snatched the watch chain in his beak, righted himself and soared to the top of one of the ceiling beams. There he set his prize upon the thick, wide oak and called down proudly, "Tempest fugit! Tempest fugit!"

"I will fugit your tempest if you do not bring that back down to me at once," called Winthrop. "That watch was given me by my mother, Nightingale, and I will have it back!"

They returned to Wicken Hall one and two at a time—the coachman, the grooms, the stable boys, the footmen, and even Jenkins, the Earl of Wickenshire's butler. Serendipity's heartache increased bit by bit as first one of them arrived and then the next and then the next, all of them without Delight on the saddle before them. "But where can she have gone that none of you should find her?" Sera whispered hoarsely, her lower lip quivering the merest bit. "She has come to some harm. She must have done or certainly one of you would have found her. Well, but there is still light remains in the sky. I shall ride out and search for her myself."

"You will do no such thing, my dear," declared the dowager Lady Wickenshire, placing a supportive arm about her daughter-in-law's shoulders. "Do you forget that you are with child? You cannot be riding off around the countryside as once you would have done. You have a responsibility to the babe within you as well as to your sister. No, do not cry, Sera," she whispered into the new countess's ear as she drew the younger woman close to her. "I shall drive out myself in my little gig. We did none of us think of it, but perhaps Delight has not gone off across the fields. Perhaps she has gone down the road to Wicken. She is a very bright child and she is in search of Lord Nightingale, after all. And since we believe him to have been stolen, not simply lost, perhaps she thinks to find the thief in the village."

"Do you think that could be so?" asked Sera. "Did any of you ride into the village?" she asked of the searchers.

"No, my lady. We have searched the meadows and the home woods and gone along the stream between Wicken Hall and Squire Peabody's lands," answered the elderly Jenkins, dismounting slowly and very gingerly. The ancient butler had not actually ridden a horse in a prodigious long time. "I shall be most obliged, madam, if you will allow me to accompany you in the gig," he added, addressing the dowager. "Two pairs of eyes are, after all, considerably better than one. Even if one of the pair are grown a bit old and nearsighted. Come, lads, stable the horses. Tripp, hitch up Dainty to the gig, quickly. We do not wish to lose the last of the light. James, light the lanterns at our gate and set the flambeaux blazing all the way along the drive. Our little Miss Delight will see Wicken Hall ablaze with light from miles away and she will find her own way home this night if we do not come upon her. I promise you that she will. She is the best of all children, smart as a whip and exceeding resourceful, our Miss Delight."

Such a very long speech from the normally reticent Jenkins, and one in which he should express such confidence in Delight, set Sera to hoping again. He was correct, of course. Delight was a most resourceful child. The shy, cringing little girl who had accompanied her to Willowsweep so very long ago, so that Sera might accept the position of singing teacher to his lordship's parrot, was the child that she had been remembering for most of the afternoon. But Delight had changed a good deal since then. Nicholas had given her an amazing confidence in herself. He had taught her to ride, to climb trees, to play pirate, and most of all to be honorable and courageous. Oh, most certainly Delight was safe and even now determined to find her way home.

It came as a great surprise to all those gathered in the front drive just then to hear horses trotting toward them, their hooves scattering gravel as they came. All heads turned in the direction of the sound.

"What on earth?" asked the dowager, peering at the vehicle as it slowed coming around the final turn and drew to a halt just beyond the little group of searchers. "Who can that be?"

Two footmen in blue-and-silver livery leaped from their perches at the rear of the vehicle. One of them hurried forward toward the crowd of people who stood staring at them, and the other rushed at once to the door of the coach, where he drew himself up and stood stock still beside it, much like a soldier at attention. A little postilion upon the inside wheeler and an enormous coachman, both of them in the same blue and silver livery as the footmen, gazed hopefully at the gathering of people in the drive.

"Does this be Wicken Hall?" asked the footman who approached. "The residence of the Earl of Wickenshire?"

"Indeed," nodded Sera. "My husband is not at home at present, I am sorry to say, but I am Lady Wickenshire. May I be of some assistance to you?"

"Aye, my lady," the footman replied, bowing quite regally before her. "We have something as belongs here, my lady." He spun about and all but ran back to the door of the coach, said a word to someone inside and then opened the coach door as the second footman lowered the steps. Stanley Blithe bounded from the vehicle, gave three quick yaps, danced in a circle, and then sat down upon his haunches, his tongue lolling, and waited.

"It is Stanley Blithe!" cried Sera in relief. "Oh, surely, Delight is with him! Do you recognize the coach?" she asked her mama-in-law anxiously. "I have never seen such a coach about Wicken before. Some kind stranger has found Delight and Stanley Blithe and brought them home to us! But why does Delight not come running out to greet us? Oh, madam, you do not think that Delight has been injured?"

The Dowager Countess of Wickenshire opened her mouth to reply and then closed it again without making one sound. She stared in silence as from the depths of the coach a hatless gentleman bent low to avoid the top of the door and stepped to the ground with Delight held carefully in his arms. He spoke a word to the dog and then strode forward, his long legs covering the ground quickly and efficiently, Stanley Blithe heeling most properly beside him. "These two reprobates belong here at Wicken Hall, I am told," the gentleman growled as he reached Serendipity and the dowager. "No, do not look so fearful, my lady. The child is not injured. Asleep, merely."

"You are the Duke of Sotherland," the dowager announced most abruptly, the cold blue of his eyes, the familiar features of his face which Lord Bradford's so resembled, not lost upon her.

"Indeed, madam," he responded. "I am Sotherland. And I am grown into an old man fond of peace and much accustomed to my own company. So you will understand precisely when I say, ladies, that I will be heartily obliged do you call upon your servants to rid me of this child and this animal at once."

SEVEN

Lord Nightingale discovered himself to be in a pleasant parrot paradise. He flapped his wings; he ruffled his feathers; he shrieked raucously and strutted about upon the ceiling beam, and everything he did and said was noted and applauded by the room full of splendid gentlemen below him. Every eye focused upon him; every hand offered him tidbits; and the magnificent gentleman who had treated him to the wonderful rides in the swinging sack even now stood on a table-top below him, attempting to bribe him with an entire dish of pine nuts. Never had Nightingale received such rousing and very welcome attention.

"Knollsmarmer!" he squawked, studying Winthrop's pine nuts. "Yo ho ho!" He stretched downward toward the dish Winthrop held in his fingertips and seized a nut from it. He transferred the nut from his beak to his foot and examined it closely. He nibbled at it, cried "Avast me hearties!" and gobbled it down. Then he picked up Winthrop's watch, sidled along the beam and dangled it from its chain above Viscount Roth's head to see what the viscount might offer him for the shiny thing.

"I have got it, I think, Butterberry," Roth called, and stepped up onto a chair, then onto a table-top. "Give over, you old pirate. You are making Butterberry extremely nervous the way you swing that watch around."

"He is dancing away from you, Roth, because you ain't got nothing to give him," Stickley laughed, waving an orange slice above his head. "Here, Nightingale. Here, you grand old thing. See what I have got for you."

"Goin' to smash the thin' upon the floor," the innkeeper told his daughter as the two of them watched the show from behind the long oak bar. "Jus' lookin' fer a place to drop it clear of all the gentlemen."

"No, he be merely encouragin' them, Pa. See the sparkle in his eyes. What a beautiful bird he be and delighted with himself, too. Likes all the attention, that one does. Proper proud o' himself for gainin' so much of it."

"Nightingale, give me that watch this instant," demanded Winthrop, stomping his foot on the tabletop and nearly tipping the table over. "I have had quite enough of this nonsense, you lunatic bird!"

"Tempest fugit!" cried the parrot gleefully, frisking back along the beam to where Winthrop yet wobbled, attempting to rebalance the table. He peered down at Winthrop through one large amber eye, wiggled his tail and bobbed his head. Then he tightened his grip on the watch chain, gave a flap of his wings and sailed off to land upon Fortescue's shoulder. He dropped the watch into Fortescue's outstretched hand, thoroughly squashing one of the grapes Fortescue had been offering him and then rubbed his red-and-white-striped cheek against Fortescue's collar. "Yo ho ho," Nightingale murmured quietly. Then he leaned down, seized upon an unsquashed grape, fluttered to a table-top and inspected his prize intently.

"Your timepiece ain't worth a pine nut, Butterberry," laughed one of the gentlemen, "but apparently it is worth a grape. By Jove, he is off again. Where is he going now?"

"Great heavens," chuckled another of the gentlemen, "he is into the rum punch again!"

"Stop him," called Winthrop, climbing down from the table. "Shoo him away from it. Rum punch cannot be good for parrots. He will make himself ill. I cannot have him ill."

" 'Course not," Fortescue agreed, and stepping forward, he attempted to remove Lord Nightingale from the punch bowl by the expedient method of picking the bird up in both hands. "Ow! Damnable bird bit me!" Fortescue exclaimed in surprise.

"He don't want you to pick him up, Fortescue. Much safer to part them this way," Stickley advised, picking up the punch bowl in both hands and moving it to the next table, sloshing the liquor and fruit concoction over himself in the process.

"Villain!" Lord Nightingale declared, glaring at Stickley. "Dastard! Rascal! Villain!"

This set Stickley and Fortescue into whoops.

"Oh, give it up, Nightingale," grinned Winthrop, tucking his timepiece safely back into his waistcoat pocket. "He is not a villain for saving you from another sip of that stuff. You cannot be drinking rum punch. It ain't good for you."

"Knollsmarmer," grumbled the parrot. And then he fluttered his wings, bobbed his head and walked pigeon-toed across the table-top until he could easily hop onto the back of a chair. There he sidled back and forth two steps one way, two steps the other and without the least warning began to sing, "Hey there mister, I saw-aw Hiramkissyer sister."

"Down in the shade of the o-o-old o-o-oak tree," joined in the gentlemen recognizing the old drinking song at once and gathering about the bird. "Hey there mister, it were not me what kissed her. I were jist awatchin', sir. It were noooot meeee!"

* * *

Miss Butterberry peeked around the corner into the public room and smiled to see them all so enthralled with song and bird both. A veritable wave of happiness surged into her heart to see Peter among them, his blue eyes laughing and the words of the naughty song slipping from between his lips just as easily as they slipped from between the lips of the other gentlemen. When Viscount Roth's hand fell companionably upon Winthrop's shoulder, Mary's smile widened considerably. This was precisely the sort of thing that her Peter required. He had been without gentlemen friends—without any friends—for so very long that he had grown most dismal. This would buck him up considerably.

With bouncing steps and rejoicing heart, Mary made her way back to the private parlor and set about eating the dinner that had been placed before her, confident that such companionship must lift the weight of grim despair from Peter's shoulders and in so doing, help him to realize how much his life in England was worth to him and how fine it could be if only this foolish notion that he had actually killed a man could be laid to rest.

Something can be done, Mary thought, cutting herself a bit of porkpie. I will go with him to India if I must, but I cannot think that India is the answer. He will not find peace in India any more than he finds peace in England. Mr. Quinn's men will not be forever chasing after him in India, but the spectre of himself as a murderer will never depart from him, no matter how far away he sails. And as long as Peter sees himself as a murderer, he will never truly find peace.

"I know you are not a murderer," she whispered, wiping her lips with the edge of the tablecloth and addressing the porkpie again. "What happened was an accident and nothing more. You were so shocked at your mama's dying that you did not so much as realize what you did. Not even

Papa would condemn you for what happened. Papa would pity you, in fact, and seek to console you, did he know the truth of it. Yes, and he would defend you from Quinn's men, too, if they insisted upon coming for you."

Miss Butterberry wondered at that moment just when her papa *would* know the truth of it. She thoroughly intended to write to him about the matter, but such action must wait until she could be certain that Peter would not be endangered by a letter. And I shall write to Lord Wickenshire as well, she told herself. As soon as I can. I will tell Nicky what has happened to Lord Nightingale. He will be heartbroken else, not knowing in which direction to look to recover his pet again.

And then it occurred to Mary that it was a most amazing thing for anyone to hire a gentleman to steal a parrot. "What on earth can someone want with Lord Nightingale?" she whispered as she took a caramel creme from the plate before her and popped it into her mouth. "And to pay such a monstrous sum for the doing of the deed! Whoever it is, the man must be mad. Yet, only look at what these fine gentlemen have paid us to be allowed merely to see the bird for a time," she added in a most bewildered voice, taking the several tankards Roth had carried in to her and spilling the gold guineas out upon the tablecloth.

With great deliberation, Mary began to count them, stacking them up before her. "Twenty-five, twenty-six," she murmured, shaking her head at the sheer folly of gentlemen and reveling in her own audacious luck. "Thirty-seven, thirty-eight, thirty-nine." Surely an angel of God is even now perched upon my shoulder, she thought as the guineas gleamed before her in the candlelight. "Fifty-two, fifty-three." Even Papa cannot stand against my decision to run away now, for has not everything gone splendidly ever since I mounted Lulubelle and turned her head toward London?

Indeed it has. All of heaven has joined up on my side, it seems, and that because I have ceased to be a gudgeon and have taken my own future into my own hands. Not only have I found Peter again, but I have been of help to him and given him solace and friendship. And he loves me just as he always did. Well, but I knew he would, for do I not love him just I always did? Love does not wither and die of its own accord, after all. Love must be trodden upon and trampled into the ground and then pulled up by its roots before it actually dies.

"One hundred and seven. One hundred and eight!" Mary's eyes grew round with wonder. "One hundred and eight guineas," she whispered. "Most certainly a passage to India and a special license can be purchased in the city of London for such a magnificent sum as one hundred and eight guineas! Oh, Mama, Papa, you need not fear for me at all, for I shall be a married woman soon, very soon and I shall be happy forever!"

There were eight of them in all, and the hostlers of the Queen's Ten Inn were nonplussed at the sight of them. "Where the devil be we goin' ta put all them 'orses?" one of the lads asked the stable master.

"Danged if I know, Jaimie. We have overflowed the stable six teams an six carriages ago. An' we 'ave overflowed the yard as well. I reckon as ye had best lead 'em 'round ta the back an' tie 'em ta the garden gate."

"Missus will rant an' rave does they nibble at 'er vege'bles," sighed another of hostlers sullenly. "Cannot ye tell 'em ta go on down the road to the Crown?"

"No, I cannot. Off ye go now, the lot of ye. Take the gen'lemen's horses an' lead 'em to the back an' look after 'em proper. Only think of the number of shillings ye've collected this day, lads," he added encouragingly. "More'n ye've seen in the past two months together, I wager. Think o' the shillings. That'll put the smiles upon yer faces."

Donovan tossed the lad who took his horse in tow a shilling. "Give her some water, lad, and just a taste of oats, eh? She's a way to go before we settle for the night."

"Aye," agreed Kelsey, nodding at another of the hostlers. "Do not be overfeeding my O'Rion. We are not done with traveling yet this evening."

The relief on the young hostlers' faces, though it escaped the notice of the eight men, brought a chuckle to the stable master. "Well, an' they 'ave been workin' 'ard," he mumbled, turning back into the stable. "They got a right fer ta be 'appy the gen'lemen ain't spendin' the night. Not hafta unsaddle them brutes, nor rub 'em down and see 'em settled neither. Tie 'em ta the garden gate, give 'em a taste o' oats an' a bit o' water an' be done wif 'em."

The gentlemen in the public room were cheerily occupied in watching Lord Nightingale roll a large colored bead about on the floor. The innkeeper's daughter had happily provided them the bead in return for a half-crown, and the gentlemen were now occupying themselves by wagering which way Lord Nightingale would turn the bead next and where he was actually bound with the thing. Stickley was certain that Nightingale would pick it up in his beak and fly with it back to the ceiling beam where he had first taken Butterberry's watch. Roth thought it more likely that the parrot would tire of the bead and desert it under a chair. Fortescue bet a pound that the bird would carry it to Butterberry in trade for a pine nut. Every gentleman, in fact, had an opinion as to what Lord Nightingale would do with the bead, and so each and every one of them was paying strict attention to Lord Nightingale and no attention at all to the door that opened into the yard. One of them would have noticed else, when the eight men entered, closed the door behind them and looked about.

"What the divil?" mumbled Donovan quietly. "William, do m'eyes deceive me or be that our lad there?"

"It does look like 'im," Kelsey replied. "But I kinnot see his face clear. Kin ye see 'im, Noble?"

"Aye," agreed the portly Noble. " 'Tis Lord Peter, kneelin' there upon the floor with a dish of nuts before 'im."

"Fancy that," whispered the smallest of Quinn's men, a person of merely average height and breadth called Dub. "An' when we ain't even lookin' for the lad!"

"Not even lookin' for him and him not so much as takin' note of us nither," muttered Quinn's head groom in amazement. "I expect the Fates be shining down upon us."

"What luck, eh?" offered the seventh of the men. "All we need do is collect the lad, have a glass and be off to home."

"Just so, Lucas," nodded the last of the group, a rather homely, red-haired fellow named Oliver. "Our luck has vastly improved. Go over, Donovan, an' give the lad a pat on the back. Ask will he have a drink with us, eh, afore we leave this place."

Donovan cocked an eyebrow at his compatriots, then shrugged and stepped into the midst of the gentlemen.

"I say, do watch where you tread," demanded Fortescue as Donovan's extremely large boots passed within stomping distance of Lord Nightingale. "You will distract the little fellow."

"Will I? What little fellow?" For the first time Donovan actually looked away from Winthrop and at the floor and discovered Lord Nightingale staring up at him. "Will ye look at that!" breathed Donovan in something approaching wonder. "What does it be then?"

Winthrop felt his heart plummet down into his left boot at the sound of that voice.

"It is a parrot," Fortescue replied. "Stand away if you will, my man. I have wagered an entire pound upon where this bird will take that bead of his in the end."

Winthrop's head came up. His hand jerked back from the bowl of pine nuts and inadvertently whacked against Roth's leg.

"Ow!" they exclaimed in unison. And then Winthrop was gaining his feet and looking about him for Nightingale's sack. Where the deuce had he left the thing?

"What is it?" Roth asked. "Butterberry? What's wrong?"

"The sack. I have got to put Nightingale back in his sack."

"But he is still pushing the bead about, Butterberry, and there are wagers placed."

"Boyo!" exclaimed Donovan, stepping carefully around the bird and directly between Roth and Winthrop. "At last we have catched ye up!"

"No, you have not," declared Winthrop, punching Donovan directly in the nose on the final word. Claret splattered everywhere. Donovan groaned and spun into Roth. Roth, simply on reflex, punched him in the stomach and sent him stumbling backward.

"Fortescue, save the bird!" shouted Stickley.

Fortescue dove for the parrot.

Lord Nightingale took wing on the instant.

The enormous Donovan slipped on the bead, danced wildly about the floor and crashed down atop Lord Fortescue with an oomph! and a groan.

"Villain! Villain!" squawked Nightingale, soaring low over the innkeeper's head just as Wadsworth turned to hand two tankards of ale across the bar. Wadsworth threw up his hands and ducked. The ale splashed wildly over Lucas and Oliver.

"Bite! Bite!" shrieked Nightingale, soaring back the other way. "Villain! Bite!"

Dub caught his hat just as one green-fringed wing grazed it. He swatted at the bird with the hat to drive it off.

"Hit a poor defenseless budgie will you?" queried Lord Mitchum and pummeled Dub with his walking stick.

Dub's hat hit the floor. His fist shot out, catching Mitchum beneath the jaw. Mitchum stumbled into Kelsey and Noble, who shoved him toward the center of the room where Donovan had risen and was busily ducking blows from Roth.

"Yo ho ho!" cried Nightingale and dove straight at Kelsey and Noble, sending them diving under the nearest table.

"I say," declared Stickley, doffing his jacket, "I do believe I will have a bit of this myself."

In the end, they all waded into the fight, Quinn's men and the Corinthians alike. Chairs flew; tables tumbled; bone whacked against bone and tankards thunked against skulls. And amidst the noise and the spreading claret, Winthrop struggled with the hope that somehow he could break free, find the sack, get the bird into it and fetch Mary out of the place. My gawd, he thought, ducking a blow from Lucas and then delivering the man a strong right uppercut, I cannot leave Mary behind in such a hubbub as this, not even if her father is within five minutes of us.

"Oof!" Winthrop grunted as an elbow connected with his midsection and sent him plummeting to the floor.

Three pairs of boots stomped on him before a hand reached down and tugged him to his feet again.

"Knollsmarmer!" Lord Nightingale shrieked from the ceiling beam. "Yo ho ho! Knollsmarmer!" as a strong, calloused hand held tight to Winthrop's lapel and the oddest pair of absolutely forest green eyes inspected Winthrop's face calmly. "You are Bradford's brother," said Wickenshire. "You remember me, no doubt. You did some work for me at Willowsweep a while back, and more recently you stole my parrot." And then Lord Nightingale came flapping wildly over the combatants to land with great precision upon one of Wickenshire's broad shoulders. "Mornin' Nicky!" Nightingale cried cheerily, pecking at the earl's dark curls. "Mornin' Nicky!"

"Wickenshire! M-Miss Butterberry," Winthrop managed, attempting to get his breath. "She is in the private parlor. You must get her out of here. Her father will be coming for her soon."

"Her father has come for her now," Wickenshire responded. "And he has every intention of blacking both your eyes as soon as these gentlemen have finished with you. And then, my good fellow, what is left of you will belong to me."

"Villain! Bite!" Lord Nightingale exclaimed, flapping again into the air just as a china platter came soaring across the room, knocking Wickenshire's hat from his head.

"Who the devil threw that?" Wickenshire roared, releasing Winthrop and spinning around to discover one of Quinn's men rushing straight at him. He seized the fellow, punched him rapidly twice in the stomach, turned him about and sent him crashing against the bar.

"Oh, I say," called Roth, picking himself up from off the body-littered floor. "Excellent jabs! Who's your friend, Butterberry?"

"Butterberry," Wickenshire said, turning back to Winthrop. "You told these men that you are Mary's brother as well, then."

Winthrop nodded and then crumpled to the floor as a chair leg descended with some violence upon his head.

"What the devil?" bellowed Wickenshire, reaching out and seizing the chair leg wielder by the shirt collar, relieving him of his weapon with one hand and tossing him half-way across the room with the other.

"Keelhaul 'em!" cried Nightingale encouragingly from the ceiling beam as an angry Wickenshire waded into the fray. "Yo ho ho! Mornin' Nicky! Avast me hearties!"

Tears streaked Miss Butterberry's face as she peered around the corner into the public room. Her Peter stretched his length upon the floor and all around him men were hitting and kicking and stomping on each other. Her fingers tightened around the handle of the coal bucket she carried as she studied the situation. She told herself that she could be as courageous as was necessary to go to her Peter's rescue. Then, taking a deep breath, Mary launched herself into the public room. "I *will* go to him," she cried, swinging the coal bucket mightily from side to side, connecting with knees and thighs and various other parts of male anatomies. "I will not let you kill him!"

Wickenshire saw her enter, but he was occupied with Lucas and Oliver and not like to be of much help until he rid himself of them. So, eschewing the values of the earl that he should have been, he allowed himself to act like the farmer he truly was and instead of fighting the men with his fists, he simply clunked their heads together and allowed the fellows to fall to the floor. He was beside Mary and relieving her of the coal bucket in a moment.

"Nicky?"

"Yes. Let me take you outside, Mary. Your papa is waiting for you in my curricle."

"No. I am going nowhere until Peter is safe from these barbarians."

"Fine," declared Wickenshire, grabbing Winthrop by the coat collar and Mary by the arm. "We will all go outside.

Nightingale, come!" And steering Mary through the tumult, dragging Winthrop along the floor behind him, Wickenshire made his way to the front door and out into the yard.

"Knollsmarmer!" Nightingale called, setting sail from the ceiling beam and flying out the door behind them. "Yo ho ho Knollsmarmer!"

"What the deuce is going on in there?" bellowed the Reverend Mr. Butterberry, leaping from the curricle and hurrying to take his wayward daughter from Wickenshire. "Mary, my dear, are you all right? What has that beast done to you? Let him up, Wickenshire, and I will lay him out flat again in the wiggle of a cat's whisker."

"No, no, remember he is your son," muttered Wickenshire as quietly as he could.

"What?"

"Your son, Butterberry. Told 'em in there that he and Mary were brother and sister just as he did at the Red Cock. Do not let on that they are not brother and sister. Not now."

"Well, I'll be deuced!"

"Deuced!" echoed Nightingale, happily clinging to Wickenshire's shoulder. "Be deuced! Yo ho ho!"

"By Jove, you did come when I said, Nightingale," Wickenshire observed, amazed. "This is the second time you have done it. I am beginning to think—no—merely relieved to see me, eh? See can you bring Lord Peter 'round, Butterberry. Mary, help your papa. I am going back inside to fetch my hat."

"N-no," groaned Winthrop, bringing Wickenshire to a halt. "Donovan. Kelsey."

"What?" asked Mr. Butterberry, glaring down at the villain who had ruined his daughter. "What does the devil say?"

"Quinn's men," gasped Winthrop. "Must get away."

"Oh, Nicky, they are Quinn's men in there," cried Miss

behind her. Keep the Duke of Sotherland, of all
s! Next she will discover something pleasant about a
ous bear and wish to keep one of those about the house
ell. "Jenkins? What on earth?" she asked, nearly col-
g with the butler as he exited the chamber across from
ight's.

Her ladyship has invited his grace to spend the night,
lady," offered the butler wearily, "and this is the only
mber not already allotted to one of the wedding guests."

"Oh, Jenkins, no. I thought the gentleman wished to
erely present Delight to us and travel on. I thought he
d a specific destination to reach this evening."

"I expect his grace's plans have altered, my lady, for he
as accepted my lady's offer."

Serendipity could not believe it. What had come over her
other-in-law? Did she not realize that the Duke of Soth-
rland had likely driven all the way into Kent with the ex-
ess purpose of stopping Eugenia's and Edward's
arriage? Of course, the gentleman *had* rescued Delight
d Stanley Blithe and brought them safely home, but that
not mean that the old curmudgeon had had any change
heart in regard to his son's matrimonial intentions. Lord
dford had not been at all reserved in telling them what
expected his father's reaction would be to his forthcom-
marriage, though he had thought that the man would
come bellowing down upon them until well after the
mony was over and done with. In fact, the portrait of
ather that Edward had painted for them had been most
lling. With considerable perturbation, Sera hurried
the staircase to the first floor and into the small draw-
oom where a fire blazed upon the hearth and the tea
ad just made an appearance.

h, Sera, my dear, there you are. Will you pour out for

Butterberry. "We must get Peter to a safe place. Somewhere
they will not think to look for him."

"Who the deuce are Quinn's men?" asked Wickenshire.

"They are—they are—they wish to kill Peter, Nicky!"

"Nothing odd in that," drawled Wickenshire, rubbing
gently at Nightingale's breast. "I wish to kill him as well,
right after your papa has blacked out both his daylights."

EIGHT

"You are never to do such a thing again," Sera murmured, tucking a sleepy Delight into bed. "You are much too small to be tramping about all over the countryside with no one but Stanley Blithe to look after you, dearest."

"We went to look for Lord Nightingale," the child replied sleepily, rubbing at her eyes.

"Yes, I know you did. And it was very brave of you, too, but you must never go off again without a grown-up beside you."

"I gived Stanley Blithe one of Lord Nightingale's feathers to sniff, jus' like Papa was used to give Rumbles a cloth, an' Stanley Blithe runned off right away af'er Lord Nightingale."

"He did? Well, then I am quite certain that Stanley Blithe tried his very best to find Lord Nightingale."

"But we didn't not find him, Sera."

"No, but Nicky will find him. I promise you that he will. He loves Lord Nightingale quite as much as you do, you know, and he would be very sad should Lord Nightingale not come back to us. It is just that Nicky must help to find Miss Butterberry first."

"Yaaarrrrr," yawned Stanley Blithe, curling up into a large furry ball upon the counterpane and resting his shaggy head on the tiny lump that was Delight's knee.

"Promise me, Delight, that you will never, dering off by yourself again."

"I promise," sighed the child, yawning might tinuing to rub at one eye with one fist. "Can me a Blithe keep him, Sera?"

"Keep him?" Serendipity leaned down and k sister's wine-stained cheek. "Keep whom, dearest

"Our duke."

Serendipity could not believe her ears. "That old gentleman? Delight! Why on earth would you keep him?"

"Because me an' Stanley Blithe founded him an' w him. He is verimost funny."

"Funny? The Duke of Sotherland?"

"Uh-huh. I like how he talks an' how he pertends to be a ol' curmudglian. An' he has the verimost bushiest eyebrows. He can make them wiggle like caterpiggles, Sera. Not even Nicky can do that. Can he?"

"No, I do not think so," grinned Sera. "But we wil Nicholas to attempt it when he returns, shall we? I am tain he will try his very best to do the thing if we r it of him. And I, for one, should like to see him atte wiggle his eyebrows like caterpiggles. But as for you darling, I am much afraid that you cannot just keep tleman you have found as you would a puppy or a Gentlemen do not belong to anyone but themselve

"We founded Nicky, an' now he belongs to yo an' Lady Wickenshire an' Sweetpea an' Stanle an'—"

"Go to sleep, Delight," Serendipity interr drowsy recital of names. "We will discuss keepi men some other time. Sweet dreams, my sweet

Truly, she is the most remarkable child, thought as she departed the chamber and clos us, darling? His grace has consented to spend a few days at Wicken Hall," the dowager announced pleasantly.

"A few days?" Serendipity asked, attempting not to sound perfectly astounded as she took a seat beside the dowager upon the flowered silk sopha and began to dispense the tea.

"It was his grace's intention to remain with Lord Bradford at Squire Peabody's," explained the dowager quietly.

"My son neglected to inform me that his lease on the property had expired and that he had departed the place," muttered the duke. "But that does not make my comfort at all your responsibility, ladies," he added with a frown. "My men and I can just as easily travel into Wicken and—"

"No, you certainly will not stay at an inn when we have any number of guest rooms standing empty," interrupted the dowager Lady Wickenshire.

"Of course you will remain with us—for as long as you require, your Grace," Serendipity said, gazing at her mother-in-law with something approaching wonder. Any number of guest rooms standing empty? Yes, but all of them awaiting wedding guests to arrive at any moment! "It is little enough to do for the gentleman who rescued my sister, and brought her safely home to us," Sera managed as pleasantly as possible. Good heavens, she thought, staring down into her tea, that we should invite Edward's father, the Devil Incarnate, to spend time with us. The things we do to appear civilized!

The Earl of Wickenshire was not feeling the least bit civilized as he deposited Winthrop, with an enormous splash, into the watering trough at the foot of the inn's porch.

"Wh-what the—?" spluttered Winthrop, fighting his way to an upright position. "Who? Where?" And just as he came to the conclusion that he had somehow fallen into a lake, another body came splashing down on top of him and began to flail wildly about. "What the devil is going on?" Winthrop shouted, shoving the semi-conscious man away from him and attempting to stand.

"You are reviving," announced Wickenshire, standing nonchalantly with one boot planted on the edge of the trough, one arm resting upon his knee and Lord Nightingale clinging possessively to his shoulder. "That is to say, I hope you are reviving, because so far this evening I have not been able to get a bit of sensical conversation out of you. And that fellow there is reviving as well. Either reviving or drowning, I cannot quite tell. Can you, Winthrop?"

Winthrop climbed dripping from the trough and stared back into it. "Donovan," he whispered hoarsely. "That is one of the men whom I particularly wish to avoid, Wickenshire. I have got to get away from here at once."

"Absolutely not. You are going nowhere at the moment," Wickenshire informed him. "You are staying right here until this fellow regains his senses. He is one of those you call Quinn's men, is he not? Mary certainly seems to think so."

"Yes, but—"

"But nothing," Wickenshire interrupted with decided authority. "We will wait right here, you and I, until this fellow can speak sanely, Winthrop. It is Winthrop I must still call you, eh, until you decide to change your name again?"

"I—I—"

"You need not explain as yet. Suffice to say that I am aware, at this point, that you are not the itinerant laborer you wished me to believe you to be when you came looking for work at Willowsweep. I know you are not the son of a carpenter from Holsbrook, Winthrop. You are the son of the Duke of Sotherland and, though you may not be aware of it, your brother has been searching everywhere for you for the past two years. His heart is set upon finding you and I agreed to help him do it, if I could. Practically my entire family, in fact, has agreed to help Bradford find you. Your brother is a very pleasant sort of a fellow. Nightingale is fond of him."

"Edward? You have *met* Edward?"

"Just so. He intends to marry my cousin, Eugenia. And I must say, Winthrop, that I am not at all amused by the thought of the brother of a murderer marrying into my family. You are a murderer, are you not? I have not heard incorrectly?"

"How? Who?"

"Mary stuttered out that particular word a few moments ago while she was attempting to convince her father and I not to part your hair with a carving knife on the spot. Wanted us to hide you away somewhere—from Quinn's men, she said. Told us quite a tale, Mary did. Of course, she did not call you a murderer herself. Not by any means. But she did say that a number of men, including yourself, believed it to be so."

"Uh, huh, uhspt!" sputtered Donovan, clinging to the sides of the trough and shaking his head, splattering droplets of water in all directions.

"What is your name, fellow?" asked Wickenshire.

"Uh? Wha?"

The earl smiled a sad smile and shoved Donovan back down into the water. "Not sufficiently revived as yet," he sighed.

Winthrop, shivering in the night air, watched in silence as Donovan popped to the surface once more.

"Now tell me your name," said Wickenshire.

"D-Donovan. P-Patrick Donovan."

"And you work for a gentleman named—?"

"Quinn. Mr. Tobias Q-Quinn."

"No, do not climb out of there as yet, Mr. Donovan. Remain where you are for a moment more if you please. Do you know this particular gentleman dripping here before us?"

"By gawd, Lord Peter!" exclaimed Donovan. "Why the devil did you punch me in the nose, laddie? I was only wishing to have a word with you. What is it that's wrong with ye? Have you not recovered your senses yet? You have been acting devilish queer for the longest time, let me tell you."

"Now you may climb out, Mr. Donovan," murmured Wickenshire. "And if I were you—or you, Winthrop—I should sit down there on that porch and empty the water out of my boots. It cannot be at all comfortable to have one's toes squishing about inside one's boots all night long, squirting water up around one's ankles. Shouldn't like it myself."

The two men warily seated themselves side by side and with Wickenshire's help, doffed their boots, emptied streams of water from them, and returned them to their proper place.

"Why the deuce do you disappear every time one of us finds ye at last?" asked Donovan petulantly as he stood and stamped his right foot into a better fit inside his boot.

"Possibly because I do not look forward with any great enthusiasm to being hanged," Winthrop replied sardonically.

"Hanged?" cried Donovan, staring down at him. "Hanged? Has that temper of yours got you into such trouble as that, then, that someone wishes to see ye hanged, boyo?"

"*You* wish to see me hanged," Winthrop pointed out quietly. "Do not be coy about it, Donovan. You wish to see me hanged for killing Quinn and there is no one can fault you for it, not even me. But I expect you must wait for a bit of time now, until the Reverend Mr. Butterberry wreaks vengeance upon me for ruining his daughter first and then Wickenshire, here, takes his pound of flesh in retribution for my stealing his confounded parrot."

Patrick Donovan stared down at the gentleman slumped dejectedly upon the porch planking in wide-eyed disbelief. "Mr. Quinn? Our Mr. Quinn? By gawd, when did ye kill Mr. Quinn, lad?" he asked in horror.

"It is a cat, your grace," replied the valet quietly.

"I can see it is a cat, Lindsey. What I wish to know is, what is a cat doing upon my bed? That is my bed, is it not? It is standing in my bedchamber and so I assume it to be my bed. However, if I am somehow mistaken—"

"You are not mistaken, your grace. It is indeed your bed."

"Then shoo the danged cat off of it, Lindsey, and chase the thing out into the corridor. I cannot abide cats. They are sneaky, rascally things made to do nothing but eat and sleep and deposit their fur about as though each thin wisp of it were a blessing. Get it out!"

Lindsey glared at the black-and-white cat, barely out of kittenhood, as it stretched across the counterpane. Sweetpea glared back at him through clear green eyes.

"Where did it come from, Lindsey? You did not pick it up somewhere along the road?"

"No, your grace!" gasped the valet. "Never!"

"Yes, well, I would not know if you had, riding back there in the second coach with not a thing to worry your head over. You might pause and steal some peasant's chicken, roast the thing and eat it, and I should notice only that you had dropped a bit farther behind than usual. Surely it is not hard to rid the bed of a cat. Pick it up and toss it into the corridor."

"Yes, your grace." Lindsey stepped forward, grasped the cat around the middle with both hands and was promptly clawed for his audacity. "Ouch! Ow! Stop that!"

"Lives here, no doubt," observed the duke. "Hold on to it, Lindsey. You are bigger than it is. Do not let the thing escape you. Watch it. Watch it. Here, I will go so far as to open the door for you. Yes, good, now toss it into the corridor."

Lindsey did exactly that and then slammed the door closed. "There," he sighed, marching over to turn down his grace's bed and pass the warming pan between his grace's sheets.

"That is quite good enough, Lindsey," muttered the duke impatiently. "It is not January. The sheets cannot be so cold as all that. Help me up into the thing and then begone. I have never been so weary as I am this night." Scowling, Sotherland took hold of the arm Lindsey offered and stepped up the three steps into the feather bed.

With careful hands, Lindsey pulled the covers up over the gentleman, bowed respectfully and, extinguishing the lamp upon the bedside table, escaped into the corridor to join the cat, who had not gone off down the corridor but taken up residence upon the opposite threshold.

"I am truly sorry, cat," Lindsey whispered. "I expect that bed is the bed on which you are accustomed to spend the night, but his grace has laid claim to it and there is no opposing him. I have been in his employ for five entire years. That is four years longer than any other valet has managed to remain, and I have yet to see anyone successfully oppose him."

"Row," commented Sweetpea with suitable disdain. "Rowrrrrowmsphft!" Whereupon she raised a most mag-

nificent black tail with a sultry white tip into the air and
paraded off down the corridor with great ceremony.
"Mrrrrspflgrsts!" she added glaring back over one sleek,
black shoulder.

"Yes, I suppose he is," Lindsey replied with a secret
smile. "I have heard him called other things just as vile,
mind you, but nothing with quite as much style in the saying
of it."

The profusion and profundity of emotions that rushed
into Winthrop's heart and mind and soul overwhelmed him
completely. For the longest time he sat like a man carved
from granite, his elbows on his knees, his head buried in
his hands. After a while, his shoulders trembled. His eyes
blurred with tears and his cheeks grew wet. His breath came
in deep, heaving gasps and then, for a moment, it did not
come at all. And in that precise moment when it did not
come, in that veritable millisecond of a moment that seemed
to him like years upon years of his lifetime passing away,
an enormous chasm deep inside him—formed when his
heart had split asunder on that most dreadful of days four
years earlier—began to alter. That foul, stinking chasm that
had filled so awfully, so relentlessly, with hatred and fear
and loathing for himself—for what he had done and what
he had discovered himself forced to do—burst open like a
festering boil and spurted forth its vile wretchedness;
spurted it out into the open where truth shone down upon
it, curdling it, shrinking it, drying it into bits and pieces of
refuse and debris. And then pure, unadulterated joy rained
down into that great ravine and rushed, churning and bubbling and splashing through it, scrubbing it clean and clear,
flushing the foulness, the vileness far from him. Grace and
gratitude blossomed and grew in the newly cleared space;

hope sent up its fresh shoots; and the oft-prayed-for but much-despaired miracle, a miracle of the most magnificent proportions, came clear and bright and shining into his mind and soul and sealed the tattered halves of Winthrop's heart together with a sweetness of salvation long denied to him.

"You are certain that I did not—I mean—Quinn is not dead, Donovan? You are not hoaxing me in order to—to—get me to accompany you to the hangman?" Winthrop managed to ask at last in a smothered voice, hope filling him completely, providing him the strength to know, to be certain, to believe in the miracle without doubt. "But it was you said Quinn was dead. I heard you call out that day. Yes, and Kelsey called it out as well."

"Oh, laddie," Donovan replied, only then realizing what had happened. "Oh, my boyo, and you thought—but it is not true, my lad. He was stunned, merely, our Mr. Quinn. And all this time you have been thinking that—oh, my lad! No wonder you did take your mama's name for your own given one. You were hoping to hide yourself away. And we chasing after you whenever we chanced to find a sign of you. No wonder you were gone every time one of us rode out to speak with you where last someone had seen your face. Lord Peter," whispered Donovan, his arm going around the young gentleman's trembling shoulders. "Peter, m'lad, all any of us were wishing to do was to say for Mr. Quinn how sorry he was about your mama and how sorry we all were as well. All any of us were wishing to do was to beg you to come home, boyo, to come home again with us and to allow us to help you through your grief and your anger as best we knew how."

"So, you are not a murderer after all," Wickenshire said quietly, seating himself upon the planking at Lord Peter's other side. "Mary had the right of it all along. I rather thought she had. I have known Mary from the day she was born, and she has always been the most opinionated, determined, audacious person; but she has seldom been wrong about the people she loves. She told her papa and I only that you thought you were a murderer, but she would not commit to that notion herself."

"I am not a murderer," Lord Peter whispered hoarsely. "By the grace of God and the luck of an Irishman called Quinn, I am not. And I shall never be," he added, lifting his head to stare out across the inn yard to where Mary waited in the curricle with her papa's arm around her. "I shall never be. I swear on my mama's grave that I will never raise my hand against another man in anger as long as I live. I vow it."

"I will hack off the boy's ears with my short sword," Sotherland muttered, allowing the draperies to fall back over the sitting room window. Unable to sleep, he had abandoned his bed, paced the bedchamber for an hour, wandered into the sitting room and stood gazing out into the darkness for a good half-hour. Now he paced across the sitting room and went to sit in the wingchair before the hearth. The cheery fire that had met him upon his first entrance into the chamber had subsided into nothing more than blinking ashes; but wrapped in his robe, his wool slippers on his feet, the duke missed the warmth of the earlier blaze not at all. The truth was, he was seldom cold, not even in the depths of winter.

"Because my blood is always boiling," he muttered, "that's why." He rested his head against the chairback and thought of a time when he had been warm because his blood had seethed with passion, but those days were long spent. Of late, it was anger and discontent that set his blood aboil. Of late, it was Edward who set it aboil from morn till night.

"Audacious puppy," grumbled the duke. "Writes me that he intends to take a bride and then commands me not to show my face at the wedding! Commands me! Me! Brat! Given him too much power too soon is what I have done. Given him cause to think that he is in charge. Well, he is not the Duke of Sotherland yet, think what he may, and I will point that out to him in no uncertain terms when I get my hands on him. He will not have the least doubt who is the duke in this family then, by Jove! No, and that gel will learn the truth of it as well.

"Boy has always been a nodcock," Sotherland fumed, rising to pour himself a glass of brandy and then making his way back to the chair and settling into it again. "But this time he has run completely mad. Marry *Miss* Eugenia Chastain! Marry some plain, pudding-faced *miss* with not so much as an honorable before her name. Why he might choose Lady Daphne Delacorte or Lady Jane Roew or Edgar's daughter Cynthia, or Cecile, or whatever it was they named that wench. Yes, he might have chosen any of them or any other titled gel on the marriage mart for that matter—chosen them and had them, too, with a nod of his head and a wink of his eye. Damnation!" he thundered abruptly. "I cannot think what has gotten into that wretched boy!"

The duke was speaking so loudly by the end of his tirade that he barely heard the knock at his sitting room door. He thought, in fact, that he must have been imagining it until it came again. He set his brandy aside, rose from the chair and made his way across the flowered carpet, wondering with each step who would have the audacity to disturb him at such an hour of the night. Certainly not Lindsey or any other of his own servants. With a degree of impatience he whipped the door open and then he stared, bewildered, at the frowning little face and worried blue eyes that gazed up at him.

"Are you all right?" asked Delight. "We hearded some-one yellin' an' we got frighted for you."

"You did?" managed Sotherland, comprehending and yet not quite comprehending that a barefooted little girl in a long white flannel gown and an enormous, spotted, shaggy dog of questionable lineage had come to provide him aid. "Well, well, that is very kind of you, but I am perfectly fine."

"Are you?"

"Yes, child, yes. I cannot sleep is all and so I was talking to myself. I am sorry to have disturbed you."

"When me an' Stanley Blithe is frighted an' cannot sleep, Nicky comes an' stays with us an' tells us a story," Delight announced, walking past Sotherland into his chambers, Stanley Blithe padding softly behind her.

"Yes, well, but I am not frightened."

"Yes, you are," Delight contradicted him soberly. "I can tell. You have gots creases all over your face because you are so very frighted, but there is nothing to be frighted about. It is only because you are in a new place."

Had he been asked, Sotherland could not have explained how it had come to be. Pixilated, he thought. Somehow, I have become pixilated. It is the rarified air of Kent, perhaps.

Rarified air of Kent or not, the Duke of Sotherland, as if in the midst of dreams, had been brought to add coals to his sitting room fire, to settle into the wingchair and take a golden-haired child in a voluminous flannel nightgown and ruffled cap upon his lap. He had been brought so far as to wrap a coverlet and his arms around her. And he had listened to her whisper of deep, dark woods and witches and wizards and dragons and a veritable army of faeries fluttering to rescue a princess from an evil spell. He had listened until Delight had fallen fast asleep with her head resting against his shoulder and her fingers curling against the lapel of his robe. With one long, tentative finger, he brushed a golden curl from her wine-stained cheek.

"Well," he whispered to the dog who lay stretched on the carpeting before them, "what am I to do now, Mr. Blithe?"

NINE

The Reverend Mr. Butterberry strolled through the public room, down the corridor and turned in through the door to the private parlor. There, just as Mary had said it would be, stood the table with the remains of her dinner upon it, and beside her place, several tankards, all of them filled to the top with golden guineas. Mr. Butterberry stared at them; he walked to the table and looked directly down into them; he touched one of the guineas with the very tip of his right index finger. "By Jove," he murmured. "And I thought Mary to be telling a farradiddle. But only look at them. By Jove!"

"Those particular guineas belong to the Reverend Mr. Butterberry," drawled a voice from the threshold. "I sincerely hope that you do not think to walk off with them, sir."

Mr. Butterberry looked up to see a disheveled young gentleman with dark brown hair and wide brown eyes—one of the eyes even now swelling closed—assessing him with a high degree of arrogance and a most disconcerting nonchalance, a tight smile creasing his handsome face.

"I have set myself to keep an eye on those guineas for Mr. and Miss Butterberry now that the brawl has ended. I expect they will return to claim them as soon as the young Mr. Butterberry has adequately regained his composure."

"How kind of you," Mr. Butterberry replied.

"Yes, is it not?"

"I am the Reverend Mr. Butterberry, you know."

"No, are you?"

"Indeed. The Reverend Mr. Butterberry from Wicken."

"You can prove that, I expect," drawled Roth.

"Well, of course I can prove who I am. I have any number of papers—" began Mr. Butterberry, fishing about in his pockets and discovering only then that he had been so very upset over his daughter's flight that he had brought nothing at all with him from the rectory, not even his purse.

If I had not already been wearing them when I learned the news, he thought amazedly, I expect I should not have brought my breeches with me either. "Apparently," he said to the gentleman, "I have not got any of my papers with me at the moment. No, wait," he added, abruptly remembering. He took his hat from his head, ignoring the amused cock of Roth's eyebrow, and pulled from the hatband a small twist of paper. "There is this," he said, with a rather sorrowful smile. "It is not a particularly praiseworthy piece of paper, but I expect it will serve to identify me since no one not myself would have cause to carry the thing about."

Roth accepted the twist, unscrewed it and read the printing upon it. Then he gave a sad shake of his head. "One pound, ten, sir, for Irish linen?"

"Yes, well, my second daughter, Clara, is to be married, you see, and there are things a girl must have—but you are not concerned with that, are you? My name, however, appears upon that dun, does it not?"

"Indeed, and the name of the establishment from which the linen was purchased in Wicken. I am pleased to make your acquaintance, Reverend Butterberry," Roth added, offering his hand. "I am Roth. I hope your son has recovered from the hit with that chair leg, sir. He has a punishing right cross, your son. Cannot think what caused him to start such a wild brawl. He just stood up and landed some fellow a remarkable facer. Wherever did a clergyman's son learn to box?"

Angry though he was with Winthrop, Mr. Butterberry was also grateful to him for the lie that had made Winthrop his son and thereby done much to protect Mary's reputation. He dare not deny that false relationship now. And besides, it was the one true sorrow of the Reverend Mr. Butterberry's life that the Good Lord had not seen fit to give him a son. He had dreamed long and often of having one boy among the flock of daughters who ruled his heart. He had dreamed of what his son would be like. And he had painted a most amazing portrait of the boy in his mind—what he would know and how he would act and how very brave and noble he would grow up to be.

"Taught the lad myself," replied Mr. Butterberry proudly, applying the portrait without the least hesitation to the man who was honor-bound by this adventure to become his son-in-law. "I am no stranger to The Fancy, you know. Not at all. When I was a much younger man, I came up to the mark once or twice myself."

"You, sir? A clergyman?"

"Well, I was not always a clergyman. I was a third son, to be sure, and must choose between the army and the church at last, but there was a time in my life when I was at university, that I was most enthralled with The Fancy. Why, once, my lord, I was so privileged as to enter the ring with Malcolm Madison."

"Malcolm Madison? You, sir? You actually went a round with The Mad Malcolm?"

"Nineteen rounds," declared the Reverend Mr. Butterberry with a proud lift of his chin and a very distinct sparkle in his eyes. "Nineteen rounds it was before I could not come up to the mark. Ah, now there was a fighter, let me tell you. The Mad Malcolm—as fine a form and style as ever you will see. A dancer of exceptional grace, he was, on that particular dance floor which he ruled."

Roth could not help but be impressed. Mr. Butterberry's face absolutely shone with the pride and, therefore, the truth of his declaration. "Well, by Jupiter, sir, I wish you will let me shake your hand again," Roth said. "My father was accustomed to speak highly of The Mad Malcolm at all times. Claimed any man who could spend more than three rounds in the ring with that fellow must be blessed by God. Oh, excuse me, sir. I did not mean—"

Mr. Butterberry shook Roth's hand again, heartily, and laughed. "No, no. No need for any apology. Perhaps your father was correct. For it did turn out that I was blessed by God, did it not? And called into His service as well."

"We could have used you in here, sir, an hour or so ago. What a brawl we had! And it was your son started the thing, too. Oh, I told you that, did I not? But I cannot think where Mr. Butterberry has got to. Some gentleman came in and took him and Miss Butterberry away right in the midst of the fun. Not that Miss Butterberry ought to have been there. We sent her into the private parlor, sir, so as to provide her properly with dinner, but she did come back in the midst of the uproar and some very large gentleman—"

"That will have been Wickenshire," Mr. Butterberry interrupted. "Fine fellow, Lord Wickenshire. Strong as an ox and not loath to throw a punch here and a punch there as he finds it necessary. Not so adept as my boy, of course. No style. Not schooled in the art. Not at all brought up to it. Well, I had best go see how my son does, eh?"

Roth, with great good will, unknotted his neckcloth, dumped the guineas from the tankards into it and wrapped them safely up. "Do not forget these guineas, Reverend

We'd Like to Invite You to Subscribe to Zebra's Regency Romance Book Club and Give You a Gift of 4 Free Books as Your Introduction! (Worth $19.96!)

If you're a Regency lover, imagine the joy of getting 4 FREE Zebra Regency Romances and then the chance to have these lovely stories delivered to your home each month at the lowest price available! Well, that's our offer to you and here's how you benefit by becoming a Regency Romance subscriber:

- **4 FREE** Introductory Regency Romances are delivered to your doorstep

- 4 BRAND NEW Regencies are then delivered each month (usually before they're available in bookstores)

- Subscribers save almost $4.00 every month

- Home delivery is always **FREE**

- You also receive a **FREE** monthly newsletter, which features author profiles, discounts, subscriber benefits, book previews and more

- No risks or obligations...in other words, you can cancel whenever you wish with no questions asked

Join the thousands of readers who enjoy the savings and convenience offered to Regency Romance subscribers. After your initial introductory shipment, you receive 4 brand-new Zebra Regency Romances each month to examine for 10 days. Then, if you decide to keep the books, you'll pay the preferred subscriber's price of just $4.00 per title. That's only $16.00 for all 4 books and there's never an extra charge for shipping and handling.

It's a no-lose proposition, so return the FREE BOOK CERTIFICATE today!

Say Yes to 4 Free Books!
Complete and return the order card to receive this $19.96 value, ABSOLUTELY FREE!

If the certificate is missing below, write to:
Zebra Home Subscription Service, Inc.,
P.O. Box 5214, Clifton, New Jersey 07015-5214
or call TOLL-FREE 1-888-345-BOOK
Visit our website at www.kensingtonbooks.com.

FREE BOOK CERTIFICATE

YES! Please rush me 4 Zebra Regency Romances without cost or obligation. I understand that each month thereafter I will be able to preview 4 brand-new Regency Romances FREE for 10 days. Then, if I should decide to keep them, I will pay the money-saving preferred subscriber's price of just $16.00 for all 4...that's a savings of almost $4 off the publisher's price with no additional charge for shipping and handling. I may return any shipment within 10 days and owe nothing, and I may cancel this subscription at any time. My 4 FREE books will be mine to keep in any case.

Name _____

Address _____ Apt. _____

City _____ State _____ Zip _____

Telephone ( ) _____

Signature _____
(If under 18, parent or guardian must sign.)

RN100A

Terms and prices subject to change. Orders subject to acceptance by Zebra Home Subscription Service, Inc. Offer valid in U.S. only.

A
$19.96
VALUE...
FREE!

No
obligation
to buy
anything,
ever!

ll...l..ll....ll.l.l..l.l.l.l..ll.l..ll..ll.l...l

REGENCY ROMANCE BOOK CLUB

Zebra Home Subscription Service, Inc.

P.O. Box 5214

Clifton NJ 07015-5214

Butterberry. They are a—contribution—to your parish from all of us. Enjoyed playing a bit with your parrot, we did."

Tucking the guineas into his coat pocket and then tucking both his hands into his breeches pockets, the Reverend Mr. Butterberry bowed to Roth and strolled from the room, back up the corridor, through the public room and out into the yard. His mind lingered upon his youthful experience with The Mad Malcolm as he made his way toward Wickenshire's curricle. There was a sprightly bounce in his step and a decidedly proud set to his shoulders. He smiled a sad, yet decidedly fascinating smile as he climbed back up to the box. And then he came suddenly out of his reverie. "Now where has that girl got to?" he muttered, looking hastily about him for his Mary.

In the shadows between a high-perch phaeton and a traveling coach, Peter stood holding Mary's hands in both of his.

"Oh, you are all wet," she said, drawing one hand away and patting his sodden coat gently. "Quite as wet as you were last night, Peter."

"Wet, but well, Mary. I cannot remember when I have felt so very well. I cannot think why. I am not the least bit deserving of it, but my prayers have been answered. Quinn is not dead. I need run from his men no longer. He is alive and well and wishes to see me. And India—I have not the least reason to attempt to purchase passage to India now. It is all called off, Mary. There is no reason at all for me to leave England. If only I had had the courage to face what I had done on the instant, I should not have wallowed in such misery and despair for so very long. I should not have despaired at all. And I would never have caused you such anxious moments."

"You were very young, Peter."

"Yes, and foolish, and very melodramatic as you are fond of pointing out to me. But I will not be melodramatic any longer, Mary, or foolish either. At least, I will attempt not to be so. There is something I must say to you," he added, his voice lowering an octave as he reclaimed both of her hands. "Indeed, there are many things I must say to you, and all of them important, too. But I cannot say them here and now. There are some tasks I must perform, to attempt to right some of the wrongs I have done to people, before I will be free to speak plainly to you. But when I have finished with all I must do, I shall make everything right between the two of us. I promise you that."

"Are you not going to hold me in your arms as you have always done, Peter? Are you not going to kiss me?" asked Mary, her eyes dark with worry, one hand gripping his tightly while the other pulled free of his grasp to flutter at his lapel.

Peter gave a shake of his dark curls. The fencing scar on his cheek stood out bleakly in the flickering light of the flambeaux. "Your papa is just beyond the phaeton, Mary. And Wickenshire and Donovan are watching us from the porch. I cannot. They would think you lost to all propriety."

"I do not care what anyone else thinks of me, only you."

"You must go home with your father now, my sweet girl," he murmured, daring only to stroke her cheek with one trembling finger. "You must return to Wicken and I must go on to London."

"No, Peter! London?"

"Only for a day or two, Mary. No longer. And when I have finished in London, I must ride to a place called Billowsgate."

"To Eugenia's? To meet with your brother at last?"

"Yes. To put an end to Edward's searching and to beg his

pardon for all the worry I have caused him and to meet his intended, too, I expect. Billowsgate is not so very far from Wicken, I am told. Perhaps a half-day's ride. Less, I am told, if one keeps a strong, steady pace. I will ride straight from Edward to you, Mary. I give you my word on it."

Tears meandered down Mary's cheeks, but she ignored them. He was correct to say what he did. She knew it to be so, but she did not *want* it to be so. "I have come so far with you, Peter," she whispered. "I have come almost to London. I have spent the night alone in your company with only Lord Nightingale to chaperon us. We have ridden cross-country, you and I, without escort. Cannot anyone understand? I have no reputation left to lose; there is no great rule of propriety that I have not already broken. Why should I not accompany you into London and on to Billowsgate?"

Lord Peter's hand tensed in hers. He longed mightily to wrap her in his arms, to taste the salt of her tears on his tongue and hold her so close that he would feel her heart beating within his own chest, but he only shook his head and nibbled at his lower lip a moment. "There is no one knows that you did anything at all untoward, Mary. No one, that is, who will say a word. Your papa will put it about that you and he spent the time at Wicken Hall, and with Wickenshire to bear him witness, who would dare gainsay your papa's words?"

"To be with you, I would gainsay them."

"No, Mary. You will not. This time you will do as I request, dearest girl, and go back home. For a brief while you will not be with me. But then, Mary, once I have done what I must, we will be together forever."

"He is saved! He is saved! He is saved!" shouted Delight over and over again, running through the Great Hall and up the stairs and down the stairs and back up the stairs again, all the way to the kitchen, Stanley Blithe prancing merrily at her heels. "He is saved!" she called to Maria, the scullery maid and to Martin the potboy. "He is saved," she announced joyously to the smiling cook. Then she and Stanley Blithe were pounding up the back staircase and skipping gleefully through the first floor corridor of the east wing. "He is saved, Martha!" she shouted in at the maid in the study. "He is saved! He is saved!" she chanted, saluting the head footman merrily as she passed him by.

"Rorarf!" added Stanley Blithe, pausing for a moment to snuffle happily at the footman's shoe. "Grrrarfwoof!"

James, who, like the rest of the staff, understood at once what was meant, grinned widely and saluted the two rascals right back and began to whistle a tune as he went about his duties.

Giggling and barking, running and jumping, Delight and Stanley Blithe covered the entire first floor of Wicken Hall from the east wing to the west, advising every servant, no matter how high or how low, of the exceedingly good news. "He is saved! He is saved!" she crowed over and over again until, at last, she discovered Serendipity and the dowager seated in the little west parlor, her sister busily making notes at the writing stand beside the window and the dowager working lethargically at the task of mending a piece of tapestry.

"He is saved!" Delight cried, skipping into the very center of the room and then cheerily hopping about in a circle.

"Wrrarf-ffarf!" reiterated Stanley Blithe, just in case either of the fine ladies whom he adored should have misunderstood Delight's message. "Wrrarf-ffarf!"

"How wonderful!" exclaimed Serendipity at once, turning from the menus she was preparing to watch her little sister hop about. "Did I not tell you that Nicky would see to all?"

"Uh-huh," nodded Delight, pausing in her celebratory hopping to acknowledge with sufficient distinction the truth of her sister's words. "You tole me 'zactly that. And you were right as truffles! He is saved, saved, saved!" she sang, changing from hopping to twirling.

"Ooph!" grunted the Duke of Sotherland as he stepped into the room and Delight twirled directly into him.

"Delight, do look where you are spinning," admonished the dowager with a twinkle in her eyes. "We are all very pleased to learn that he is safe, but is it necessary, dearest, to set his grace to staggering because of it? Come in, your grace, and join us. We thought you had gone for a ride about the grounds this afternoon and so did not worry our heads about you."

"Yes, yes," grumbled Sotherland, "I have been riding about a bit. Is there a copy of *The Times* to be had, or does it not reach you here in the hinterlands until the evening? Who is saved?" he added, his hands upon Delight's shoulders preventing her from running off to spin again.

"Lord Nightingale." Delight smiled proudly up at him. "He is safe as houses. The Reverend Mr. Butterberry came right up to our front door an' tole Mr. Jenkins so. An' Mr. Jenkins allowed as I might have the priv'lege to tell everyone in the whole house."

"I see. And who is this Lord Nightingale? Is he a relative of yours, madam?" the duke asked, glancing at the dowager. "And from what has he been saved, if I may be so bold as to inquire."

"He is the verimost finest parrot in all of England and Lord Bradford's verimost best friend," Delight answered at once, diverting the duke's gaze from an abruptly coughing Lady Wickenshire and a blushing Serendipity. "An' he is going to be groomsman at Lord Bradford's wedding," Delight announced grandly, "which Genia an' Lord Bradford are going to have right here in our very own house just as soon as Genia's papa gives them permission. Oh, an' as soon as Lord Bradford has got the special license that says that they do not got to wait like ordinary people nor do not got to have it in the church."

"Delight! Cease and desist! And Lord Nightingale is not going to be Lord Bradford's groomsman!" Serendipity exclaimed, taking note of an abrupt straightening of the Duke of Sotherland's shoulders and the filtering of a perfectly freezing light into that nobleman's eyes.

"Yes, he is too going to be Lord Bradford's groomsman," Delight contradicted. "But just when I had been started to make up his morning dress for him to wear," she explained, turning to look up at the duke, "Lord Nightingale was stoled!" She lowered her voice in the most dramatic fashion and tugged the duke insistently down to her own level by the expeditious method of pulling on the bottom of his coat until he must bend forward. "Lord Nightingale was stoled away from us in the very middle of a storm-tossed night amist thunner an' lightnin'," she whispered most dramatically. "Ever'one was overcomed by the sheer audacidy of the crime."

"As am I," responded his grace darkly. "Have you told everyone that Lord Nightingale is safe?"

"Yes," replied Delight confidently.

"The coachman and the grooms and the boys in the stable?"

"Oh! No! Just ever'one in the house."

"Well then, run and tell the lads in the stable at once," urged the duke. "They will be greatly relieved to know. And take Mr. Blithe with you."

Greatly pleased that her duke should think of it, Delight

released him from her grasp, made a dip of a curtsy and veritably flew out the door with Stanley Blithe at her heels.

Not so much as glancing over his shoulder to see her go, the Duke of Sotherland straightened himself until he stood so stiffly upright that Sera quite expected to see him fall over backward. His blue eyes turned to bits of blue ice and the very tips of his ears reddened considerably. "Madam!" he bellowed, causing both the dowager countess and Serendipity to jump the tiniest bit. "How dare you? To tell me that Edward had gone off to a place called Billowsgate without so much as a word about—about—"

"His wedding?" asked the dowager, as Serendipity gulped.

"You *know* this Miss Eugenia Chastain?"

"Indeed. She is my niece, your grace."

"Your niece? My Edward is to marry your niece and you said nothing of it to me?"

"You did not refer to the event, your grace, and so I thought it wise not to refer to it either," the dowager replied.

"Bah!"

"Come and sit down and we will discuss it now, if you like."

"There is nothing to be discussed, madam. My son will *not* marry your niece! I have come to Kent for one reason only—to bring this nonsensical marriage to a stuttering halt, and I will do it, too. I shall pack my things and be gone from here in a quarter-hour, but I shall return, madam. You may believe that I shall return. And believe also that no wedding ceremony will take place in this house—at least no ceremony in which Edward will take part!"

"You are making a complete jackass of yourself, you know," the dowager replied, sitting primly in her chair, her hands folded across the tapestry.

"What!"

"You heard me, your grace."

Serendipity could not think what to do. The Duke of Sotherland glared at the dowager countess as though he would wind his fingers around her throat and strangle her at any moment.

"Oh, do cease muttering under your breath and sit down, your grace," urged the dowager. "Can you not see that it would be most uncircumspect of you to pack up your trunk and drive off. Where would you go? Lord Bradford and Eugenia are at Billowsgate with my brother-in-law, Robert. If you go there now to confront your son, you will lose every battle. Robert loves his daughter beyond measure and he will *not* tremble at your bellowing. He will see you swept from his doorstep and your Edward will not so much as note that you are anywhere about."

"Ha!"

"You think it cannot be, but it can. Eugenia's papa is not a gentleman to be threatened or browbeaten or bribed."

"I have no cause to so much as speak to the man. It is my son with whom I will have words."

"I do not think so. Unless I am sadly mistaken, your son does not so much as care to see your face at his wedding."

"I will disown the boy."

"He would undoubtedly be grateful, though you cannot disinherit him, you know. Once you die, he must inherit. Is that not truth?"

The duke scowled. The duke mumbled. The duke stomped about the room and kicked at a table leg.

"Am I mistaken, your grace? I have never known an eldest son who could be disinherited yet. Disowned. Sent off to foreign climes, ignored—but in the end, when his papa is set into the ground, it is the eldest son who inherits the title and all attached directly to it."

"Yes, yes, yes," roared the duke, smashing his fist down

upon a tabletop. "But I will not have Edward married to a perfect nobody!"

Serendipity thought for a moment that her mother-in-law was about to rise from her chair, cross the room, and jab her sewing needle into a rather prominent portion of the duke's anatomy. "Eugenia is a wonderful young woman and Edward is beyond lucky to have her," she interjected on the dowager's behalf.

"Good lord, another quarter heard from!"

"Yes, and if you were one-half as sensible as you are hot-tempered, you would be pleased to see him married to Eugenia. She has made a happy, pleasant man of him."

"I would be pleased? Pleased?" roared the duke.

"Oh, very well then. I can see that you *do* intend to confront your son, no matter what anyone tells you, your grace," sighed Serendipity.

"I *shall* confront Edward."

"Just so. Then you had best remain here. You will not gain his ear at Billowsgate. Lady Wickenshire is correct in that. You will not so much as be admitted into the house. Nicky's Uncle Robert is not a gentleman impressed by titles or reputations. And there is no way at all to threaten him or to bribe him. Besides, Edward and Eugenia may not even *be* at Billowsgate when you reach the place. They could well be driving back here by the time you get there."

"So you are telling me what, my lady?" grumbled Sotherland.

"She is advising you to cease acting like a fool, to continue to accept our hospitality a bit longer and to say what you must say to your son right here in this establishment," huffed the dowager, sinking her needle back into the tapestry where it belonged. "But I warn you, your grace, that if you persist in displaying such a vile temperament as this too often, I shall have Jenkins throw you out of Wicken

Hall on your ear. I am very close to doing it this minute. And then you will be forced to take up rooms at the inn in Wicken if ever you are to face your son."

"Balderdash!" the duke protested.

"You will see if it is balderdash do you try me once too often. You will not like to abide at the Red Rose Inn. The chambers are small, the fireplaces all puff soot, and the food is most unpalatable."

"And there are bedbugs," added Serendipity softly, but loud enough for the duke to hear.

"Well, I will consider remaining here for the time being," puffed the duke, his tone much depressed from its earlier volume.

"By all means," nodded the dowager. "And do let me know what you decide. *The Times* is always to be found upon the largest of the sideboards in the breakfast room by a quarter of three in the afternoon. You do remember where you breakfasted, your grace?"

"Precisely," grumbled Sotherland, exiting the room without so much as a nod to either of them.

"The bedbugs were a marvelous touch, Sera," said the dowager once the duke was heard to slam the breakfast room door. "I do wish I had thought of them."

"But why do you wish him to remain here, my lady? I should think it would be much better to send him off in a different direction so he would not find Edward and Eugenia until after they are married."

"No, no. He cannot stop the wedding. Lord Bradford is not such a coward as to abandon Eugenia because his papa says that he must. Had his grace made such a display of himself last evening, I would have been perfectly willing to see him chase all about the countryside to no purpose. But today, I have been made privy to something that has quite altered my opinion of the man."

"You have?"

"Yes, my dear. According to Jenkins, the duke's valet went to wake him this morning only to discover him fast asleep in a chair before the hearth with Delight wrapped in one of his comforters and curled up on his lap and Stanley Blithe dozing at his feet."

"Oh, my!"

"And did you see how Delight spoke to him, and he to her, a few moments ago? And did you note how he sent ⬛⬛⬛⬛⬛⬛⬛ to the stables before he began to bellow?"

⬛⬛⬛⬛⬛⬛⬛⬛⬛⬛⬛⬛, there is not a bone in ⬛⬛⬛⬛⬛⬛⬛⬛⬛ body that is not perfectly despicable, Sera. And so says Lady Vermont as well. And because you and I and Nicky had no experience with the gentleman, we believed every word they each said. But I think now that Lord Bradford is wrong. And I think that Lady Vermont, who vows Sotherland is the Devil Incarnate, is wrong as well. And I am most curious, Sera, to see if I will be proved correct in the matter. And if I am to be proved correct, only think what it will mean. It will mean a fine father-in-law for Eugenia, instead of a devilish old man who will not acknowledge her, and two loving grandfathers for their children instead of only Robert. So I wish to keep him here and see if there is not some way to make the heart that is so careful of Delight come out of hiding and participate in the world again."

TEN

...n speak of him... the win...
...ody the min her sister Clara, and ga...
ternoon. In the cerulean sky she saw Peter's eyes, blue and
bright and free of self-loathing at last. In the twirling puff
of a cloud she recognized his hesitant, flickering smile. She
pushed the casements outward and heard his whisper in the
wind, felt his finger wander slowly, tenderly along her
cheek. One great teardrop formed in the corner of Mary's
eye and she dashed it away with impatience.

I will not cry, she told herself silently. There is nothing
to cry about. Peter *will* come to me just as he promised,
and he will ask Papa for my hand and Papa will give it
him. "Only—only I fear for his safety in London," she
whispered to the elm beside her window. "I cannot think
why. All that threatened him has ceased to do so and Nicky
is with him besides, but still, I cannot believe him to be
safe. What is it that he intends to do in London? How is
it that he thinks to right the wrongs he has done? And what
wrongs does he imagine himself to have done? He has such
a very vivid imagination. I cannot believe that he has done
anything wrong at all."

Well, he did steal Lord Nightingale, she reminded herself,
but certainly, now that Nicky has the bird back, that wrong
is righted, and what else can there be?

Mary rubbed at the tip of her nose and sighed. It was the most frustrating thing. To have worn the willow for the gentleman for two entire years; to have longed for him so much that she must, at last, run away to London to find him; and then to be with him for an entire night and an entire day, each moment reveling in the realization that it was truly his face she saw and his voice she heard, that he was no longer merely a memory; and then to be torn from him again.

"I do hope you are not completely overcome with sorrow, Miss Butterberry," offered a voice from the threshold, "because there is something quite important that I must discuss with you."

"Lady Wickenshire?"

"No, no, you must call me Sera just as Eugenia does, and I hope that you will allow me to call you Mary. We have not had much opportunity to come to know each other as yet, but Eugenia has told me ever so much about you. And my husband, of course, has known you since you were in your cradle and so has told tale after tale about you."

"He has?"

"Oh, yes. You are the heroine of any number of his tales, because he thinks you so very intrepid, you know. May I come in?"

"Oh! Yes, of course. Unless you would rather go downstairs to the parlor."

"No. I requested that your mama give us time alone together, and so she is keeping all of your sisters quite occupied by dusting and sweeping and polishing up the parlor." Serendipity closed the door behind her, crossed the room and settled onto the edge of the bed. "I expect she thinks that I have come to speak to you about your escapade, but I have not."

"What have you come to speak to me about?"

"This gentleman who calls himself Mr. Peter Winthrop. He is Lord Peter, Lord Bradford's brother, is he not?"

"Indeed."

"He did not come back with you to Wicken?"

"He has gone on to London with Nicky to make something right, though I cannot think what."

"Do you expect him, Mary, to return here soon?"

"Yes, I do. He has promised to come as soon as possible. He stops in Billowsgate to reunite with Lord Bradford and to meet Eugenia, and he will come to me immediately after that."

"And you intend to marry him?"

"Yes," Mary replied grudingly. "You *have* come to lecture me about what you think to be my total lack of morality in running away to search for a gentleman, and it is not a bit of it your business, you know. It is no one's business but my own."

"No, you mistake me, Mary. I only wish to know your feelings about Lord Peter because—because—"

"Because what?" asked Mary, fingering the wide sash upon her jonquille morning dress nervously. "You are not going to tell me about anything else dastardly that Peter has done? I will not believe you if you do because Peter is not at all dastardly. He has been frightened and confused and very, very sad for a long, long time, but there is not a truly dastardly bone in his body."

Serendipity took a deep breath, gave a little shake of her head and smoothed the soft muslin of her skirt. "I shall trust you are correct in all that you say, for I have never met the gentleman. But I have come here to tell you that Lord Peter's papa has come to Kent and, at the moment, resides with us at Wicken Hall."

"The Duke of Sotherland? That—that—beast? At Wicken Hall? How can you possibly have allowed that wretched scoundrel to so much as set foot upon your doorstep?"

"I would not have done, but Nicholas' mama—"

"Oh, dear! Does she not know—is she not aware what sort of person the Duke of Sotherland is?"

"That is just the thing," sighed Serendipity. "Nicholas' mama thinks that the duke is not near the villain everyone makes him out to be. She views him in the same fashion that you apparently viewed Lord Peter even when so many others persisted in seeing Lord Peter differently. Your view has been proved to be the correct one now, I should think."

"Yes, indeed. I think that even Papa must accept that Peter is good and kind and true now, though he was very angry and talked and talked with Peter for ever so long before he would set him free to go on to London."

"Well, the dowager countess has determined to discover if her view of the duke is more correct than the view that everyone else holds of him. And so, she has invited his grace to remain with us. And I think she may be right, Mary. It is possible that under all his bluff and bluster, the Duke of Sotherland has a heart. Somewhere. But I cannot think it will be at all an easy task to discover it and—"

"Well, I know just how to discover if that beast has a heart," interrupted Mary, rising from the windowseat and placing her hands upon her hips. "Only show me where Nicky keeps his dueling pistols and I will give you an answer to that particular puzzle in a matter of moments."

That evening a heavy fog slithered relentlessly over London, walling up the city in a thick, yellowish gray mist; sealing it off street by street, alleyway by alleyway, building by building. Slowly, silently, with grim determination, the stuporous vapor wrapped itself around street lamps and coaches, gobbled up doorways, seeped down deep into gentlemen's bones.

Like walking corpses in winding sheets of mist, two figures equally as determined as the fog—one of them carrying a hopping, swinging, wiggling, muttering sack—paused before the barely discernible flambeaux of Number 66 Pickering Place.

"Are you certain this is it?" asked Wickenshire quietly.

"Yes. Trump was clear enough about it. Number 66 Pickering Place, at ten o'clock. The gentleman I am to meet will be wearing a blue flower in his buttonhole."

"Well, here then," Wickenshire said, offering the sack to Lord Peter. "Do be careful with him, will you not?"

"Scuttle the blackguards," mumbled the sack.

"Nightingale, do be quiet. You have been muttering and mumbling the entire way. Lord Peter does not require you to draw everyone's attention to him."

"Mornin' Nicky. Yo ho ho. Knollsmarmer."

Lord Peter grinned, though it was barely visible through the fog even to Wickenshire. "He is the most incorrigible parrot I have ever met. Of course, he is the only parrot I have ever met. You will remain within hailing distance of us, eh?"

"Keep you in sight no matter what. Only give me time enough to fade into the background before you enter, eh?"

The tobacco smoke within the gaming hell proved as thick as the fog without. Wickenshire closed the door tightly behind himself and gazed about. There were no dandies here, no delicate sniffers of snuff. Here the Corinthians came to be shed of such nonsense, to smoke their pipes and the new cigarillos. Here Blue Ruin flowed as freely as wine and the talk was of gaming, racing, pistols, cock fights, bear-baiting and most usually The Fancy.

Wickenshire wound his way through the crowd, his bea-

ver low upon his brow, his coat collar high, his hands stuffed
into his pockets, until he found himself a position at the
rear of the main gaming room from which he could see the
front door and most of the tables clearly. He rested his broad
shoulders nonchalantly against the flowered wallpaper and
gazed down at the game of whist going on at the table
immediately before him, apparently becoming engrossed in
studying the varying skills of the players.

As he swaggered into the gaming hell a mere three minutes after Wickenshire had found himself a vantage point,
Lord Peter might well have been mistaken for a practitioner
of The Fancy. With his broad shoulders and lean hips, his
dark curls, piercing blue eyes and the thin scar that marred
his otherwise startlingly handsome face, he had the look of
the fighter about him, a look greatly enhanced by the wool
hunting jacket he wore and the scarlet cravat tied negli-
gently around his neck.

Holding tightly to the sack, he peered through the gathering of gamesters, at last spying a gentleman with a blue
flower in his buttonhole playing at E.O. "That will be the
man," he muttered under his breath.

"Villain! Bite!"

"Nightingale, be quiet," Lord Peter hissed, giving the bag
a gentle shake. He worked his way through the crowded
room until he reached the left shoulder of the gentleman
he sought. There he halted, watched the play for four turns
of the wheel, then hissed, "Knollsmarmer." The gentleman
jerked back from the table as though he had been burned.
He turned quickly, took note of the flamboyant cravat and
the wiggling sack, nodded, and strolled directly out of the
gaming room into an adjoining chamber. The man in the
scarlet cravat followed in silence.

"Close the door and join me at the fire, eh? Damnable
fog chills a man through."

"Let us just get on with it," growled Lord Peter, closing the door and resting his shoulders against it.

"Yes, well, we will. I was expecting that Trump fellow."

"He sent a message 'round to one of your dandy clubs. Said you were to wear that flower and I this particular cravat so that we would recognize each other."

"Indeed, but—"

"Villain! Bite!" called Lord Nightingale raucously.

"You *have* got him!" exclaimed the gentleman. "I would recognize that wretched bird's voice anywhere. He is in that sack you hold? Give him to me at once."

"The money first," muttered Lord Peter.

"Yes, yes indeed," responded the gentleman excitedly, withdrawing his purse from his inside pocket and counting out a number of bank notes. "Fifteen hundred in all was the price. I gave Trump two hundred when he agreed to find someone to do the job. That makes it thirteen hundred you are owed, eh?"

"Precisely," nodded Lord Peter, stepping toward the gentleman and giving the door a kick with his heel as he did so.

The gentleman with the blue flower in his buttonhole placed the bank notes into Lord Peter's hand and grasped the sack eagerly. And then he scowled as the brighter light of the fire flickered across Peter's face. And then he squinted. And then he stepped back and stared. "By Jove, it cannot be! Bradford!" He was so totally astounded that he did not notice the door ease open and Wickenshire slip into the room.

"Villain!" Nightingale squawked and sent the sack in the gentleman's hand to swinging. "Villain! Bite!"

"Bradford, how on earth? Why in heaven's name should you—"

"He is not Bradford, Neil," interrupted Wickenshire, stepping forward and seizing the sack. "He is Bradford's twin. Calls himself Peter Winthrop at the moment. Winthrop, may I present to you my cousin, Neil Spelling. A gentleman who has just managed to bring me to the very end of my tether."

They stepped out of Number 66 Pickering Place onto the flagstones, Wickenshire and Lord Peter, each holding fast to one of Mr. Spelling's arms as that gentleman marched between them.

"Villain. Villain," muttered Lord Nightingale, bouncing about in the sack Wickenshire held in his left hand.

"Yes, I know, Nightingale," Wickenshire replied. "And we are going to do something about this particular villain shortly."

"You do not understand, Nicky," whispered Spelling hoarsely. "I must have Nightingale. There is no other way. It is a matter of life and death."

"It certainly is now, Neil," Wickenshire replied.

The fog gathered them into itself, swallowing them completely from sight as they walked off down the street, bootheels shuddering against the flagstones.

"Wh-where are we going?" Spelling asked, his voice quivering through the mist.

"To your house, Neil. Wickenshire House is closed and shuttered and empty of staff at present, but you are intending to invite Winthrop and myself and Lord Nightingale to spend the night with you."

"Yes. Of course."

"We have abandoned our horses and the few things we brought with us at Grillon's, but you will send one of your footmen and a groom for them."

"I will."

"Just so. And then you will dismiss your servants for the

rest of the evening and we will all settle down in your parlor and discuss which of your arms I am to break first."

"Wickenshire," Lord Peter chuckled.

"No, I mean it. I have had all I am going to take of this—this—scoundrel for the rest of my life. And to think that Mama was so very pleased with you this summer, Neil, that she wrote me three entire pages on how she was certain you had changed your ways and would never prove nefarious again! Yes, and Eugenia has invited you to her wedding! After I break both of your arms, I ought to address myself to your nose and your jaw as well. Perhaps that will teach you a thing or two."

They turned at the corner instead of crossing and set their feet to wandering in the direction of Hanover Square.

"Wetwetwet," protested Lord Nightingale.

"It is only damp, Nightingale. You will be warm soon," replied Wickenshire. "I ought to stuff you into this very sack and drown you in the Thames, Neil," he added with a glare at his cousin. "You may detest Nightingale, but to send a perfect stranger after him, with no way to transport him but a sack—Damnation, you have no heart at all!"

"I do have a heart," mumbled Spelling. "I would not have agreed to it if I did not have a heart and wished it to go on beating. And I cannot think that he means to hurt the wretched bird, Nicky. If I thought he meant to actually harm Nightingale, I would have—I would have—well, I cannot be certain what I would have done, because I did not take that into consideration."

"He?" asked Lord Peter. "He who? Do you mean to say that you are not the one wants Lord Nightingale?"

"Come, Neil, at least be truthful," Wickenshire grumbled. "You were the one Winthrop met just now. You were the one handed him the money."

"Yes, but only because I need the wretched bird to trade

to Upton for the deed, Nicky. I would never have done it, else."

Mary, in robe and slippers, sat beside Serendipity, who was likewise attired. They sipped hot chocolate before the hearth in the sitting room of the master's suite at Wicken Hall.

"I am so very glad that you decided to come," Serendipity said, gazing into the fire.

"Did you think I would refuse? I am beyond anything grateful to you for telling Mama that you required my assistance for a day or two. I had begun to fear, you know, that Mama and Papa might think to hold me prisoner in the rectory until my thirty-first birthday after all the excitement I have given them."

Sera laughed. "Never. But they were most upset when you ran off, you know. Your mama and papa both. You ought to have seen the way your papa came flying up the drive, and heard how he pounded upon our door the morning they got your note. Not that I blame him at all. I would have been equally as upset if my daughter had gone off to London all on her own. And Nicholas would certainly have gone dashing after her with precisely the same urgency that he went dashing after you."

"Do you wish to have a daughter or a son first?" asked Mary, her eyes twinkling.

"Oh, dear, is it so very obvious?"

"Yes," smiled Mary. "You forget that I have five younger sisters. I have become accustomed to noticing when a lady is in the family way."

"I hope it is a son," confessed Serendipity. "I should like to have a son who is the image of Nicholas. And then, of course, the problem of an heir will be solved upon the spot, so that Nicholas' mama need not worry about that particular aspect of life ever again."

"And what does Nicky say?"

"That he does not care in the least, so long as I and the baby both survive the ordeal in the best of health. But what do you think about the Duke of Sotherland, Mary, now that you have made his acquaintance?"

Mary took another sip of her chocolate and squinted her eyes the least bit in thought. "I have not changed my mind at all. I still think he would benefit nicely from the proper application of a dueling pistol."

"No, really? You think Nicholas' mama is incorrect and the duke is precisely as black and heartless as he has been painted?"

Mary shook her shining midnight curls. "I think he is much blacker than anyone can ever paint him, and that he was born with a piece of coal where his heart ought to be. And I cannot believe that such a man as that sired my Peter."

"Or Lord Bradford."

"Or Lord Bradford. What a horrible thing for Eugenia, to come here with her papa and Lord Bradford expecting to share a pleasant wedding day with family and friends, and to meet with the Duke of Sotherland first thing."

"However, he has been extraordinarily kind to Delight."

"Well, I cannot account for that at all. It is some sort of temporary aberration, I think."

"He did speak to her at table as if she were a real dinner partner this evening," Serendipity offered hopefully.

"But we have no idea what he said."

"No, but whatever he said, he did not make her cry."

"He made her giggle rather," agreed Mary. "I was surprised to see it. Still, there is something most frightening about him. Did you not notice, Sera, how like ice his eyes

seemed. There was not one sparkle of warmth in them the
entire evening."

"There was at least one."

"There was? I did not take note of it."

"I chanced to look up and catch just the hint of warmth."

"When?"

"When he began to pace the drawing room as you played
upon the pianoforte. Delight jumped up and began to pace
behind him. His eyes flashed when he took note of her
following in his every footstep with her hands clasped behind her back in perfect imitation of him. I vow that I saw
something very warm in those eyes for just that moment."

Mary set her cup of chocolate aside and turned to face
Sera directly. "So, you think that her ladyship is correct."

"I do not know," Sera replied, setting her own cup down
upon the cricket table beside the sopha and taking Mary's
hands into her own. "But I asked you here for a particular
reason, Mary. I think that we must attempt, you and I, to
discover a living, beating heart that is good and decent in
that gentleman. After all the tales I have heard of him, I
cannot but think that if any heart is left, it must be buried
beneath innumerable layers of crust and soot. But if my
mama-in-law and Delight—for Delight has developed a distinct fondness for him—if my mama-in-law and Delight are
correct, then we must set ourselves to release this imprisoned heart of his and bring his better nature to the forefront,
and quickly too."

"Why?" asked Mary bluntly. "I should think we would
do best to drive him to distraction so that he leaves Wicken
Hall before Eugenia and Edward return."

"No. He will merely await news of them at the Red Rose
Inn and come crashing into this house, demanding that Lord
Bradford call off the ceremony and accompany him home
at once. He has no care for propriety, I think, and so will

not find any fault with himself for doing precisely that. And only think, Mary, what decency and sweetness lie in Lord Bradford and Lord Peter, both. And then remember what a bad impression they both made on people at first. And this is the very gentleman who gave them life. If that same sweetness and kindness has somehow been buried deep within the duke's heart and cannot escape—"

"I still cannot make myself believe that he has a heart."

"But Mary, he will be your father-in-law and grandfather to your children. You will be forced to deal with him once he learns you will be Peter's bride. Should not you like to know for certain and if he has a heart to—"

"He does not give a fig about Peter," Mary protested. "Peter has stood in dire need of him for the longest time and the man did not once seek him out. He will not care if Peter marries me or a cleaning wench because Peter is not his heir."

"Not his heir, but Peter is still his son and deserves a kinder father just as Edward does. And if there is a kinder father buried inside this old curmudgeon, Mary—"

"Eugenia told the truth about you," Mary said softly. "You are beyond anything compassionate, Sera."

"Then you *will* help me? Surely, if there is goodness in the gentleman, you and I between us can discover a way to break it free and let it rise to his surface."

Mary nodded. "Have you a plan how to do it?"

"No, but I have every confidence that between you and me, we shall think of one. I have a notion that Delight must be involved in it, for if Nicholas' mama and I are not mistaken, Delight is the one who has managed to bring at least a feeble flicker of warmth about in him."

"Well," sighed Mary, standing to take her leave and giving Sera's knee a reassuring pat, "I will give it a deal of thought before I fall asleep, and you must do likewise. It

Butterberry. "We must get Peter to a safe place. Somewhere they will not think to look for him."

"Who the deuce are Quinn's men?" asked Wickenshire.

"They are—they are—they wish to kill Peter, Nicky!"

"Nothing odd in that," drawled Wickenshire, rubbing gently at Nightingale's breast. "I wish to kill him as well, right after your papa has blacked out both his daylights."

EIGHT

"You are never to do such a thing again," Sera murmured, tucking a sleepy Delight into bed. "You are much too small to be tramping about all over the countryside with no one but Stanley Blithe to look after you, dearest."

"We went to look for Lord Nightingale," the child replied sleepily, rubbing at her eyes.

"Yes, I know you did. And it was very brave of you, too, but you must never go off again without a grown-up beside you."

"I gived Stanley Blithe one of Lord Nightingale's feathers to sniff, jus' like Papa was used to give Rumbles a cloth, an' Stanley Blithe runned off right away af'er Lord Nightingale."

"He did? Well, then I am quite certain that Stanley Blithe tried his very best to find Lord Nightingale."

"But we didn't not find him, Sera."

"No, but Nicky will find him. I promise you that he will. He loves Lord Nightingale quite as much as you do, you know, and he would be very sad should Lord Nightingale not come back to us. It is just that Nicky must help to find Miss Butterberry first."

"Yaaarrrrr," yawned Stanley Blithe, curling up into a large furry ball upon the counterpane and resting his shaggy head on the tiny lump that was Delight's knee.

"Promise me, Delight, that you will never, ever go wandering off by yourself again."

"I promise," sighed the child, yawning mightily and continuing to rub at one eye with one fist. "Can me and Stanley Blithe keep him, Sera?"

"Keep him?" Serendipity leaned down and kissed her sister's wine-stained cheek. "Keep whom, dearest?"

"Our duke."

Serendipity could not believe her ears. "That grouchy old gentleman? Delight! Why on earth would you wish to keep him?"

"Because me an' Stanley Blithe founded him an' we like him. He is verimost funny."

"Funny? The Duke of Sotherland?"

"Uh-huh. I like how he talks an' how he pertends to be a ol' curmudglian. An' he has the verimost bushiest eyebrows. He can make them wiggle like caterpiggles, Sera. Not even Nicky can do that. Can he?"

"No, I do not think so," grinned Sera. "But we will ask Nicholas to attempt it when he returns, shall we? I am certain he will try his very best to do the thing if we request it of him. And I, for one, should like to see him attempt to wiggle his eyebrows like caterpiggles. But as for your duke, darling, I am much afraid that you cannot just keep a gentleman you have found as you would a puppy or a kitten. Gentlemen do not belong to anyone but themselves."

"We founded Nicky, an' now he belongs to you an' me an' Lady Wickenshire an' Sweetpea an' Stanley Blithe an'—"

"Go to sleep, Delight," Serendipity interrupted the drowsy recital of names. "We will discuss keeping gentlemen some other time. Sweet dreams, my sweet girl."

Truly, she is the most remarkable child, Serendipity thought as she departed the chamber and closed the door softly behind her. Keep the Duke of Sotherland, of all things! Next she will discover something pleasant about a ravenous bear and wish to keep one of those about the house as well. "Jenkins? What on earth?" she asked, nearly colliding with the butler as he exited the chamber across from Delight's.

"Her ladyship has invited his grace to spend the night, my lady," offered the butler wearily, "and this is the only chamber not already allotted to one of the wedding guests."

"Oh, Jenkins, no. I thought the gentleman wished to merely present Delight to us and travel on. I thought he had a specific destination to reach this evening."

"I expect his grace's plans have altered, my lady, for he has accepted my lady's offer."

Serendipity could not believe it. What had come over her mother-in-law? Did she not realize that the Duke of Sotherland had likely driven all the way into Kent with the express purpose of stopping Eugenia's and Edward's marriage? Of course, the gentleman *had* rescued Delight and Stanley Blithe and brought them safely home, but that did not mean that the old curmudgeon had had any change of heart in regard to his son's matrimonial intentions. Lord Bradford had not been at all reserved in telling them what he expected his father's reaction would be to his forthcoming marriage, though he had thought that the man would not come bellowing down upon them until well after the ceremony was over and done with. In fact, the portrait of his father that Edward had painted for them had been most appalling. With considerable perturbation, Sera hurried down the staircase to the first floor and into the small drawing room where a fire blazed upon the hearth and the tea tray had just made an appearance.

"Oh, Sera, my dear, there you are. Will you pour out for

would be a wondrous thing to see Peter and Lord Bradford clutched happily in that old fiend's embrace. We must discuss whatever ideas come to us the very first thing tomorrow morning. But I warn you, Sera, if we find it is not possible to change the Duke of Sotherland from beast to best, I may well discover the whereabouts of Nicky's dueling pistols and put all discussion of that particular gentleman's heart to an end."

ELEVEN

Lord Peter was nothing if not confused. He stretched his long legs out before him, sipped at the glass of brandy he held in his hand and attempted to sort it all out.

"Villain!" squawked Lord Nightingale, who was presently swinging upside down from the chandelier in the center of Spelling's parlor. "Bitevillain!"

"No, you may not bite him, Nightingale," Wickenshire declared, staring down at Spelling, who was stretched his length upon the flowered carpeting. "Do get up, Neil."

"No."

"I did not hit you so hard that you cannot stand back up."

"My noth ith bleeding," mumbled Spelling, holding his hand gingerly over that throbbing appendage.

"Here then," grumbled Wickenshire, tugging his handkerchief from a pocket and tossing it down to his cousin. "Staunch the flow, Neil, and then get up off the floor. Your nose ain't broken. I did not hit you smack upon it. I was careful not to."

"Ow!" cried Spelling, abruptly rolling about on the floor like a man gone mad. "Ouch! Thtop! Thtop, you wretch!"

Laughter tickled at the back of Lord Peter's throat as he watched Spelling roll and dodge and then curl himself into a smaller target as Wickenshire sighed loudly and gazed placidly up at the chandelier.

"My dear Lord Nightingale," Wickenshire drawled. "I understand your feelings in the matter, but we have discussed this precise use of candles before, you and I, and I have not altered my opinion on it."

"Badbadbad," the parrot replied, plucking another of the candles from its holder and tossing it straight down at Wickenshire. "Badbadbadbad! Villain!"

"Indeed," the earl agreed, catching the candle, hefting it for a moment in his hand with the most thoughtful expression on his face, and then tossing it at Neil's head himself.

"Now that is setting the bird an excellent example," Lord Peter observed. "I should get up, Spelling, if I were you, and move out of range of them both."

"Yeth," agreed Spelling, handkerchief pressed tightly against his nose as he attempted to gain his feet. "Do not hit me again, Nicky. It ain't like you."

"No, but hiring someone to steal Lord Nightingale without the least thought as to what Upton wanted with him is exactly like you. You are totally without conscience, Neil."

"Am not. Have a conscienth. Tried to do the right thing all thummer long. Did, too."

"And then September came and you could resist being obnoxious and nefarious no longer? Is that it?"

"Arnthworth choth to marry Clara Butterberry!" Mr. Spelling shouted in his own defense, sinking down upon the mauve silk sopha. "He choth to marry Clara and it would have been cruel to talk him out of it. Bethides, I tried and tried to talk him out of it, and he would not lithen!"

"Clara Butterberry?" murmured Lord Peter. "Mary's sister?"

"Gilly Arnsworth, do you mean, Neil?" asked Wickenshire. "What has Arnsworth to do with any of this?"

"It wath a bet," whined Spelling, dabbing tenderly at his nose. "I bet Carey that I could marry Arnthworth off to one of the debutantheth thith Theathon, but he choth Clara. I lotht. I lotht the deed to Tivally Grange, Nicky!"

"Oh glory!" Wickenshire exclaimed, sinking down on the edge of a lyre-back chair whose seat was upholstered in puce brocade, and whose bottom barely supported his weight.

"Juth tho."

"What?" Lord Peter queried, looking from one to the other of them, his confusion mounting. "This is adequate justification for stealing the bird, Wickenshire? That he lost a bet?"

"And then Carey lotht the deed to Upton," Spelling continued. "And Upton offered to trade it back to me for Nightingale. I wath dethperate! And now it doth not matter what you do to me, Nicky. Not at all. Becauth now I am a dead man," he finished in despair.

Wickenshire leaned forward, his arms resting on his thighs, his hands clasped between his knees. "Perhaps Uncle Ezra will not kill you, Neil," he offered quietly.

"Of courth he will. You know he will. If I do not get that deed back before he learnth of it, he will kill me without the leatht thought, and you know it, too!"

"Who the devil is Uncle Ezra?" Lord Peter asked. Confused beyond bearing, he set his brandy glass aside, stood and began to pace. "I came to London to spring this trap for you, Wickenshire, as reparation for my stealing Lord Nightingale in the first place. And we have caught this rabbit in it. But I am demmed if I understand anything he—or you—have said in the past ten minutes. What I mean to say is—are you done with needing my help? Because, if you are, I wish you will say as much, because I have got to find Trump and deliver him the most of this blunt. I should like to give him the entire fifteen hundred. I owe him much more than that in a way, but I must keep five hundred of it, else I have nothing at all to offer Mary's father on my side of the marriage contract. And I have got to see Edward and—and—set his mind to rest. And to tell truth, I do not like that I had to abandon Mary so abruptly, and I wish to attend to particular matters concerning her as soon as I can."

"Knollsmarmer, wetwetwet," observed Lord Nightingale, swooping to the floor and bobbling along, flat-footed and pigeon-toed behind the pacing Lord Peter. "Yo ho ho. Howdedo. Mornin' Genia. Baaaad Nightingale. Woof!"

Wickenshire roared into laughter at the sight of the both of them pacing. "D-do not g-go yet," he managed. "I will help you, Winthrop, with all the rest, if you will h-help Neil and I with but one more thing."

Viscount Upton glared down his nose at Spelling and the wiggling sack. "For the life of me, Spelling, I cannot think why you should drag me all the way out here to the mews."

"Because I thought your thtable would be the thafest place."

Upton cocked an eyebrow in the flickering lantern light. "Since when have you taken to affecting a lisp? Don't become you, Spelling. Take my word for it."

"Not affecting a lithp. Hit in the noth. Thatth why I thent for you to come here."

"Because you were hit in the nose?"

"Thactly. Blighter wanted more money for the blathted bird. Fought him. Afraid he might thteal it back if he theeth me taking it to your houth. Have you brought the deed?"

"Yes, yes, I have brought the deed," muttered Upton, fishing about in his pocket. "You are such a coward, Spelling. Let the fellow attempt to steal Nightingale back from me. I will give the blighter a pounding he will not forget. Here. Take it."

Spelling took the deed to Tivally Grange into his hand with tremendous relief and then handed the sack to Upton. "You are not going to kill the beatht?"

"No, of course not."

"What are you going to do with him then?"

"That is not your concern," Upton replied haughtily, swinging the sack over his shoulder. The sack squawked loudly at such uncouth treatment. "Cease and desist, you blasted fowl. You are mine now, and I shall do with you what I will."

"So you think," murmured a voice directly behind him.

"But you are sadly mistaken," added an oddly familiar voice from the shadows at his left side. "That bird is ours until we see another five hundred pounds. No, I should not protest. I have a pistol aimed straight at your heart, my lord. Winthrop, take the blasted thing away from the gent."

"Damnathon," groaned Spelling. "He did follow me, and brought along thome help. You are a toad, thir, a motht unthcrupuloth fellow!"

"Indeed," grinned Lord Peter, stepping around to face Upton. "I will have the sack. Now!"

"No," protested Upton. "Spelling will give you another five hundred pounds."

"No, I will not," protested Spelling.

"Then I will give you five hundred pounds."

"When?" Lord Peter asked, the lantern light causing the scar on his face to stand out considerably.

"Tomorrow. The very first thing tomorrow."

"In which case," the voice from the shadows proclaimed,

"the bird will be spending the night with us. Take it, Winthrop."

Lord Peter took Upton's arm at once and pried the sack from his grasp finger by finger.

"Knollsmarmer. Yohoho," muttered the sack.

"We will meet you tomorrow night at nine, at the base of London Bridge," Lord Peter murmured. "You bring the blunt an' we will bring the bird. Count to one hundred, my lord, before you move from this place or you will be dead before you get three paces into the open air, I promise you that. Where do you think you're going?" he called over his shoulder.

"I am leaving right now," Spelling declared. "Thith arrangement hath got nothing to do with me."

"Go then," growled Lord Peter.

"Spelling! Do not you dare! Give me that deed back at once. Our bargain was the bird for the deed," Upton protested as Mr. Spelling dashed for the stable door.

"I gave you the bird," Spelling called back. "The bargain ith kept. What happenth to him now ith between you and thoth fellowth," and he was gone off into the night.

"I have no idea why you chose to help Spelling," Lord Peter said, as he and Wickenshire advanced carefully through the fog toward St. Giles, "but I did enjoy the look on that villain's face when Spelling dodged out of the stable with the deed."

"A family matter," Wickenshire replied. "Tivally Grange does not actually belong to Neil."

"But he holds the deed?"

"Yes, well, it is a peculiar arrangement at best. I believe Neil is meant to be a cover of sorts."

"A cover?"

"A seemingly disinterested party, in case the excisemen should ever connect—"

"Excisemen?" Lord Peter interrupted.

"Um-hmm. You are not the only gentleman involved in . . . a bit of illegal business. If I have figured it all out correctly, the theory is that the excisemen will not be so certain, you see, that their conclusions are accurate if they should ever link Uncle Ezra to Tivally Grange. Because they will then discover that the Grange does not belong to Uncle Ezra, but to Neil. And believe me, it would be highly impractical and impossible to prove that Neil is connected with any smuggling operation. Also highly illogical to suppose that Uncle Ezra would use someone else's property to stow his goods."

"Your Uncle Ezra is a smuggler?"

"Our Uncle Ezra is a madman. Might actually have killed Neil had he lost the Grange. Never know. Mad as a hatter, Uncle Ezra."

"What does he smuggle?" asked Lord Peter, most interested.

"Well, he does not actually *sail* the ship across the channel or anything, Winthrop. He has an arrangement with a group of fellows is all."

"No, but what does he smuggle, Wickenshire?"

"Soap," whispered the earl.

"Soap?"

"Not so loud, Winthrop," Wickenshire chuckled, hitting his companion lightly on the arm.

"You have a mad uncle who smuggles soap?"

"Irish soap. Gave Sera and I an entire case of the stuff for a wedding gift. We accepted it, too. Well, what could we do? He is my uncle, after all, and quite proud of his soap. This Trump fellow is the one helped us trap Neil, eh? Care to confide in me more fully what it is he did for you that makes us go seeking him out to give him a share of the money?"

"Well, I would not ordinarily tell you this, Wickenshire, but since you have confided in me about the s-soap—"

"Cease laughing, if you will. We do all of us have family members who are not particularly acceptable."

"Yes, well, Trump is not family. But he has done me several great favors in the past few months. Rescued me from the gutter and kept me from starving, for one. Attempted to teach me his trade so I could survive, for another."

"Burglary?"

"No. I was a complete failure at Trump's trade, you see, so when he got wind of your cousin's little project, he arranged with Spelling for me to do the thing. Trump was near certain that I *could* do the thing. And he knew the money would be enough to get me safely out of England, which was all that I desired."

"Which tells me that Trump is a man who gives a care about someone he likes, but does not at all tell me who he is or why you wish to give him fifteen hundred pounds. I agreed to get the extra five hundred out of Upton so that you might do so and keep five for yourself as well, but fifteen hundred pounds is a veritable fortune, Winthrop."

"But it must be divided among three of them. And I am thinking that Trump and his partners will use it to—to—set themselves up in a more acceptable and prestigious sort of business, you know. Or perhaps they will each choose to go into business separately."

"More prestigious than what?" asked Wickenshire, his curiosity highly aroused.

Lord Peter stuffed his hands deep into his pockets and stared down into the fog swirling about his feet. "Trump is a Resurrection Man."

"Oh, my gawd," Wickenshire half-laughed, half-groaned. "You made an attempt at becoming a Resurrection Man? Poor Edward! And I was concerned over having a soap smuggler in the family!"

The sun rose at Wicken Hall and the Duke of Sotherland rose at Wicken Hall, and there all similarity between the two ended. Mary had spent the night tossing and turning upon her bed, staving off nightmares of her precious Peter being trampled beneath iron-shod hooves in some London street or attacked and beaten to death by footpads; and so she welcomed the subtle, soothing rise of the sun. She did not, however, welcome the pandemonium of the duke's rising, though he did so with such great hubbub that she could not ignore the fact that he *had* risen.

"Lindsey!" he shouted so loudly as to be heard in echoes all the way from his chamber in the west wing to the breakfast room in the east wing. "Lindsey, come at once!" The sound of the bell ringing in the kitchen as he yanked violently upon it again and again, filtered up through the chimney pieces and made Mary frown. The hurried stomping of Sotherland's valet's feet upon the servants' staircase did not go unnoted by Mary's ears either.

"We must be mad to think there is any saving grace about that man," she mumbled to herself as she walked to the sideboard to fetch herself a rasher of bacon. "He cannot so much as wake in the morning in an acceptable manner."

But I shall attempt to forgive him for it, she told herself silently, sitting back down at the table. He is Peter's papa after all, and so I must make the attempt to find some goodness in him. Sera was correct about that. How much happier Peter and Lord Bradford both would be, could they but form some more fortunate bond with their papa than the one they have now. And Eugenia and I would be far better off as well. And our children—they will want to have a pleasant sort of grandfather on both sides of the family. I am certain they will not understand if we do never go to visit their grandpapa the duke. We could, though, neglect to mention that they *have* a grandpapa the duke, she thought, a smile tugging her lovely lips upward.

"What are you smiling about, Miss Butterberry?" asked a tiny voice, rousing Mary from her thoughts.

"Oh, Delight, I did not so much as hear you enter. I thought you had already eaten, my dear."

"Yes, I did, but I am hungry again," explained the child, balancing a dish against a sideboard that was taller than she, and reaching blindly upward to fill it with whatever might come to hand.

"Here, let me help," offered Mary instantly. "You cannot even see what you are taking."

"No. Most usually Mr. Jenkins helps me, but he is busy. An' James an' Charles are busy too. Ever'one is busy. I think it is because our duke is making such a awful fuss."

"Eggs?" Mary asked. "Toast? Kippers? Bacon? Ham?"

"Uh-uh," replied Delight to each. "Is there any gruel?"

"Gruel? Do you mean to say that you actually like gruel?"

"I don't know. I have never had any. But I heard our duke say that it was probably 'zactly what he would be served for breakfast an' so I wish to try it, too."

Mary grinned. "Did he truly say that?"

"Uh-huh."

"Well, he was wrong, I fear, for there is no gruel on the sideboard. Perhaps we ought to ask cook to make him some."

"Do you think?" asked Delight.

"Well, if he is expecting it."

"I will run an' ask her right away," declared Delight with

great enthusiasm, and off she ran toward the kitchen and cook.

I ought to be thoroughly ashamed of myself, Mary thought, a smile lingering upon her lips. Sending that innocent child off to request gruel for his grace. What a perfectly awful thing to do. "But I could not resist," she murmured, sitting down once again to her breakfast.

She wondered what Peter was having for breakfast. She wondered if he had even broken his fast as yet. Does he rise early or late? she mused. I shall need to grow accustomed to it if he rises late, because I am most usually up with the dawn. Except for days like this when I have spent the entire night worrying about Peter. But soon I will not need to worry about him at all. Soon we will be together forever and I will not wonder where he is at night, because he will be right beside me.

"Cook is making it!" cried Delight, dashing into the room. "She says it is an odd thing for our duke to want, but she is making him some right away. I hope it willn't come too late."

"I do not think that the duke will come down for some time yet, Delight. Did he not just rise?"

"Uh-huh. Didn't you not hear him? He was terrible grumpy."

"Would you like something to eat before your gruel comes?"

"Uh-huh, but I can get it." With a hop, skip and a jump, she made her way to the sideboard, reached up and swiped a piece of toast from under one of the covers, plopped it down on a plate and carried it carefully back to the table. "An' I would like a cup of hot chocolate, please," she smiled angelically up at Mary.

"Of course," Mary grinned, pouring her one from the

pot on the table. "What was the duke so grumpy about, do you know?"

"Uh-huh. Sweetpea was sleeping on his chest, an' that maked him grumpy."

"Sweetpea? But she is the friendliest little thing."

"Yes. But our duke does not like cats, Mr. Lindsey says. Of course, that is not true at all, I don't think. Our duke just does not know anything about cats an' so he thinks that he does not like them."

"I expect he sent Sweetpea running and yelled at Mr. Lindsey for letting her into his chamber."

"Yes, he did," nodded Delight, picking off a piece of her toast between thumb and forefinger and nibbling at it thoughtfully. "But I told him that it wasn't not Mr. Lindsey's fault, because Sweetpea knows how to open doors all by herself."

"You told him? Were you up there?"

"Uh-huh. I runned up right away when I heard all the rumgumption going on. An' he said what was I doing there, an' I said he was makin' such a terrible rumgumption that I could not help but be curious."

"And what did he say to that?"

"That I was a brazened rapscalpion an' ought to be kept in the nursery where I belonged."

"And what did you say?"

"That he was a big ol' baby 'cause he was afraid of cats an' he was the one ought to be in a nursery, not me. But I ought not to have said that. That was verimost unkind. An' so I said I begged his pardon at once an' that I would teach him to like Sweetpea whenever he wished. An' then I jumped up an' down on his bed five times an' he catched me when I jumped off. An' then I came here to see what gruel was."

Mary had quite finished her morning meal but chose to

linger at the table with Delight until the duke should descend to break his fast. She was on her third cup of chocolate by the time his grace arrived in the breakfast room.

"Oh, good, you have comed at last!" exclaimed Delight. "We have been waiting an' waiting."

"You have?" asked the duke with a decided glare at Mary. "Good morning Miss—Butterberry, is it not?"

"Indeed. Good morning, your grace."

"Well, and why have you been waiting for me, imp?" the duke muttered, wandering over to the sideboard and lifting innumerable covers without putting one thing on his plate.

"I was not goin' to, but it took so verimost long for cook to make it that I thought I would just wait an' eat it right along with you," Delight explained, slipping out of her chair and skipping over to him. "It is in that big silver bowl right over there," she offered, pointing.

"What is?" queried the duke, reaching forward and lifting the lid.

Mary held her breath and waited for the storm to break.

"Gruel?" his grace managed in the most suffocated voice.

" 'Zactly," confirmed Delight proudly, attempting not to jump up and down with excitement. "We did not have any at first, but I told Miss Butterberry just what you said, about having gruel for breakfast, an' she said why did I not go ask cook to make you some. An' I did! An' I am going to eat it with you because I have never haved it before in my whole entire life!"

The Duke of Sotherland turned about, the silver cover of the enormous silver bowl still in his hand, and he glared silently, but most speakingly, at Mary.

I ought to have known that Delight would tell the man it was my idea, Miss Butterberry thought, lowering her gaze to the cup of cooling chocolate before her. Her cheeks turned pink with embarrassment. Oh, I do wish I had not done the thing. But it did seem such a perfect jest.

If Mary could have melted away at that moment, she would have done so most willingly. But then she reminded herself with righteous indignation that this particular gentleman whose glare caused her such ready embarrassment was the Duke of Sotherland—Peter's father—the very man who had dismissed Peter from his life, sent him off to the hinterlands when he was merely eight and had not so much as written him one letter to this very day. To be forced to eat a dish of gruel was the least of the punishments the duke deserved.

Mary's shoulders straightened and her chin lifted and she turned her beautiful sea-colored eyes full upon the gentleman. "You will pardon me, your grace," she said most clearly, her eyes boldly daring him to take her on, "but I thought it only proper that your grace's openly expressed expectations of breakfast at Wicken Hall should be met."

The Duke of Sotherland's gaze shifted from Mary to Delight and back again. The tips of his ears grew so very red that Mary could see the change in their color from where she sat. His freshly shaved cheeks puffed up to the most intimidating size. The veins in his neck began to pulse noticeably. And then his eyebrows wiggled.

"Oh, you are doing it," cried Delight, clapping her hands happily together. "You are the verimost funniest gentleman in all the whole world."

"Enough with your Spanish coin, you rapscallion," growled the duke, his gaze fastened on Mary. "Fetch us bowls, imp. We cannot eat gruel without bowls to put it in. Fetch three of them. It would be most cruel of us not to allow Miss Butterberry to join us in such a delightful treat, do not you think?"

TWELVE

Lord Nightingale perched merrily upon Wickenshire's shoulder, securely tethered to one end of the leather lead that Bobby Tripp had fashioned for him. Wickenshire had cavalierly tied the other end of the lead through the top buttonhole of his burgundy riding coat.

"What happens if the old pirate should decide to fly?" Lord Peter grinned.

"I expect he will take me with him. I have never done this before, but Delight assures me that Nightingale is quite accustomed to go roaming about the countryside latched to a lead."

"Who is Delight?"

"My little sister-in-law. You will meet her at Bradford's wedding if you do not have cause to visit us at Wicken Hall before then. A regular rascal, Delight. Always makes me smile. Why the sudden scowl, Winthrop? You were grinning a moment ago."

"Nothing. I am wishing we were bound directly for Wicken instead of stopping at this—Billowsgate. I have not seen Edward since we were eight years old and—"

"You are worried about meeting your brother?"

"I expect so. I cannot think of the first thing to say to him. What *do* you say to someone whom you ought to know just as well as you know yourself, but whom you do not know at all?"

"Yo ho ho! Knollsmarmer!" crowed Lord Nightingale cheerily.

"No, do not say that," laughed Wickenshire. "You merely say, 'Hello, Edward,' and then Bradford will make all the rest as easy for you as eating a cherry tart. I thought his heart would break when we went down to Willowsweep only to find that you had departed Frost Pool Cottage a se'ennight before without leaving the least clue where you were bound. He and Eugenia are both determined to find you. They have planned their wedding trip around places you might be."

"Their wedding trip? They intend to spend their wedding trip searching for—"

"You," nodded Wickenshire. "You will understand once we reach Billowsgate and you meet my cousin. Eugenia is the sweetest, kindest person on the face of this earth. You will like to have her as a sister-in-law, I promise you that."

"Mornin' Genia!" offered Lord Nightingale, shifting from one foot to another and nibbling at the brim of Wickenshire's hat. "Mornin' Genia. Mornin' Nightingale. Mornin' Nicky."

"He rides the most amazing old horse, Bradford does," Wickenshire said. "A strawberry roan. Delight is madly in love with the thing. Bradford told me that he had vowed upon a bible and his honor as a gentleman to . . ."

". . . prevent any harm ever coming to Nod even if Edward must die himself to prevent it," Lord Peter completed the thought for him softly. "I remember. I insisted Edward vow it because I was to go away with Mama and he and Nod to remain at Northridge. I thought then that for so long as Edward managed to keep Nod well and with him, he would not forget about me. So, Nod is yet alive and prancing?"

"And dancing," nodded Wickenshire, observing with great understanding the winsome look that had come to sit on Lord Peter's face and the pensiveness that lingered in his eyes.

"Nodnodnodwetwetwet," mumbled Nightingale, still occupied with Wickenshire's hat brim.

"He is the most remarkable bird," Lord Peter observed, changing the subject abruptly. "I did never think a macaw could speak so many words and so very clearly."

"I do not think most of them can. I have been told of late that Nightingale is quite exceptional. But I don't know that for a fact. I had never so much as seen a macaw before I inherited Lord Nightingale."

"You inherited him?"

"Um-hmmm. He belonged to my Aunt Winifred, Spelling's stepmother. And before that to my Uncle Albert, Spelling's father. And before that to someone else, but I have no idea who it might have been. A sailor, I think, from some of the things he says, though I cannot prove it."

"He must be very old, then, eh?"

"Well, he is necessarily older than Neil. Uncle Albert had him before Neil was born. And Neil is—let me think—twenty-five, I believe. How long do macaws live, do you know?"

"Not the foggiest. Twenty-five is a goodly number of years though, and you know him to be older than that. But he does not at all look as though he is upon his last legs."

"No, apparently he is just reaching his prime," laughed Wickenshire, flicking his finger at Nightingale, who had switched from nibbling on his hat brim to tugging at his cravat. "Nightingale, behave. You will have me looking a perfect ragbag by the time we arrive at Billowsgate. Uncle

Robert's butler will make me enter through the kitchen door."

The Duke of Sotherland had discovered Wickenshire's billiards room and, cue in hand, had set about entertaining himself for the afternoon. Ought to drive to this Billowsgate and pull Edward out by his hair, he thought, frowning over the baize-covered table. If I did not know that he intended to come here soon, I would, too. Damnable puppy! More trouble than he is worth. He glared at the balls spread out before him, selected his shot with great care and lowered the cue.

"Oh, here you are!" exclaimed a pleasant voice just as Sotherland stroked the cue forward, the unexpected sound causing him to miss the cue ball completely and bounce the tip of the cue off the baize.

"Damnation!" he muttered, looking up.

"Did I make you miss? I am sorry. I did not intend it."

"You did not, Miss Butterberry? How extraordinary. I should think it precisely what you intended."

"You would? Why?" asked Mary, stepping across the threshold.

"Perhaps because it is so obvious how much you despise me."

"Balderdash. I do not know you well enough, sir, to actually despise you. That is not an attitude assumed lightly."

"I see. And so then the gruel was because—"

Mary's piquant little face lit with laughter. "Oh, dear! I simply could not resist. But you did repay me for it, if you will remember. And very nicely, too."

A faint light of amusement flickered in the duke's cool blue eyes and Mary caught it upon the instant. Her heart stuttered a bit with hope. She had thought this morning as they sat at the breakfast table—the duke, Delight and herself, all determinedly eating the gruel—that she had discovered the source of Delight's power over the gentleman and a means to assume that power herself. She had shared her observations with Sera, and now she and Sera intended to give her idea a try. "Can you believe," she smiled, "that Delight actually enjoyed her portion?"

"She would, the little minx."

"Yes. Is billiards a game that gentlemen generally play by themselves?"

"Sometimes, but not generally."

"I thought not. Would you care to have me play against you?"

"You play billiards, Miss Butterberry?"

"Well, I do not know the rules of it, precisely, but—"

"Mary, here you are," interrupted Serendipity, stepping into view. "I wondered where you had gone. Good afternoon, your grace. You are playing billiards."

"I was," drawled the duke coldly.

"It cannot be a great deal of fun without an opponent."

"Just what I thought," nodded Mary.

"Allow us to give you some competition," Sera smiled, sweeping into the room and taking cues down from the case for Mary and herself. "You will enjoy the game so much more with people to play against you. Here, Mary, you may have this stick and I shall use this other. Now, you must just remind us how to go about it, your grace, and we shall begin."

"Remind you how to go about it?"

"Yes. Well, I know that you are to use this stick to knock that ball into one of the red balls. I have seen Nicholas do it."

"I have seen him do it, too," agreed Mary, placing her cue on the edge of the table, wrong end forward. "It is something like this." Whereupon she aimed the cue at the cream-colored ball, gave it a mighty shove with both hands, missed the ball completely and sent the cue whacking across the table and into the opposite wall. "Oops," she murmured. "I expect that was not quite right."

"Not quite right?" grumbled the duke. "Not quite right? That was appalling!"

"No, was it?" asked Sera, widening her eyes in feigned innocence. "I thought it was rather nicely done. Although, Mary, I do not think that when Nicholas does it, the stick goes flying out of his hands so. One must hold onto the stick, I think. Only the balls are to go flying."

"Saints preserve us!" cried his grace. "It is not a stick, ladies, it is a cue. And the cue must not leave your hands and go flying into the wall and the balls are not to go flying into the wall either. Are you both mad? This is billiards, not cricket!"

"Now you are upset," sighed Mary. "Oh, dear."

"Oh, dear?" echoed the duke, his eyebrows rising.

"No, he is not upset. Gentlemen merely get excited when they play at games. Step aside, Mary, and let me take a whack at it," urged Sera, approaching the table.

"Turn the blasted thing around!" cried the duke impatiently.

"Are you certain?"

"Yes, yes, turn the blasted thing around!"

"Well, if you say so."

"No, not the ball! The cue! Turn the cue around!"

Sera did as she was told, stared at the cue and then stared at the duke.

"Wait, Sera," Mary said. "That cannot be correct, your grace, to have the stick that way. Just look at the difference in the size of the stick at that end. One cannot possibly send one of those balls thawacking about the table with that little end of the stick. I doubt you can hit a ball with that end at all."

"Well, by gawd!" declared his grace, his eyebrows definitely wiggling. "Of all the things I have ever—you are laughing at me, Miss Butterberry!"

"Well, perhaps a bit, your grace," Mary conceded, her lips pursed, her eyes sparkling. "Because you are so very serious. But I am laughing at myself as well."

"Nicholas always says that playing at billiards helps him to relax," declared Sera. "In a matter of moments, we shall all be at ease and most companionable."

"Companionable," muttered the duke, shoving them aside and taking a shot. "That is how it is done, ladies."

"Oh, I see. Sera, did you watch? We must do just as his grace did. And he did it with the small end of the stick, too."

"The *cue!*" exclaimed Sotherland.

"The cue. Like this." Mary attempted to do the thing properly and managed only to send the cue jerking across the baize once more.

"Great heavens, Miss Butterberry, you are a disaster!" bellowed the duke. "You ought not be allowed to set foot in any billiards room anywhere."

"Well, perhaps not," Sera smiled. "But I am just as terrible at it. Nicholas did never actually have time to teach me."

"And papa does not have a billiards table," confessed Mary. "He is only a poor clergyman, after all. But now we have got you to teach us, your grace!"

"Oh," groaned Sotherland.

"Only think what a surprise it will be for Nicholas when he returns to discover that I actually know how to play billards," Sera said, resting her chin upon the top of her cue.

"And I shall thoroughly impress my intended," Mary de-

r flat upon the ground. He stood with his
:kets and his shoulders leaning against the
ie tree and saw and heard and thought only
then she ceased to laugh. Her eyes widened
rim of her straw bonnet, and she struggled
ig as quickly as she could.

at is it?" Bradford asked, stepping forward
; the swing to a halt. "You are not ill?"
vard. Oh, I cannot believe it! Edward, turn
look down the path."

ith?" He helped her from the swing, then
irms around her and followed her gaze. His
ggedly in his throat.

together along the flower-bordered path in
Jightingale fluttered and muttered and
on Wickenshire's shoulder, but neither of
iose to speak a word or so much as breathe

io had left his hat behind him in the stable,
he ground as he walked, his hands fisting
iis dark curls tossing about in the breeze.
· had overcome him, covering him over as
ning's fog. He felt it seep ever downward
reached in and froze the very marrow of
tomach lurched and fluttered and lurched
:oreness in his throat had become an ex-
imp. He peered up from beneath his thick,
:an the path in front of him and came to

ere," Wickenshire whispered. "It is merely
her twenty feet or so. You can walk that
n you not? Only think how far you have

clared, wrapping her small hands tightly around her cue,
and smiling her most beguiling smile.

"We will be ever so proud and we will owe it all to you,
your grace," added Sera, fluttering her lashes at him.

"You *are* going to teach us, are you not, duke?" asked
Mary, her gaze fastened upon him, her eyes bubbling with
good humor. "Of course you are. It will be the finest way
to spend an afternoon and you will not be at all bored, we
promise you that."

"Minxes," mumbled the duke.

Billowsgate was a house of moderate proportions set in
a park of conservative size and surrounded by an estate
neither too large nor too small. It possessed a home wood
which one could wander through from one side to the other
in a matter of ten minutes, three meadows given over to a
healthy sprinkling of cattle; one paddock, a stable of four
horses with space for ten, and two fields planted alternately
in wheat and mangel-wurzels. One entered the place by a
long, curving drive precisely bordered by elms—all of them
of one height, one width, and spaced evenly apart. There
were no ruts in the drive, no weeds, and the gravel was
freshly turned every month. Lord Peter smiled to see it.

"This one of your uncles, unlike the mad one, is a moderate type gentleman, eh, Wickenshire?"

"Determinedly moderate as regards almost everything.
Uncle Robert is the sort of gentleman who is never too
loud, too forward, too boring, too generous, too clutchfisted."

"Moderate," nodded Lord Peter, managing a slow smile
behind which he hoped to conceal his rising panic at the
thought of meeting his brother. Actually, his heart was kicking at his ribs in the most unreasonable fashion. His hands

were sweating in his gloves. His neck ached and his throat had grown suddenly sore. Of all the things in the world his features wished to do, smiling was not one of them. But he did not wish to betray such emotional turmoil as assaulted him to Wickenshire, and so he forced himself to maintain the smile. But the closer they drew to the end of the drive, the tighter Lord Peter pulled Leprechaun's reins, until the poor horse was forced to slow to practically a tiptoe.

Wickenshire could not help but guess what was happening behind that pasted-on smile, especially when Lord Peter's horse began to tiptoe, but he pretended, with great good will, not to notice. Without comment, he slowed Gracie to the unusual pace and remained steadily beside the gentleman. Gracie threatened to trip twice going at such a sluggish speed, but Wickenshire merely patted her neck supportively and said nothing about it. "Uncle Robert is a scholar of sorts," he offered as they halted before the front entrance. "He generally keeps his nose in his books and out of his fields. Hired a gentleman by the name of Seabrook to oversee his fields for him and never interferes in any of the decisions, which is why, I think, his fields prosper."

"Uh-huh," murmured Lord Peter, dismounting.

"Just tie him to the post. There is only one groom. Snead is his name. He will come 'round and take the horses to the stable once he learns that we are staying for a bit."

"Perhaps we are not staying for a bit."

"Of course we are staying, Winthrop. Spend the night, I imagine."

"Awwwk, mrrrrow, rrrrarf," muttered Nightingale as Wickenshire dismounted.

"Quiet, you old feather duster." Wickenshire tucked an arm through Lord Peter's and led him up to the door. He

turned the bell. "Good afte door opened. "Is anyone at

"Master Nicky! I mean, is at work in his stud Eugenia—"

"Yes, Tolliver? Miss Eu

"Is swinging—upon meadow," finished the bu astonishment upon Lord believe."

"We shall go around to deliver our horses to Snea and visit with Eugenia fo dig Uncle Robert out of

"J-just so, Master Nic take the—to take Lord N

"No, I will keep him he whispered in the elder and started back toward

"Indeed," replied the two peas in a pod. I the things."

Eugenia was laughin as delicate as the whisp the breeze. Bradford co and sound of her filled somehow, despite all h he had come at last to ture, and wonder that, have him for her husba as she swung up into booted foot rested upo

oak and the hands in hi rough trunk of Eugenia. under the w to slow the

"Eugenia, to help her

"No, no, around do, a

"Down th turned with h breath caugh

They trudg silence. Lor preened hims the gentlemen loudly.

Lord Peter, stared down a in his pockets The greatest f thick as last e into him until his bones. His again. And th ceedingly large dark lashes to an abrupt halt.

"Do not sto a matter of an much farther,

traveled alone, Winthrop, and for how many years. But twenty feet more, my friend, and you will never need to travel alone again."

"What if he does not truly wish me to return to him?" whispered Lord Peter hoarsely. "What if I am not all that he expects me to be? What if he is sadly disappointed in me?"

"He has been searching for you for years."

"No, he has not. He has been searching for a dream. For a brother he remembers from another time. I am not the same as I was when we were eight years old. I do not even recall much about the sort of boy I was then, and that is precisely the brother Edward has been longing to have restored to him—not me, not what I have become. He will be grieved to see what I have become."

Wickenshire's lips parted in an attempt to dispel the gentleman's fears, but before he could say so much as one more word, Lord Nightingale danced wildly upon his shoulder, began to flap his great wings and shrieked, "Knollsmarmer! Yo ho ho! Knollsmarmer!"

And then a voice that was almost an exact reproduction of Lord Peter's—a hoarse, frightened and yet eagerly hopeful voice—sounded across that twenty foot space between them. "Peter," it said. And again, "Peter!"

In but a slip of time, a passage of breath, a beat of two hearts with one rhythm, Bradford was with them. His arms engulfed Lord Peter and drew him so close that not even a bit of the breeze that rustled the leaves above their heads could pass between the two.

Lord Peter's arms came slowly, tentatively up around Bradford and then they clutched at him with all the strength they possessed. "Edward," he whispered. And tears blurred the clear blue of his eyes as they filled with an awesome wonder.

Wickenshire took hold of the parrot's lead and brought the bird to stand on his gloved hand as he backed away from the two gentlemen. "Not just now, Nightingale," he murmured. "You will have your chance with Bradford, but not just at this moment. You have missed him, eh? Well, just look right over there, old spit and feathers, and see who else we have found again."

Lord Nightingale, forced thus to turn away from the brothers, set one large amber eye to viewing the landscape before him. His head began to bob and his chest to swell. "Mornin' Genia!" he called in his merriest tone. "Mornin' Genia!"

"Good morning, my lord," Eugenia called, strolling to meet them before they ever reached the swing. She stroked the parrot's chest gently, ruffling his feathers, which set him to posing and preening and muttering, and at the last, to stepping from Wickenshire's hand onto her shoulder, where he set about nibbling happily upon the brim of her bonnet.

Wickenshire untied the end of the lead from his button-hole and gave it to Eugenia. Then he tucked her arm through his own and smiled down at her with the most triumphant look in his eyes.

"I cannot believe that you actually found him, Nicky," Eugenia said, her smile as bright as the sky above. "I thought for a moment, when first I noticed you, that I was seeing things. Where did you find him? How?"

"It is a very long story, my girl, and believe it or not, that feathered fiend on your shoulder played a large part in it. I will tell it all to you once I have a cup of tea in one hand and a tart in the other. Shall I escort you back to the house, do you think? Those two will not so much as notice that we have left them."

"No, they will not. Oh, Nicky, just see how tightly Edward holds him, as though Lord Peter would disappear did

Edward give him space to take so much as a decent breath. I thought Edward would faint when he saw him walking beside you up the path. He grew so still and so pale all at once. Yes, let us go back to the house. Tolliver has likely told Papa that you are here and Papa has yet to congratulate you upon—"

"Upon what, minx? Why are you smiling that particular smile?"

"I told Papa that Sera was in the family way, Nicky, and I thought that he would tumble right out of his chair. He is determined to break out the finest wine in our cellar and toast you with it. After he teaches you to tie your cravat, that is," she added with a mischievous grin.

"Unfair. It was tied perfectly. Nightingale destroyed it."

"Did you, Nightingale? What a bad boy."

"Bad," Lord Nightingale intoned quite seriously as the cousins made their way slowly back toward the house. "Bad. Bite. Villain. Wetwetwet. Mornin' Genia. Knoooooooollsmaaarmer."

THIRTEEN

Upton shivered in the rising, billowing fog at the base of London Bridge. He had arrived as instructed, at nine o'clock, with the five hundred pounds wrapped in oilskin in his greatcoat pocket. That had been well over a quarter of an hour ago, and still no one had appeared to collect the money and restore Lord Nightingale to him. "Demmed nit-witted scoundrels have probably lost the bird," he muttered, stamping his feet in a fruitless effort to warm them.

"Nope, we 'aven't lost 'im," replied a deep, gravelly voice from just beyond his left shoulder.

The voice was so close and so unexpected that Upton actually jumped at the sound of it. He spun about and squinted into the fog-whitened night. "About time you showed yourselves! Where the devil are you?"

"I be right 'ere," replied the man, stepping out from behind a tangle of brush. "An' m'boys be all around ye, so ye'll not be thinkin' of causin' us any trouble, eh? Ye've brought the blunt wif ye, have ye not?"

"Yes," grumbled Upton.

"All five hunnerd of it?"

"Yes. I told you, yes. I have it right in my pocket."

"Good. Excellent. Ye'll perduce it, if ye please."

" 'E'll perduce it even if 'e don't please," laughed a voice at Upton's back.

"You are not the same men who took the parrot from me last night," protested Upton. "I cannot see you clearly, but your voices are not at all the same."

"Ah, a smart cove! A bright cove! A 'telligent cove! Right ye are, m'lad. We bean't the same atall. Still, m'dear, we be the blokes what is relievin' ye o' yer five hunnerd pounds this night, eh? Give it 'ere," the man standing before him directed, wiggling his raggedly gloved fingers extremely close beneath Upton's nose. "Be handin' it right over, if ye please."

"Not until I see the bird," scowled Upton. "I am not so stupid as to give you the money and then be left with nothing."

"Oh, the bird! Why certain-sure ye shall see the bird if ye be wishin' it. 'enry, bring the bird."

Another man stepped into Upton's sight from his right with a hopping, wiggling sack in hand and began to untie the rope from around the top of it. "Jus' a minit. I gots to git this 'ere knot out. Bloody knot! Done been tied too forceful."

"No, do not open it up!" exclaimed Upton. "Are you mad? The blasted bird will fly away and I shall never get him back."

"So's we thought areselfs," agreed the first of the men. "But then, ye did arsk ta see the beastie."

"No, no, it is enough to see the sack. It is the same sack that he was in last night. Here, take your money and be gone," growled Upton, thrusting the wrapped bank notes at the man in the raggedy gloves.

"Aye, an' ye take yer bird, m'dandy. 'enry, be givin' 'im the sack. There's m'lad. An' a good day ta ye, sir. 'Twere a pleasure doin' bidniss wif ye."

There was a rustling of brush, the sound of hushed voices and laughter, and in but a moment, the men—how many of them, Upton could not guess—had faded away into the fog.

Angry because he had been forced to pay five hundred pounds out of his own pocket—the original fifteen hundred had been Spelling's contribution—Upton nevertheless refrained from doing anything at all rash, like chasing after the villains. Instead, he tossed the heavy sack over his shoulder and trudged back up the hill from the bridge abutment to the place his carriage and driver waited. "Home, John," he ordered, stuffing the sack inside the vehicle and climbing hastily in after it. He stared at the wiggling sack on the seat opposite him, watched it hop about, and the scowl on his face faded, to be replaced by a most contented grin. "I have got you now, you old bit of feathers, and you are going to make me rich," he snickered softly. "By Jove, had I known the worth of you when first we met at Willowsweep, I would have done a good deal more to help Spelling in his attempt to spirit you away. But there I was, all unsuspecting and interested only in getting my hands on my cousin Serendipity and that scraggly little sister of hers. What a mistake that was, eh? What a sorry lack of intelligence. When you were sitting right there before my eyes."

It did occur to Upton that Lord Nightingale was not giving out with his usual and generally annoying chatter, but he thought he could well understand why the parrot did not. "Likely kept you in that sack all night and day, did they not? Likely have not fed you a thing, either, since they took you from Wickenshire. Well, you will feel more the thing when I get you home, Nightingale. I have a cage waiting for you, my friend, and all the pine nuts and bits of fruit you can possibly desire."

As Upton's coach rolled hastily toward Marlborough Street and Upton House, the three men who had relieved him of his money were laughing and whispering and scurrying across London Bridge, intent on gaining Tooley Street and the safety of a tiny pub called the Cat and the Cradle. "Gawd bless the boy," the man with the raggedy gloves proclaimed. "I tole ye Winthrop'd be worf are trouble ta take 'im in, didn't I not?"

"Aye, ye did, Trump," agreed the second of the men enthusiastically. "An' right ye were about it too. Gived us a thousand pounds, he 'as, by gawd, right out of his own pocket. He didn't not ha'f ta do that. An' then 'e puts us in the way o' another five hunnerd!"

"The boy be a blessed saint," mumbled the third man. "He has maked us rich!"

"Five hunnerd pounds apiece it come to," observed Trump. "I asked my Elsie fer ta figger it out. A man may raise up 'is childern an' care fer 'is woman wifout no worries fer years wif five hunnerd pounds in 'is pocket. Aye, an' not be havin' ta resurrect no un ever agin, lads!"

They all laughed long and hard at that as they strolled into the Cat and the Cradle, ordered themselves ale all around and crowded into the pub's only private booth, pulling the curtain closed after them.

"Thank gawd word o' that job come filterin' down ta me," grinned Trump when the ale was brought them. " 'ere's ta Winthrop. Gawd bless the boy an' 'is weak stomach! If 'e woulda took to resurrectin', we wouldn't none o' us be no richer at all fer it."

They began then to reminisce about Winthrop and his first encounter with the trade—Mr. Withers—The dearly deceased upon whom Winthrop had undergone his first and last lesson had been called Mr. Withers.

" 'E were a heavin' an' agaspin' so hard by the time we pried open that coffin! I do remember! And when 'e begun atuggin' out the freshly deceased, I thought as how I would break out into whoops!" laughed Trump, gulping at his ale.

"Aye," chuckled Henry Tolliver. " 'E be a sweet lad, Winthrop, an' he were willin' all right, but do ye remember how white 'e turned when we done 'splained ta him as we hadda take orf the grave clothes afore we put Mr. Withers into the coach?"

"Couldn't not conceive of it," provided Charter Covern, almost spilling his ale down his chin. "Couldn't not conceive how a bloke could be gaoled fer ridin' aroun' wif a corpse what 'ad clothes on, but how nobody'd say nuff'in were the corpse naked!"

"Aye, an' we near ta lost 'im," winked Trump, "makin' 'im ride about in that stinkin' coach wif that stinkin' corpse all over Lunnon. Kept gittin' greener an' greener 'e did. Barely maked it ta the surgeon's back door afore 'e cast up 'is accounts."

"Weren't not made fer it, Winthrop weren't," agreed Tolliver. "Not made fer it atall. Takes a strong stomach it does and a certain lack o' pretensions, resurrectin'. Not that Winthrop has got pretensions 'zactly, but there do be a bit o' the aristocrat about the boy, an' it did not fit atall good wif robbin' graves. That it didn't."

"Aye," nodded Trump. "Still, the boy gived resurrectin' the best 'e had. An' 'e done gived this burglar thin' the best as well, I think, 'cause lookit all what he got from it. Musta proved ta be a excellent burglar, eh? An' he be a fine lad, ta think ta share his profits wif us!"

Charter Covern was just proposing to start up a bakery shop with his share of the money when, far across town, Lord Upton stepped into his parlor, set the sack they had given him upon the carpeting before the cage he had had fashioned for the express purpose of housing Lord Nightingale and began to undo the knotted rope that kept the sack closed.

"Hold on, Nightingale," he whispered. "I shall have you

out in a moment. There is a fire lit in here for you to warm away the chill. What a fine fellow you are," he murmured reaching down carefully into the sack. "What a good bird."

He felt the bird peck at his gloved hand, remembered the bite it had once given Spelling and, thinking that two hands would make capturing the parrot safer by far, dropped the top of the sack and knelt down on the floor to fish the parrot out.

"Is there some way in which I may be of assistance, my lord?" asked a voice from the threshold.

"Oh! Lansing!" Upton had not expected his butler, but it occurred to him at once that he could use the man's help. "I have just got my bird, Lansing. The one for whom I had that cage crafted. I wonder, would you mind holding open the cage door? Will not do to have it swing closed when both my hands are around the creature."

"I should be pleased to do so, my lord," replied Lansing, crossing to the cage.

There was a bit of a struggle as Upton's hands closed upon the bird and the bird's claws clung to the cloth of the sack. But then, in a rush, the bird was out and Upton standing with it and turning toward the cage. A fluttering. A fluff and puff of feathers. And the cage door snapped shut.

"There!" cried Upton triumphantly, looking down and brushing several feathers from his coat. "You are in your new home at last, my fine, feathered friend!" And then Upton looked up, to smile in at Lord Nightingale.

Upton stared. His jaw dropped. He made the oddest squeaking sound deep in his throat.

"It is—a most remarkable bird, my lord," offered Lansing after a very long, silent moment. "Quite pretty, actually."

"It is a demmed pigeon!" whispered Upton hoarsely, beginning to tremble with fury.

"A remarkably large pigeon," intoned Lansing, wondering what his employer could possibly want with a pigeon. Still, he was not a man to criticize the eccentricities of those who paid his salary. "And very nicely colored as well," he added. "All in all, a fine bird, I should think. Tea, my lord?"

"You will pardon me, sir," Mr. Spelling's valet murmured, sorting through the clothes his employer was hurling onto the bed and attempting to fold them decently into a trunk, "but I understood that our visit to Wicken Hall was not to occur until next Tuesday. I would have had you all packed and ready to depart else. I cannot understand how I could have been so very wrong about the date."

"You were not wrong about the date," Spelling replied. "Not at all. It is none of it your fault, Carson. I have changed my mind, is the thing. We are leaving London the very moment the sun peers over the horizon tomorrow morning and not a second later. I have told Nathan to have the curricle ready and at the door."

"Yes, sir. Am I still to accompany you?"

"What?" asked Spelling, leaning deep into his armoire. "I did not hear you properly, Carson."

"I merely wondered if I were still to accompany you, Mr. Spelling, or if you had, perhaps, changed your mind about that as well—since you propose to drive the curricle, Mr. Spelling."

"No, I have not changed my mind about that. You are not afraid to accompany me, Carson?"

"Of course not, Mr. Spelling."

"Good. Because I shall have need of you."

"Well, perhaps I am a bit afraid, sir," Carson conceded quietly. "But that is only because every time you and Lord Wickenshire come together something dreadful happens to someone. I shall never forget poor Mr. Arnsworth, Mr. Spelling."

"Wickenshire had nothing at all to do with that, Carson. Lord Wickenshire was not even in England at the time."

"No sir, but we were at Wicken Hall at the time. And Mr. Arnsworth's nose was broken, Mr. Spelling. And the time before, when you visited Willowsweep without me—"

"I remember, Carson."

"And last evening, sir, when Lord Wickenshire and his friend accompanied you home. Well, your nose is still a bit swollen, Mr. Spelling. I cannot help but think that perhaps it is not such a very good idea for us to be driving out to Wicken Hall again, especially when we are not expected until next Tuesday. There is no telling what may happen."

Spelling could not help himself. He ceased ferreting about in his armoire and clothespress and chest of drawers and collapsed into the wide, overstuffed chair before the window. He leaned back and then he leaned forward. He rested his arms upon his thighs and clasped his hands between his knees. He lowered his head and muttered something that the valet could not at all comprehend, then looked up at Carson with the most sorrowful eyes. "I am in a bit of a bind, Carson," he confessed quietly.

"You are, sir?"

"Indeed. Do you recall that great pounding on our front door an hour ago?"

"I do, indeed, sir. Do you mean to tell me that Lord Wickenshire and his friend—"

"No, no, it was not Nicky pounding. It was Lord Upton."

"Lord Upton?" asked Carson, amazed. "We have not been privileged by a visit from Lord Upton since—"

"Since he accompanied me to Willowsweep. I know, Carson. At any rate, something dire has happened. There was— Lord Wickenshire and I were—well, what happened is not something to be shared with you, but apparently Lord Upton sat down this evening and set his mind to remembering everyone he knew, and has recalled Nicky's voice. He has connected my cousin to what happened."

"Recalled his lordship's voice, sir? Connected Lord Wickenshire to what happened? And because of this we must rush off to Wicken Hall?"

"Yes. Wickenshire may be in danger, and I am obliged to warn him of it, because what he did, he did for me. Now pack, Carson, as fast as humanly possible. We must be gone from London as soon as the morning dawns."

Mary sang softly to herself as she sat braiding her long midnight tresses before the small vanity mirror. It was a very old song. One her mama often sang, about a young woman who lost her heart to a highwayman and how she waited at the window each evening for him to come riding up. And then, one evening, he did not come. He never came again. They found him dead upon the road and the young woman in the song wasted away of a broken heart.

How very sad, thought Mary, as she completed the final verse and the last of the braid at one and the same time. How very sad to pine away for someone you can never have. Thank goodness I am not in that same horrible state— though I thought I well might be for the longest time. But Peter does not lie dead on some highway and he will be back in Wicken soon. Perhaps even as soon as tomorrow. Oh, I hope it is tomorrow.

"What ought I to do?" she whispered to her reflection in the mirror. "Ought I to go home tomorrow and await Peter there? Or ought I to remain here?"

Well, I know I ought to remain here, she mused, because I did agree to help Sera with the duke. But if Mama and

Papa tell Peter that I am a guest at Wicken Hall, he will ride out here and no doubt be confronted by a father he has not seen since he was a boy—a father whom he believes cares nothing about him and worse, a father who despises him so much that he did never bother to write him one letter in all the years they were separated. No, I cannot put Peter through such a meeting without warning him to expect it first. I shall go home tomorrow and remain there until Peter arrives.

But what if he waits to accompany Lord Bradford and Eugenia and Nicky from Billowsgate? What if he chooses to make one of their party? They will expect him to remain here as a wedding guest. Most likely he will be called on to be Lord Bradford's groomsman. And then I will be at home with Mama and Papa and he will be here and forced to meet his father without me.

"He will have Lord Bradford with him, if that is the case," Mary murmured, standing and crossing to her window. "Peter will not be alone. Lord Bradford will be standing right beside him and Lord Bradford has lived with the Duke of Sotherland his whole life long. Surely Edward will not allow the duke to hurt Peter all over again. No, he will not allow that any more than he will allow his father to interfere with his own marriage to Eugenia."

The thing of it is, Mary thought, I wish to go home, and yet I do not. I am beginning to believe that the dowager countess is correct, that the duke is not as black as we all thought him, and that Sera and I and Delight together may be able to make him into at least an acceptable human being. He did come near to laughing when Sera at last hit the ball with her stick. With her cue, I mean. And he did call me a remarkable lass when I banked that wretched ball correctly after the fifteenth attempt. And if Peter does not come tomorrow and we have another entire day to work on his father—

With a shrug and a sigh, Mary turned from the window, snuffed the candles and lowered the lamp wick, doffed her robe and stepped up into her bed. She did not wish to think about any of it further. She was tired and making everything much more difficult than it needed to be. Tugging the coverlet up to her chin, Mary closed her eyes and struggled toward sleep. She attempted to count sheep, but that did no good at all, because they all turned into little wine-colored balls, which the Duke of Sotherland plucked from a baize-covered table with his bare hands and squeezed until little droplets of wine-colored blood dripped out of them. Mary muttered and giggled a bit at that and attempted to count her blessings instead. But she only got as far as one blessing. Peter. She discovered that she could proceed no further. His face filled her mind; his voice filled her ears; the most incredible longing for him filled her heart; and without so much as thinking any more about it, she fell asleep counting the number of sweet kisses he had given her in the time before he had fled Wicken with Tobias Quinn's men at his heels.

In one of the two guest chambers at Billowsgate, Lord Peter lay on his back staring upward at the dark ceiling. Beside him Bradford chuckled. "It has been near fourteen years since we were forced to share a bedchamber, Peter. And I cannot recall that we ever had to actually share a bed."

"This is why your Eugenia chooses to be married at Wicken Hall, eh?"

"Indeed. We both thought it would nice if our guests had

beds to call their own while they were with us. Do you ride on to Wicken tomorrow?"

"Yes. I have left Mary in the most preposterous position and I cannot allow her to linger there."

"Well, I will ride with you then."

"You will?"

"Um-hmmm. I have settled everything here and have the special license stowed safely away. Wickenshire and I will keep you company as far as Wicken Hall."

"But Eugenia—"

"She will follow in the coach with her Papa in a day or so. There are things, she says, that she must do before the wedding, and she does not need me around to keep her from them. You will not mind to have my company?"

"Mind? Mind to have your company? When I feared for so very long that you would never so much as wish to hear my name again? By gawd, Edward, I shall rejoice whenever I have the good fortune of your company for the rest of my life."

"So, you and I and Wickenshire, then. We will leave after breakfast. Now go to sleep, eh? You have had a very busy week from all I hear, and there are weeks and months and years ahead of us to be together, little brother. And we will be together. Forever and ever. I give you my word on it."

In less than three minutes Bradford was snoring softly, but Lord Peter could not find sleep. His heart rejoiced in his brother beside him, but his soul knew that his rejoicing was not so fine a thing as it might have been.

It would all be finer still were you here to share the joy with me, Mary, he thought, envisioning the emotions of this day reflected back at him in her ever-changing sea-colored eyes. His heart began to ache with longing as memories of her—stubborn, insistent, thoroughly determined and un-bending in her love, in her belief in his goodness—flashed through his mind. You believed in me, Mary, when I did not even have the good grace to believe in myself, he thought. It is you who brought me to this place and this time. Had you not run away and found me, had you not refused to leave me that morning at Wicken Hall, I would likely be boarding an Indiaman this very night and watching my soul drown on its way to some foreign shore.

The Duke of Sotherland had climbed up into his bed and fallen soundly asleep without the need for one sip of brandy, without finding it at all necessary to pace or mumble or mutter at the coals upon the hearth. He did recollect for a moment or two, before he began to snore, how very angry he was at Edward and what he intended to do to his son for choosing to marry this untitled niece of the dowager Countess of Wickenshire. But the recollection of it did nothing at all to keep him awake.

The fact was that for the first time in many years, the Duke of Sotherland had lain down between the sheets with a smile upon his face. He had not allowed Lindsey to see it, of course. He had kept his scowl firmly in place until his valet had departed for the night. But then the smile had slipped out, and it had lingered, without the least effort on his part, until he had heard his chamber door open softly and tiny footsteps patter across the floor. In a moment, two white paws were clinging to the mattress near his pillow and two pea green eyes were blinking up into his own.

"Mrrrrr?" the cat had asked quite politely.

"Absolutely not," the duke had replied. And then a cold, pink nose had pressed against his own and a rough red tongue had begun to lick at his upper lip.

"Mrrrr?" the cat had asked again, after it had thoroughly washed the particular spot it had deemed unacceptable.

"Oh, why not," the duke had muttered. "I have taught two incorrigible gels to play billiards, had a battle of wits with the dowager all through dinner, been kissed good night by a faerie princess *and* her dog; why should I vacillate at having a cat to sleep upon my bed. Come up, then."

"Mrrrrrphspt," Sweetpea had thanked him, leaping across him and kneading herself a place at his side. "Murglespritmrrrrow."

"Yes, well, you are welcome. But I know, now, that you can open doors on your own, so you must be gone before Lindsey comes to wake me in the morning, do you understand?"

"Mrrrrrrrrrow."

"Good, because it would not do to have him discover that I have allowed you to sleep on this bed after all. He will be certain that my brain has turned to mush."

And then the Duke of Sotherland had closed his eyes and wiggled just a bit and had fallen off to sleep, with the smile still lingering upon his face.

FOURTEEN

Mary could not contain her eagerness any longer than it took her to dress and pack and eat her breakfast. "I did think that perhaps I would remain until this afternoon," she explained to Serendipity as they stood beside the phaeton in which John Coachman was to drive her home, "but I fear that I will not be of the least help in dealing with his grace today. Peter promised to arrive in Wicken today or tomorrow at the very latest, and my mind overflows with thoughts of him this morning. I cannot seem to concentrate on anyone or anything else."

"I can see that plainly," Sera smiled. "But I do believe that we have chipped away a bit at his grace's blackness, Mary. Enough to prove that it may be done. Still, for all we know, to bring him around far enough to accept all that he must with good grace may be a project requiring months, even years."

"Yes, but now that we know it is possible, I shall attempt to convince Peter to give his papa the benefit of the doubt just as we did," replied Mary, her fingers playing impatiently with the strings of her reticule. "Perhaps I shall even be able to convince Peter to come here and speak plainly to the duke. He has neither seen nor heard from his papa in fourteen years. But I think now that such a thing did not happen because his papa is so very black. I think, perhaps, that his papa became black because of whatever happened to separate them."

"If you can convince Peter so, to come and speak with his papa, then you ought to accompany him, Mary. It will make all easier for both of them. His grace is fast developing a fondness for you, I think. But he does not at all realize that you and Lord Peter are betrothed."

"We are not betrothed as yet, Sera."

"No, but you will be as soon as Lord Peter speaks with your papa. I am certain of that. And then, if the two of you come and speak with his grace, I cannot think but that he will make an effort to reconcile with Peter, and perhaps he will speak of all that happened to separate them for such a great length of time. I believe his grace will do it, Mary, if only to please you."

"To please me? Do you think so?"

"Yes, you made him come so very close to laughing any number of times yesterday. You could never have done so if he were not in the midst of developing a fondness for you."

"I do wish he would develop such a fondness for Eugenia," Mary sighed. "And quickly, too. That would make everything very much easier for everyone."

"Yes, but I cannot think that he will unless he takes the time to come to know her. Eugenia is so very shy sometimes and quiet, one cannot measure her worth at first sight, or even second. And his grace, you know, is determined to make a great commotion over Edward marrying Eugenia. It was his sole reason for driving all the way into Kent, after all. And he is so very stubborn that he *will* bellow the moment he sees Edward's face. Still, I will take Eugenia and Edward aside before he descends upon them, I promise you that. And I will tell them both what we have discovered—that beneath all of his grace's scowls and bellows and angry words, there lies a heart not thoroughly black. And you must be certain to convince Lord Peter of the same, Mary."

"I will, and I thank you, Sera, for rescuing me from Mama and Papa for a time. I know that that was a part of the reason you came to fetch me, and it was most kind of you."

Serendipity gave Mary a hug and a kiss on the cheek. "We shall become the best of friends," she said. "I know it. You must remember to be extra patient with your mama and papa, Mary. And kind. Especially when Lord Peter arrives on your doorstep. They will be upon pins and needles, I think. Especially your mama."

"Indeed, and I must play the pincushion. Well, I will. I can do nothing else. I will have Peter to be my husband whether Mama and Papa wish it to be so or not, but it would be so much better if they did wish it. Goodbye, Sera," she added, accepting the footman's hand and stepping up into the phaeton. "And if you find that you require my aid—or Peter's aid—you must only send word to the rectory by one of your footmen."

Serendipity watched as the vehicle disappeared down the drive. She could not imagine what would happen when Lord Peter appeared on the Butterberrys' doorstep, but she knew beyond a doubt that Mary would have her Peter for husband in the end, in spite of any and all objections. "I do hope that all goes well for you, Mary, from the very moment that you see him again," she whispered. "I wish you nothing but happiness with all my heart."

Lord Nightingale could not be pleased that morning as the three gentlemen rode toward Wicken. First he must sit on Wickenshire's shoulder and then Bradford's and then Lord Peter's and then Wickenshire's again.

"Do cease fluttering about, you old pirate," Wickenshire protested as the bird came back to him for a third time.

"Yo ho ho! Tempest fugit!" replied Nightingale with great good will. "Gentlethoughtsan' tenderheart. Ca-a-a-ringkind andtrue—ue—ue," he sang then, joyously.

"Gentle thoughts and tender heart? Where the devil did he learn that?" asked Wickenshire. "He never ceases to amaze me."

"I taught him," admitted Bradford, the tips of his ears reddening. "It was—I—he sang it for Eugenia, you see. The night I proposed marriage to her."

"Surely you jest," Lord Peter drawled with the most amazed look in his wide blue eyes. "You proposed marriage with the help of this incorrigible parrot, Edward?"

"Yes. And with Nod's help, too."

"Well, I can understand wishing Nod to be there." Lord Peter grinned fondly at his brother's horse. "Every time I look at him, Edward, I remember how excited we were the day he was born."

"He is the one has kept me sane all these years," Bradford admitted. "Nod and Stanley. Without them to remind me what it is to be loved and to love in return, I should have grown to be exactly like father."

"Stanley is still with you?"

"Uh-huh. He is the grandest old gentleman, Peter. Likely he will come entirely undone to see you face-to-face once more."

"Where is he?"

"Where?"

"Yes. He was not at Billowsgate. He would have helped me to borrow even more of your clothes than I already have had he been there. Stanley was always the best of gentle-men."

"He would likely have tied your cravat for you too," drawled Wickenshire, cocking an eyebrow at the raggedly tied article. "He wishes to know where Stanley is, Bradford. Do we dare to confide in this fellow?"

Bradford grinned. "I cannot think why not. Peter was used to be good at keeping secrets."

"And I still am," offered Lord Peter.

"I have sent Stanley to London, Peter," Bradford said.

"To London? When? Was he there when Wickenshire and I—?"

"Yes, there the whole time," nodded Bradford. "Putting up at Pultney's. Doing me the most enormous favor. I traveled to London two weeks ago to purchase a special license at the Archbishop of Canterbury's office in Doctor's Commons, y'see. Because Eugenia wished to be married at Wicken Hall instead of in the church, and in the afternoon rather than the morning. And we did not wish to wait for the banns to be called in both of our parishes, and—"

"Tell the truth, Edward. You wished to tie the knot before our father got wind of it and mustered his forces to drive into Kent to stop you, eh?"

"Precisely. I wrote him that I intended to marry a young woman he knew nothing about—a young woman without title or fortune. I can imagine how that must have set him to bellowing. He has told me time and time again that because I am his heir, I must marry *both* title and fortune. He did not take it lightly when he learned that I had chosen Eugenia. I am certain of it. I fully expect he has decided to drive down into Kent and break up our wedding, but he has no idea when the wedding is."

"And a good thing, too," Lord Peter responded.

"Yes. I expect he will wait until he hears the first of the banns called in Northridge parish."

"Which means that he will wait forever," murmured Wickenshire. "Or at least until he remembers that there are such things as special licenses."

"And by the time he does remember that," Bradford added, "Eugenia and I will already have done the deed."

"He will throttle you once he gets his hands on you," Lord Peter warned. "I have not forgot so much about Papa as all that."

"He will likely try," nodded Bradford. "But he is not at all fond of traveling these days, Peter. And he will believe that the banns must be called, so I doubt that he will come raging down upon us before the end of November at the soonest, and we shall be married a month by then. At any rate, when I went to get the license, I happened to pass a particular shop in Marley Street, and in the window—"

"Was a pattern for a dress," Wickenshire took up the tale, smiling. "And your brother, brave as he can stare, marched right inside and arranged to have the pattern made up in a Florence satin of a soft rose color—whatever a Florence satin of a soft rose-color may be—because he thought that it would make an excellent wedding dress for Eugenia."

"And it will fit her, too, because when I got back to Billowsgate, I convinced her papa to take one of her gowns of this past Season from her armoire, and I sent Stanley back to London with it so that the seamstress could use it to size the new gown correctly."

"She will be flabbergasted when she learns of it," grinned Wickenshire. "And also very thankful that I and her father had nothing to do with the choosing of it."

"Eugenia has been searching everywhere for the gown her father took ever since," laughed Bradford. "I did never once see her in that gown, but let it be spirited away, and she must have it the very next day."

They parted late in the afternoon on the high road at the drive to Wicken Hall. Wickenshire and Bradford turned in to the drive. Lord Peter urged Leprechaun onward toward the village of Wicken and the rectory. The closer he got to the village, however, the more he reined in the horse, because he was beginning to feel quite ill. The closer he got to Wicken, the more unaccountably heavy his heart grew and the more intensely his stomach ached. As he neared a particularly familiar turning in the road, visions of rose wedding gowns began to float about in his brain and he began to grow extraordinarily warm. He slowed Leprechaun to a walk and swiped the back of his hand across his brow, knocking the hat he had borrowed from his brother far back upon his head. "I cannot do this," he murmured, so softly that Leprechaun pricked his ears back in an effort to determine what his master wished of him. "No, I am not speaking to you, Chaun. I am merely muttering to myself. It comes of being born a Finlay. We do all of us talk aloud to ourselves. At least Mama always complained that we all did."

He bit his lip then and felt the first rustlings of terror rising up within him. What a fool I am, he thought. I know that Mary loves me. Has she not shown me so time and time again? And I love her. I love her with all my heart.

But what good is love? he thought then. Did not Mama and Papa love each other? And only think what happened to them. Mama became a shrew and Papa a tyrant. And Mama ran off to live with Tobias Quinn and Papa—well, I do not precisely know what happened to Papa. I only know what Edward says, that Papa became an old curmudgeon and hid himself away and made Edward subject to his every whim and fancy. Still, Edward is not the least bit afraid to marry Eugenia despite what Papa may do. No, and Eugenia is not afraid to marry Edward, either. They believe that love can overcome any obstacle or ill or misfortune.

"I believe that love can overcome any obstacle or ill or misfortune," he whispered to himself. "I must believe that love can overcome any of those. I must, because I am even now on my way to speak to Mary's father and to propose marriage to the gel. I have gone so far as to borrow Edward's best riding coat and breeches. I am decked out in my brother's best hat and gloves and one of his finest cravats. I am dressed to the nines in borrowed togs and all for Mary's sake, so as not to disgrace her again before her parents."

He came to the small wood that stood just north of Wicken and he brought Leprechaun to a halt. He sat for a time in the saddle and stared down at the ground; then he dismounted and led the horse off the road and into the wood. He stumbled awkwardly. His feet did not seem to know where they were going and the most dreadful dizziness came over him. The soft, warm breeze that rippled the leaves above his head chilled him to the marrow. He stopped, clutched at the nearest tree trunk with a shaking hand and abruptly cast up his accounts.

"Love? Overcome every obstacle and ill and misfortune? Love? What is love but a noose around one's neck?" his mother's voice hissed at the very back of his mind. "Love is a badly fashioned noose, too. One that does not break your neck swiftly and mercifully, but chokes you bit by bit until you pray for death, and even when you are praying and praying, death does not come!"

"No," Peter muttered, the bitter taste of bile lingering in

his throat. "No. You are wrong, Mama. It is not so. Love is not a noose, badly fashioned or otherwise!"

"Peter?"

The sound of his name caused him to look up.

"Peter, you have come!" Like a lovely wraith of a woman, her bonnet hanging by its ribands on her shoulders, her hair loosed from the most of its pins by the breeze, Mary came to him through the dappled landscape amidst the sun and shadow of the trees, smiling, her arms open wide.

"Mary? Is it truly you?" He could not be certain. He thought perhaps she was some vision conjured up by his imagination, for why else would she appear to him here, in this stand of trees, when she ought to be awaiting him in the rectory at Wicken?

"Peter, you are ill." Mary stopped before him and studied him, nibbling nervously at her lower lip to see him so very discomposed. She stepped up to him and took his brother's hat from his head and smoothed the dark curls back from his perspiring brow. "You *are* ill. Come. Just a bit further. You may sit down and rest on the rock at the foot of The Conqueror's Tree, and rest for a time."

"The Conqueror's Tree," murmured Peter as she took his hand and led him deeper into the wood. "I had almost forgotten about The Conqueror's Tree."

"Had you? But it is where we used to meet, Peter, whenever I could sneak away without Papa and Mama knowing. Here. Here we are. Sit down, my darling. Let me unbutton your coat and loosen the knot in your cravat. There. Now you will be able to breathe a deal easier. Peter, do let go of your horse's reins. If you fear he will run off, I will tie him for you."

"No, no, Chaun will not go without me. Mary, is it truly

you? You are not some vision risen whole from my damnable imagination?"

"Yes, of course it is me. You are very late in coming. I waited and waited and then I thought that perhaps you would not come until tomorrow, so I saddled Lulubelle and came here to the wood to dream of you for awhile. It is not so very easy, you know, to dream of the man you love when you live in the same house with five sisters," she added softly, taking Leprechaun's reins from his hand and letting them dangle to the ground. Then she sat down beside him on the large white rock at the base of the ancient oak and tucked her arm through his. "Do you remember, Peter, how we used to sit here and watch the stars flicker through the treetops?"

"I remember," Peter replied, leaning forward and resting his head in his hands. "I remember. I compromised you each time by the doing of it, too. And I ruined you all over again by allowing you to spend the night with me in that barn and then, when I allowed you to accompany me toward London, the two of us alone."

"No. No, you did not compromise me. If I have been compromised, then it is I who have done it to myself. If I am ruined, then it is I who am responsible. Peter? What is it? Why do you speak of these things now? Do you feel faint? Have you a fever?" Mary asked fearfully, stripping off her glove and pressing her hand to his brow.

"I am—lightheaded."

"But not feverish, thank goodness."

"No. Mary? Do you believe that love can overcome any obstacle or ill or misfortune? Do you?"

His voice quavered so when he said it that Mary knew immediately how important her answer must be to him. "Do you wish me to answer truthfully, Peter?"

"Yes."

"Well, it seems most absurd after all I have said and done for the love of you to say so, but no, Peter, I do not believe that love can overcome everything you mention. Not precisely."

Lord Peter straightened slowly and looked at her. His face had grown pale above the white cravat and his eyes had darkened to a blue the color of a midnight sky. "You do not?"

"No. But I believe that love is the best position from which to battle the obstacles and ills and misfortunes that assault us. I believe that love gives us an advantage, Peter, in all the battles we face. But at the same time, I believe that without love, everything in the world would eventually despair and wither and die. Most especially people."

"People can despair and wither and die even when they have love. I have been witness to it."

"Oh, their bodies do, of course, but not their souls. Their souls soar up into heaven to meet triumphantly again some day."

"Not every soul. If my mother's soul were ever to meet my father's soul in heaven there would be the most enormous uproar. The sky would likely fall, and yet, they loved each other."

Mary felt her heart sink down, seeking refuge somewhere deep inside her. Both her arms circled around him, holding him tightly. "What is it, Peter?" she whispered. "What is it that you are attempting to tell me?"

"I am afraid, Mary."

"Of what, my dear?"

"I am afraid to love you. I have loved you from that first day when I caught you peering in at me as I worked on the pews in your father's church. And I wanted to marry you soon after, but I could not because I knew Quinn's men to be searching for me and it would have been unconscionable to ask you to flee with me to some foreign shore. And now, when all has been addressed and I am free to do as I please, I still love you and I still wish to marry you, but I am afraid of—of—"

"Of what, Peter?"

"You think me a fool, do you not? But I cannot help myself. The closer I came to Wicken, Mary, and the more I heard Edward speak of his approaching marriage to Eugenia, the more I remembered how terrible it was."

"How terrible what was?"

"Love. Mama's love for Papa and Papa's love for her. The more Edward said about how he had come so close to becoming a Turk like Papa and living out his life grumbling and grouching, and never finding anything satisfactory with anyone, the more I feared that if Eugenia's love made Edward better and Mama's love made Papa worse, then it was all Mama's fault what happened. And I am the one, Mary. I am the one."

"The one?" Mary released him and stood to peer down at him. "The one what, Peter?"

"The one who is like Mama. Well, I must be, Mary, because I am the one Papa dismissed from his life, just as he did Mama. And I am afraid that because I am like Mama, my love will not overcome anything at all. Because I am like her, my love will prove to be the worst terrain upon which to battle against obstacles and ills and misfortunes."

"You believe it was your mama's love for him that made your papa so—so—dreadful? And you think that you—"

"Yes, that's what I am saying, Mary, do not you see? Perhaps if Papa, like Edward, had fallen in love with a woman like Eugenia, he would have changed for the better just as Edward has. Perhaps, had he not been bound to Mama, he would have been a different sort of gentleman entirely."

Mary sat back down and thought the thing through in silence. "You believe," she said at last, "that it was the way your Mama loved your Papa that changed his life and made him into a veritable Devil Incarnate."

Peter nodded slowly. "I do. I have come to believe exactly that. And if it is true, and if I am truly so like Mama that Papa must dismiss me entirely from his mind, then—"

"Then you will turn the person you love into a replica of your father."

"Oh gawd, Mary, I am a madman! A madman and a fool! How can I believe such a thing? How can I even think such a thing? And how can I sit here and say it—say it aloud—to *you*?"

"Because you are good and kind and true, Peter."

"What?"

"Because you do not wish to hurt me, nor yourself. But I think it is especially because you do not wish to hurt me."

"No, you are the one who is good and kind and true. You ought to be picking up one of those branches and cracking me over the head with it right this very minute. Yes, and then riding home to your father and urging him to come out here into the wood and shoot me for a paltry poltroon."

"Never. Papa may shoot you, of course, but it will not be because I urge him to do it. In fact, I expect I will be quite angry with him if he does."

For the first time since she had found him there in the wood, Lord Peter smiled. It was not a wide, happy smile, but it was a smile nonetheless.

"Are you feeling better now, Peter? Can you ride as far as Wicken, do you think?"

"Yes," nodded Peter.

"Good. We shall go to the inn and get you a room. I will not tell Mama and Papa that you have arrived. I will let them think that you have remained at Billowsgate for another day. And the very first thing tomorrow, we will discover just what did make your papa a veritable tyrant. And if it was your mama and the way she loved him, Peter, then we will discover why she could not love him in any but the terrible way that you seem to remember. We will discover if you are as like to her as you imagine and if you are, we will learn if there is some way to guard yourself and me against a similar fate."

"How are we going to do that? Discover those things?"

"Well, that will be a bit of a problem, perhaps, because Edward has gone with Nicky to Wicken Hall, has he not? I assume he has, since you said that he accompanied you most of the way."

"Yes, they have both gone to Wicken Hall."

"Well, there is nothing can be done about that now. We shall just have to hope that all the shouting and bellowing and roaring is over by tomorrow and that he is not in such a very foul mood that there is no speaking to him. Because he is the one who will know all of the answers, Peter. And if only we can reach him—if we can touch his heart, which is not truly black—why, he can tell us all that we need to know."

"Who? Edward? But Edward has no more idea than what—"

"No, not Edward, my dearest, your papa. Your papa is at Wicken Hall. And tomorrow, you and I shall go and tell him all that you told me, and ask him to explain what happened between him and your mama to make them each so very unhappy."

FIFTEEN

Wickenshire and Sera stood in the very center of the summer parlor, listening. They could not help but listen, the Duke of Sotherland bellowed so loudly in the room next door. "Oh Nicholas, do you truly think we ought?" Serendipity asked as, with his arm lovingly around her waist, Wickenshire whispered in her ear again. "He sounds so very angry. I cannot think that it will do any good at all."

"You did say that Delight had chipped a small crack in the old tyrant's armor," he pointed out.

"Yes, I did say that," nodded Sera, "but I am not certain, you know, whether or not Delight will have any effect upon him at all in such a state as he is in."

"Well, it cannot hurt to attempt the thing, Sera. I will ask the rascal, and if she is not afraid to do it, and it does work, think how grateful Bradford will be, not to mention how grateful the rest of us will be. Our ears are burning just as badly as are Bradford's, I think. Delight, come here for a moment, my girl."

Delight jumped up from the sopha beside the dowager and skipped across the carpeting to them. "What, Nicky?"

"You are not afraid of the Duke of Sotherland, are you, Delight?" Wickenshire asked, kneeling down before her.

"Uh-uh. I am not afraid of him at all. He is shouting verimost loud, Nicky. Like an old bear."

"Yes, well, the duke is Lord Bradford's papa, you see, and he is angry with Lord Bradford and so he—"

"But why is he so very angry with Lord Bradford? Was Lord Bradford bad?"

"No, not actually. Delight, I should like to attempt to get the duke to cease bellowing."

"Yes, you can do it, Nicky. You must just go right in there and tell him to stop," Delight declared. "This is your house."

"Yes, well, but I doubt that the duke will pay me the least heed. Likely he will bellow even more loudly if I so much as peer around the door frame."

"He will?"

"Indeed. He is not much happier with me than he is with Lord Bradford at the moment. But I was thinking that you could get him to quieten down, Delight."

"Me?"

"Uh-huh."

"How?"

"Well, you must just—" Wickenshire whispered the rest into his little sister-in-law's ear. "Do you think you can do that?" he asked aloud.

Delight giggled and nodded and hopped on one foot. "Shall I do it right now? Right this very minute, Nicky?"

"By all rights I ought to box your ears! What gives you the audacity to suppose that I will take orders from you? Command me not to come into Kent and disrupt your wedding, will you, boy?"

Lord Bradford sat in the big wingchair, the calmest look upon his face, and watched his father pace the floor.

"Have you nothing to say to me? Nothing at all? You do not think that I am owed some apology?"

"Oh, yes sir," nodded Bradford. "You are perfectly correct. It was most audacious of me to think to command you not to come."

"Yes, well, that is the least of it, and well you know it too. Marry Miss Eugenia Chastain! What sort of a beetle-headed thing is that to do? What has a plain miss to offer a marquis? She compromised you in some way, forced you into it, did she not, boy? Tell me! I will see the woman is set in her place directly. You may trust me to do it."

"Are you mad? Compromised me? Father, I am in love with Eugenia. I *begged* her to marry me!"

"Damnation! I let you out of my sight for more than one week at a time and you turn into a veritable fleabrain! Love. A perfect nobody. I vow, if you do not call off this wedding at once, Edward, I will drag you kicking and shouting back to Northridge and not let you out of the place again until you are fifty and likely to have some common sense!"

"You have threatened me with that already."

"Have I? Have I? Audacious puppy! What if I threaten you with the loss of all you have? Will that make some sort of a dent in your skull? Eh? And do not say that I cannot, because I can. I can refuse ever to lay my eyes on you again. I can refuse to make so much as a shilling available to you from my estates. I can cut you off at the knees, my boy! What will this fortune-hunting miss think of you then, eh? How will your Miss Chastain like to be married to you when you must find a way to support her all on your own? She will not like it one bit, that is how she will like it! Toss you away, she will, and never look back!"

"No, she will not. Eugenia is not a fortune hunter, Father. And I shall inherit when you die, you know, regardless."

"I will refuse to die!"

Bradford parted his lips to suggest that such a threat as his father refusing to die might be put to the proof if the old squire did not cease at once to insult his intended, but not so much as one more word passed his lips because the door across the way opened at just that moment, and Delight, her pale golden curls bouncing against her shoulders, came determinedly into the room. She had a hand pressed over each ear and she stomped up before the duke like a soldier on parade.

Sotherland ceased to pace at once and glared down at her. "Well, what do you want, imp?"

"You is talkin' much too loud," Delight shouted up at him. "My ears are hurtin' and I am way in the other room. An' Stanley Blithe has got his head hid under one of the sopha pillows."

"He has, has he?"

"What?"

"I said, he has, has he?"

"What?"

Sotherland seized hold of the child's wrists and tugged her hands away from her ears. "I said, he has, has he?"

"Who has what?"

"Mr. Blithe," declared the duke, fighting a smile. "He has hidden his head beneath one of the sopha pillows to avoid my bellowing?"

"Oh. Uh-huh. He has. Are you almost done roaring at poor Lord Bradford? Because I have got someone for you to meet."

"I have not so much as gotten a good start roaring at Bradford," declared the duke, placing his hands on his hips and frowning down at Delight. "Now run away like a good girl and play with your doll and leave us alone."

"I don't have a doll."

"Of course you do. All little girls have dolls."

"Not me. I don't like dolls. But I like pirates," Delight offered hopefully. "If you would be done roaring at Lord

Bradford, you an' me an' Lord Nightingale could play pirates."

"Lord Nightingale? The one who was saved?"

"Yes, he is the one I got for you to meet. Yo ho ho!" Delight added in as husky a voice as she could manage, sticking out her chin and swaggering about in a circle before the duke. "Scuttle them blaggards; lift them mensels! That is the kind of things pirates say. Lord Nightingale says them excellent. We can teach you ever'thing you need to know."

Lord Bradford, who was just as angry with his father as his father was with him—and with more reason—observed the duke's reaction to Delight with considerable disbelief. A bit of warmth flickered up into the old man's frigid eyes. The corners of the duke's mouth tilted slowly upward. One of the duke's hands hovered over the golden halo of Delight's hair as if not certain whether to pat her on the head or not.

What the devil has gotten into the Old Squire? Bradford wondered with amazement.

"You will like Lord Nightingale immensely," Delight assured the duke hopefully. "He is the verimost best pirate in all the world. Better even than Nicky. An' he squawks perfect."

The Duke of Sotherland's right eyebrow cocked. Then his left eyebrow cocked. Then both of them began to wiggle. And Bradford abruptly remembered something from very long ago. *Why, he was used to make his eyebrows do that for us,* Bradford thought. *I am certain he did. By gawd, yes! Whenever Peter or I were frightened or crying over something, he was used to tug us up on his lap and make his eyebrows wiggle about just like that until our sobs turned into giggles. How could I have forgotten such a thing about him?*

"Well," grumbled Sotherland, "I expect you will give me

no peace until I go with you to meet this Lord Nightingale, eh?"

"You is absolutely correct," Delight declared.

"Very well, then. I expect I will cease bellowing at this reprobate for a time. But do not you think that this discussion is closed, Edward. I have not finished with you, boy. No, I have not. We shall speak on this matter again." And with a scowl for Bradford, the duke reached down and took Delight's hand into his own and allowed her to lead him from the room.

"Well, I'll be deviled," muttered Bradford, watching them depart. "I expected him to send the child packing without so much as a nod or a 'pardon me.' What the deuce has got into Father?"

Carson closed his eyes and held tightly to the side of the curricle. A southerly wind whipped against his face, and despite the fact that it was rather warm, the very feel of it caused him to shiver. "Can we not go just a wee bit slower, Mr. Spelling?" he asked through lips grown grim with fear.

"Slower? I think not, Carson. I expect we are barely ahead of Upton as it is. Thank gawd I have my own teams posted along the road to Wicken. If we were forced to depend on those to be had at the posting houses, we should not be near this far by now, and Upton would have passed us by."

"But, Mr. Spelling, sir, we are near to flying. Only see how the road flashes by beneath us. One misjudgement and we shall be killed at such a speed as this."

Spelling gave a shake of his head and glanced with some understanding at the little valet beside him. "The lads are not running full-out, Carson. I realize that to someone who has never ridden in a curricle, it seems as though we are going at the most incredible rate, but it ain't so. The lads are merely traveling at a steady gallop. I did give them their heads a while back, but then you made the most horrid gurgling sound in your throat and I thought you about to have an apoplexy, so I reined them in a bit and have kept them to a slower pace."

"A slower pace?" gulped Carson, clutching the seat more tightly. "We are already going at a slower pace?"

"Yes, Carson. And I promise I will not give the lads their heads again. Buck up, Carson. We are very close to our destination now. One more change of horses and we will be within easy driving distance of Wicken Hall. But we shall not drive any slower than this until I have the Hall in sight. I warn you of that. The trunk remains secure, does it not? I have never attempted to tie one to a tiger's perch before."

"I—I do not know, sir."

"Well, take a look, Carson."

The little valet groaned, inhaled deeply and darted a quick glance back over his shoulder. "Yes, sir. It is still there," he managed, hunching his shoulders against the wind.

Carson was well aware that his employer found this driving about at breakneck speed exhilarating, but never before had Carson been forced to participate in such a wild ride. Always he had followed along behind, in the lumbering old traveling coach with the trunks. Traveling was pleasant in the well-sprung, completely enclosed traveling coach. A man did not so much as notice whether the road whizzed by beneath him or not. No, and there was a structure around one to protect one if the coach should wander from the road or overturn. "I th-think I am g-going to be ill, Mr. Spelling," Carson confessed ashamedly. "I think I am. I truly th-think that I am."

Spelling, glancing to the side, noted the white line forming around his valet's lips and an increasingly greenish tinge to Carson's countenance and so drew back slowly on the ribbons until the team came at last to a standstill. "There. Climb down then, Carson. Do you need my help?"

"N-no, sir," managed the valet, stumbling to the ground and taking only three steps before what little of the nuncheon he had been able to get down in the brief stop they had made at one of the coaching inns, came cascading up and splattered around him.

"I am sorry, Carson," called Spelling. "I know I ought to have allowed you to follow me in the traveling coach with the rest of the trunks, but it occurred to me that it might be a deal better to have two of us arrive at Wicken Hall before Upton did and not just one, just in case. I cannot guess what Upton intends, but it will be something vile because he was scathingly angry when I confessed that Wickenshire had likely taken that featherbrained—well, never mind that—Upton was scathingly angry and there is no telling but what he may hire some rather uncouth gentlemen to attempt to—and I do not know who is at Wicken Hall. I doubt any of the wedding guests have arrived there as yet, so it is likely just Nicky, Sera, Delight and Aunt Diana are present—and Jenkins and the footmen, of course. But Jenkins is ancient, and the footmen new to Nicky and perhaps not so loyal as they should be. And so, Carson, well, two more men might come in very handy, you know."

"Y-yes, Mr. Spelling," groaned Carson, taking his handkerchief from his pocket and wiping at his lips and his chin and his brow. It is a curse, he thought, as he made his way back up into the curricle. It is some sort of a family curse. Whenever Mr. Spelling comes into contact with Lord Wickenshire, something particularly horrible happens to someone. Dearest God, do not let it be me. Please, please, do not let the something particularly horrible happen to me.

"But, Peter," Mary began, most taken aback, "I thought that we had agreed that you—"

"No. We did not agree, Mary," Lord Peter replied, stepping down from Leprechaun's back before the Red Rose Inn. "Remain here. I shall go inside and request Neville Dothan to provide me a room for a day or two. He will not like to do it. He thinks me a thief to this day, I expect. Still, I must face him down. I expect I must face the entire village down sooner or later and convince them that I had nothing at all to do with the theft from the rectory. But for now, Dothan is the only one I must deal with. Then, Mary, once I have convinced him to rent me a room, you and I are going directly to your home and I am going to speak plainly with your father."

"There is no need, Peter, to call upon my papa so soon. He does not expect you now until tomorrow."

Lord Peter stepped up beside Mary's Lulubelle and placed his hand on the mare's withers, stroking the old horse gently. "I will procure a room and then I will accompany you home, Mary," he repeated, gazing up at her from beneath thick, dark, lashes.

"But *your* papa, Peter. What about speaking to *your* papa first as we discussed."

Enough of this, Lord Peter thought to himself, gazing up at her spirited little face and noting the distinct uneasiness in her eyes. I have sworn to control my temper, and by gawd, I am going to control my tendency for melodrama as well. "I shall speak with my father just as soon as I have finished speaking with yours, Mary. Why do you look so distressed? Are you frightened that I will say something most unacceptable to your father? I promise you that I will not. What tumbled from my lips beneath The Conqueror's Tree was all nonsense, my gel. The melodramatic blathering of a confused little boy. Well, that child has ruled my life quite long enough. It is time he made way for the grown man. Never fear, Mary. Not only do I love you, but I am in honor *bound* to marry you and I *will* marry you, and whatever fears haunt me will prove to be just that—spectres from my childhood."

Mary gazed down at him pensively, her eyes darkening with thought. Somewhere deep inside, her heart throbbed dully. To be his wife—it was all that she cared to be—but to be his wife because he considered himself duty-bound to take her? Well, there were any number of things she could say to him about that.

"I do not care the least bit about your honor," she murmured. "No more than I care about my reputation."

"I know, Mary," Lord Peter sighed. "It was a stupid thing to say. I am always saying the most stupid things of late. Only believe this. I love you. Even if I had not loved you from the first—which I did. You have given me every reason to love and admire you since. You have stood by me and believed in me—and during the worst times of my life, too. Even when I stole Lord Nightingale, you did not shun me for it. I cannot understand, Mary, how I have come to be deserving such love. I am not worthy of it in any way. But I am not such a dolt as to brush it aside. I vow I am not. Everything will work out for us, m'dear. It will. Catguts!"

"What?" asked Mary, startled.

"Mary, let me lift you down. Hurry," Lord Peter urged, reaching for her, lifting her to the ground and then bending over her and whispering in her ear. "There is a gentleman has just rode up, Mary. He has dismounted and is strolling this way. He cannot be allowed to see me."

Without further thought Mary wrapped her arms around Peter's neck and kissed him mightily. Boot heels rattled against the planking as a gentleman bounded up onto the porch, passing them by with a snort and a chuckle. Still Mary's lips pressed tightly against Peter's and her arms clung to him. Not until she heard the door to the inn open, those particular boots tramp inside, and the door close again, did she release Peter and attempt to catch her breath.

"Ouch," Peter murmured, touching his lips gingerly. "You bit me, I think."

"Who is he? Why must he not see you?" asked Mary, hands on her hips, bending forward at the waist and inhaling deeply.

"Are you all right, Mary?"

"Yes, yes, I am fine. I merely forgot to breathe for a moment or two. A very long moment. Well, I could not breathe, actually. Did I bite you? Let me see. Oh, dear, I did."

"Mary, you must ride home at once," declared Lord Peter, glancing over her shoulder.

"Why? Peter, who was it you saw?"

"It is a gentleman I met in London, Mary. Lord Upton, he is called. And just behind you are four fierce-looking fellows who rode in with him. I cannot imagine how he found us out, but he has, and come here, I think, to settle a score with Wickenshire. He will be asking Dothan for directions to Wicken Hall at this very moment."

"To settle a score? With Nicky?" Mary could not quite comprehend the thought. "Peter, you must be mistaken. Nicky is the most unassuming, quiet sort of gentleman. He never does anything untoward. He never has in all his life. One may rely upon him never to start a bit of trouble. There can be no reason for anyone to have conceived a grievance of any consequence against Nicky. Certainly no reason for a gentleman to come riding into Wicken with a band of fierce-looking—"

"Mary," Lord Peter interrupted, grasping her about the waist and lifting her back into the saddle, "I am not mistaken. I was present when it all began. That particular gentleman took a—jest—very badly, I think. He would not be in Wicken now if he were not determined to repay Wickenshire for it in some way. Do not think to argue with me, Mary. Perhaps all will come to nothing, but I must at the least warn Wickenshire to expect the man and his vile-looking companions. Now go home like a good girl and I will come to you as soon as I can."

With that, Lord Peter went to Leprechaun, mounted and, turning the horse's head back the way they had come, rode off at a gallop in the direction of Wicken Hall.

Mary did not precisely know what she ought to do. She turned Lulubelle about and rode her slowly past the four men of whom Peter had spoken, to have a look at them for herself. They made the most disgusting noises at her as she did so. And one of them made the most outrageous suggestion in a gruff, annoying tone. Mary's face flamed at his voicing of it.

Of all things! she thought angrily. Certainly there is not one of them may lay claim to being a gentleman. Of course, they likely do not think me to be anything but a hoydenish milkmaid, pretending to kiss Peter so very passionately as I did, and right on the main street in front of the inn, too. Oh! she thought then. I hope no one who knows me saw it. If Papa and Mama should hear of it—Oh, my goodness, just see how that Lord Upton person stomps out of the inn. As though he would strangle someone.

And then Mary's eyes widened and her heart began to beat at twice its normal speed, for she watched Lord Upton step up into his saddle and pull a pistol from a pouch that hung from his saddle bow. He appeared to check it for something, then stuffed it back into the pouch and turned himself, his horse and his companions in the direction of Wicken Hall.

"Yo ho ho! Tempest fugit!" cried Lord Nightingale shuffling about the top of his cage and peering at the duke suspiciously. "Avast, maties!"

"Scuttle them blaggards! Lift up them mensels!" cried Delight, hopping up and down joyously with the duke's hand clasped tightly in her own. "Now it is your turn, duke! An' you must try to sound as much like a pirate as you can."

The Duke of Sotherland tilted his head slightly to one side and stared at the parrot. "Batten the hatches. Stand clear, me laddies," he growled.

Lord Nightingale came trundling down to the very edge of the cage top and cocked his head at the gentleman. "Shivermetimbers," he muttered all in one breath.

"I have never heard Lord Nightingale say that precise thing before, Nicholas," Serendipity observed from across the room where they both stood, amazed that Delight should actually prove to have such influence over Sotherland as to lure him away from his haranguing of Bradford to play at being a pirate with a macaw.

"No, neither have I. I wonder who taught him that? Ah, there's Bradford." Wickenshire motioned for the gentleman to join them where they stood. "Bought you a bit of breathing room, Delight has, eh, Bradford? Only listen. Apparently, your father and Lord Nightingale are well matched."

"Father and that old peacock? Never. Lord Nightingale is much too much of a gentleman to be compared with my father."

"Edward!" Serendipity exclaimed softly.

"What?"

"She does not think that you ought to speak of your father in such unglowing terms," provided the dowager from behind her embroidery ring.

"Oh, pardon me, my lady. I did not see you there."

"No, I am hiding."

"Mama," grinned Wickenshire.

"I *am* hiding," replied the dowager. "The very best place to hide is right out in the open where no one expects to see you, because since they do not expect to, they generally do not. Your father, Edward, has not yet noticed me."

"No, he has not noticed any of us, he is so occupied with Delight and Nightingale," agreed Wickenshire.

"He most generally never notices anyone but himself," Bradford murmured. "But he will take note of me from now on—and Eugenia. And he will behave properly toward Eugenia, too. And I will see that Father takes note of Peter, as well. You may believe that. I have had quite enough of his dictatorial ways. Do you know that he did never once write to Peter? Not once in fourteen years! My gawd! Peter is his son as much as I! Well, I am not frightened by that old Turk any longer and I will tell him just what I think of him and all that he has done before one more day is out. I vow it!"

"Avast ye harpies!" Delight shouted then, recalling everyone's attention to the three pirates.

"Awwrk. Avast me hearties!" echoed Nightingale.

The old duke tilted his head to the side and considered Lord Nightingale again, very thoughtfully. Then he took a step closer to the cage, and another, Delight still clinging to his hand. "Yo ho ho," he said in a gruff whisper. "Treasure dead ahead."

Lord Nightingale stood straight up as high as he could

stand. He wiggled his tailfeathers and fluttered his wings. He rocked back and forth without moving his feet.

"Yo ho ho," whispered Sotherland gruffly once again. "Treasure dead ahead."

"Yo ho ho! Knollsmarmer!" exclaimed the macaw, and in a burst of excitement, Lord Nightingale soared from his cage and made three perfect circles around the room. "Knollsmarmer!" he squawked raucously. "YohohoKnollsmarmer! Deadahead! Treasuredeadahead! Knollsmarmer!"

"By Jove, it *is* the same bird!" the Duke of Sotherland exclaimed loudly, capturing everyone's attention. "I thought it looked the same, and by Jove, it is! But it has been—it has been—almost thirty years! I cannot believe it!"

SIXTEEN

Mrs. Emily Butterberry collapsed into the nearest chair with one hand at her bosom and the other flopping uselessly across the chair arm. She made little gasping noises, none of which were at all understandable to Mary or to any of her sisters as they gathered around the woman. It was Clara who at last thought to fetch her mama's bottle of sal volatile and wave it under that lady's nose. "Shhh, Mama," she murmured. "Mary cannot help that she met Lord Peter in the wood. She was there, and he was there. People meet one another quite by accident all the time. You must only think of it as a chance encounter."

"That is exactly what it was," nodded Mary, "a chance encounter. Please, Mama, there is no time to be lost. That Lord Upton person had a pistol. I saw him take it out. Peter spoke of a jest the gentleman had taken badly. He has ridden out to Wicken Hall to warn Nicky that Lord Upton is here and a group of ruffians with him. But I am certain that Peter has not given one thought to the man's having a pistol!"

"Ooooooh!" groaned Mrs. Butterberry loudly. "That it should come to this. In our dear little village. Ruffians and a pistol! Is there no one who does not find it necessary to murder this Winthrop fellow of yours, Mary?"

"No, Mama, you do not understand. Lord Upton does not wish to murder Peter. He has come to confront Nicky!"

Mrs. Butterberry blinked in disbelief. "Lord Wickenshire? A gentleman with a pistol and he seeks our Nicky?"

"Yes, Mama."

"But Constable Leptforth is not to be had, Mary. He and your papa have gone off to Lady Vermont at Wilderly Crossroads. I cannot think how long it will be until they return." Mrs. Butterberry gave herself a shake and straightened in her chair. "You must unsaddle Lulubelle, Mary, and hitch her to the cart and then you and I must drive out to Wicken Hall ourselves. We shall interrupt this confrontation before any such thing as a pistol enters into it."

"Mama, you will both be killed!" exclaimed Clara.

"No, we will not. Ruffians do not take it upon themselves to murder women and children. The more women who are present at Wicken Hall, the more likely it is that whatever the cause, the conclusion to this—this—ruckus—will be reached sensibly."

"Then we should all of us go," declared Clara, glancing at her younger sisters.

"No, you will remain here, Clara, and watch over the other girls. And when Papa and Constable Leptforth return, you must send them after us directly."

Jenkins tramped through the Great Hall in answer to the pounding of the heavy knocker on the door and the insistent twisting of the bell. "Never a footman around when you need one," he sighed to himself. "Such impatience. If Lord Bradford were not upstairs, I would think it were he at the door." Jenkins smiled, remembering his first encounter with the impatient, ill-tempered Lord Bradford. "Now *there* is a gentleman who has altered greatly," he murmured to himself as he tramped across the stone floor. "Our Miss Eugenia did change that gentleman for the better. That she did. And both of them are the happier for it."

As he reached the enormous double doors, Jenkins adjusted his features into a virtual mask of placidity and swung one of them open. It did give him a jolt to see the gentleman who had raised such an impatient ruckus. But then he noticed the long, thin scar on the gentleman's face and knew at once that Lord Bradford had not fallen out the window of the summer parlor and come around to demand reentrance. This must be Lord Bradford's twin, of whom he had heard a word here and a word there.

"I must speak to Lord Wickenshire at once," the gentleman demanded. "He is here, is he not?"

Jenkins looked him up and down calmly. The gentleman's neckcloth was undone, his coat unbuttoned, his gloves nowhere within sight and his hat missing as well. His dark curls had been blown about in the most distressing manner all over his head; his boots were covered with dust and grime; and a leaf and three twigs had caught in the kerseymere of his breeches.

"Whom shall I say is calling?" asked Jenkins, his eyes flickering in silent judgement upon the gentleman's dishevelment.

"You must say that it is Lord Peter and that it is imperative I see Wickenshire at once. No, no, do not say anything. Lead me to him directly, if you will. It is likely a matter of life and death."

"Life and death, sir?" Jenkins stood back from the door and allowed Lord Peter entrance.

"Well, perhaps I exaggerate a bit. I cannot think the fellow would actually kill Wickenshire over it. But it is most serious and your employer must be warned."

"If you will follow me," Jenkins intoned calmly, and proceeded to lead Lord Peter up the main staircase to the east wing. They reached the first landing and turned to the right. Jenkins intended to precede the gentleman all the way to the summer parlor and introduce him properly into the company present there, but another great pounding came upon the door. Jenkins halted in his tracks.

"Do not answer it," Lord Peter said. "If it is the person I believe it to be and he has his men with him, it will be a great deal better not to answer the door at all."

"And if it is not the person you believe it to be?" asked Jenkins. "What then, sir?"

"It is. It must be Upton."

"Lord Upton?" Jenkins' mask of placidity tilted noticeably. What would cause Lord Upton, who had been effectively driven from his lordship's estate at Willowsweep, to come knocking on the door at Wicken Hall? "You did say Lord Upton, did you not?"

"Yes, and it must be him, because he was not far behind me. He had just gone into the inn to get directions."

"Well, but the door must be answered, Lord Upton or not," murmured Jenkins, mostly to himself. "His lordship and the others are in the summer parlor, Lord Peter. That is straight down this corridor, the third door on the left. You will pardon me, but the footmen are otherwise occupied, so I must return to the Hall to answer the door. I must answer it, regardless who stands upon the other side. It is my duty. Oh! Your brother, sir, and your father are in the summer parlor as well, I believe."

Without pausing to hear the further protest against his answering the door, which he could very well see was about to come out of Lord Peter's mouth, Jenkins turned upon his heel and hurried back down the staircase.

Well, this Upton fellow will not likely take out his frustrations on such an elderly old butler, Peter thought. No, he will not. Best if I go ahead and warn Wickenshire so that at least he will be expecting the man and his minions. He strode determinedly forward down the corridor, his spurs jangling as a great lump of anxiety rose in his throat at the thought that he was finally to see his father after fourteen years. But Wickenshire's welfare was a most pressing matter. His worries about a face-to-face meeting with his father must necessarily take second place to it.

Mr. Spelling was aware that he was not one of Jenkins' favorite visitors, but the look on that ancient's face when that worthy opened the door and spied Spelling standing there quite overwhelmed Neil. "Come now, Jenkins. I will allow that I am a few days early, but I was invited."

"Mr. Spelling. I do beg your pardon." Jenkins schooled his features, which he only then realized had slipped into disdain, back into a calm, orderly expression. "I expected you to be Lord Upton, sir. I was misinformed."

"Upton? You are *expecting* Upton, Jenkins?"

"Yes, Mr. Spelling. That is, a particular gentleman who arrived moments ago indicated to me that it might well be Lord Upton at the door."

"Oh? Carson, do not be fiddling with that trunk. You will get it free and it will fall on you and kill you straight off," Spelling called as he glanced over his shoulder. "Come with me and leave off all that fussing. You will send a footman or two for the trunk, eh, Jenkins?"

Mr. Jenkins peered out, noted the trunk tied with rope to the curricle's perch and glanced at Mr. Spelling with something approaching wonder. "However did you—Why would you—I shall," he replied. "If I may take your hat and gloves, Mr. Spelling."

"Indeed, you may. And take Carson's, too, Jenkins, will

you? We are both of us going up to speak with Nicky. He is upstairs, is he not?"

"In the summer parlor," nodded Jenkins, appalled that Mr. Carson, a mere valet, should be taken up into the summer parlor and stand before his lordship as though he were a welcomed guest. But just then Carson stepped over the threshold and the paleness of that poor gentleman's face, the odd cant to his features, and the tremble in his hands convinced Jenkins to think otherwise. Something most unorthodox going forward, Jenkins thought. The poor man is frightened half to death. "I shall take you up, sir," Jenkins said, setting hats and gloves and Spelling's cane aside and preceding the two up the main staircase to the east wing. He managed this time to lead the visitors as far as the first door that opened into the corridor when the front bell began to jangle again.

"Do not open it, Jenkins. It will be Upton," advised Mr. Spelling. "Well, I expect you must open it, but tell him that no one is at home."

"If you will remember, Mr. Spelling, the summer parlor is merely two more doors down upon your left," Jenkins advised, turning about on his heel, bestowing upon Mr. Carson what he hoped to be a supportive look, and starting back down the staircase. "I am coming as fast as I can manage," muttered Jenkins, making his way down the staircase with one hand holding tightly to the rail. "I am a deal older now than I was five minutes ago after all this rushing up and down. The next time I request the footmen to turn the wine bottles and clean the lamps, I shall be certain to recall this day and do the things myself."

"By Jove, Delight, run and look out the window. It is raining people, I dare say," observed Wickenshire. "First

Lord Peter and now Cousin Neil. Come in, Neil. You know everyone, I think, except perhaps his grace. Sotherland, my cousin, Neil Spelling. Neil, the Duke of Sotherland."

The Duke of Sotherland, standing before the parrot's cage and staring in surprise at his youngest son, who stood immobile beside Wickenshire, glared for a moment at Spelling and nodded once, most imperiously.

"Villain!" Nightingale squawked raucously. "Bite! Villain!"

"No, I am not the villain, you pompous old bag of feathers," sighed Spelling. "G'afternoon Winthrop, Aunt Diana, Sera, Bradford—Winthrop? What the devil are you doing here? Well, I expect it is good you are here. Nicky, Upton is on his way to Wicken Hall. Likely downstairs this very moment. Bell rang just as we reached the corridor. Most out of sorts with us, Upton was, over—well, you know. Recognized your voice, Nicky. Said he recognized your voice in the stables."

"So, that's what gave us away. Good memory Upton has, eh? Lord Peter came to warn us as well. Caught sight of Upton in the village. Accompanied by four ruffians, Peter says."

"Oh, Winthrop is Lord Peter now? Devil of a thing when you do not know what to call a man. Upton brought ruffians with him? It is a good thing we came, then. We shall be as much help as we can if it comes to a fight, shall we not, Carson?"

"Carson? Carson, I thought it was you," offered Wickenshire. "Neil, surely you do not expect your valet to—take up arms on my behalf?"

"Indeed I do. Though with so many gentlemen present, I doubt he will be required to do very much for the cause. Of course, the duke likely cannot fight but—"

"What was that? The duke cannot *what?*" roared Sotherland.

"I only mean to say that you are old, your grace."

"Neil," hissed the dowager and Sera simultaneously.

"Well, he is old," declared Bradford from beside the fireplace. "Practically as ancient as your butler."

"No, he ain't," Lord Peter contradicted, still standing beside Wickenshire, still staring at his father. "He does not look nearly as old as I expected him to look, Edward."

"I am in the prime of my life!" bellowed the duke. "If there is fighting to be done, I shall be the first into the fray. You may believe that!"

"Good, because I shall not be in the fray at all," Lord Peter said. "But I did think I ought to warn you, Wickenshire. If I had known that your cousin was coming to warn you—"

"Warn him? Not be in the fray at all?" Sotherland interrupted, astounded. "What is this? Have I sired a coward?"

"No, you have not," Bradford protested. "Let him be, Father. He has vowed not to lift his hand against another man in anger ever again. He told me so."

"To protect a gentleman—a friend and his family—to keep them safe in their own home, has nothing to do with anger," the duke growled. "It has to do with honor. That will be the scurvy villain, eh?" asked Sotherland just as Lord Upton stepped into the summer parlor, gazed about and bowed quite politely to the gathering in general.

"Your butler pointed the way, Wickenshire. He had to run back down and answer the door. Footmen are otherwise occupied, he says," explained Upton quietly. "Interrupted a house party, have I? Beg your pardon for that, but I must have a word with you. Really, I must. It is quite important."

"Certainly, Upton," Wickenshire nodded. "What the devil is all that racket?"

"Stand away!" cried a voice from the corridor. "He has a pistol!" and Mary rushed into the room, Mr. Jenkins at her heels and Mrs. Butterberry not very far behind.

"Mary, do not be so melodramatic," ordered Mrs. Butterberry. "You do not know that the man has brought the thing with him into this house, much less into this room. He has left his ruffians standing about in the Great Hall. Perhaps he has left his pistol there as well. Good afternoon," Mrs. Butterberry added, her voice fading away as she noted the number of people present.

"A pistol? Upton, have you brought a pistol with you?" asked Wickenshire with a frown.

"Delight, run across to the west wing, dearest, and see can you find my sewing box. And take Sweetpea with you," urged Serendipity from the sopha beside the dowager.

"You go as well, Sera, and you, Mama, and Mrs. Butterberry and Mary. Yes, all of you go and have yourselves a bit of tea in the west wing, while we gentlemen discuss this."

"Why send them off?" interrupted Upton. "Do you think I am going to shoot someone, Wickenshire?"

"Yes," replied everyone at one and the same time.

"How very discerning you are," Upton murmured, slipping the pistol from his pocket and pressing the muzzle of it directly against Lord Peter's side. "This is the fellow helped you take the bird from me the evening before last, is it not?" he asked, forcing Lord Peter to accompany him to the far side of the room, away from the lot of them. "You will not like to see your friend's blood spilled all over this very fine carpet, will you, Wickenshire?"

"Upton, do be sensible," Spelling began.

"I am being sensible, Spelling," Upton replied quietly. "I do not threaten the ladies or the child or the ancient butler or your valet. I have no idea who these other gen-

tlemen are and so do not know whether their lives are sig
nificant to Wickenshire or not—though that one is brothe
to this one, I see. And Wickenshire must be free to move
about, because he must capture that damnable bird for me
and truss it up so that it can be carried away on horseback
And that leaves me with you and this fellow here, Spelling
And I know perfectly well that your cousin would not care
in the least were I to spill your blood all over his carpeting."

"You cannot," Mary whispered, taking three steps and
sinking down on a ladder-back chair. "Oh, my dearest God
you cannot! Only think what you are about to do!"

"I am going to faint dead away," groaned Mrs. Butterberry, grasping Spelling's arm with both hands.

"Henry Wiggins," declared Serendipity, gathering De
light onto her lap and glaring at Upton over her shoulder
"you are the most vile and stupid man in the entire world
Did you not cause us trouble enough at Willowsweep? And
what did you gain by it?"

"Nothing," snickered Lord Upton. "I gained nothing a
Willowsweep. But I might have done had I known more
m'dear cousin, about that bird. I might have gained mysel
a fortune."

"Do not threaten my brother's life," Bradford mumbled
taking a step in Upton's direction.

"Halt at once," warned Upton. "Your brother will be
dead before you take one step more, sir. And once this pisto
shot is heard below, my men will come dashing up those
stairs and none of you will be safe, not even the ladies and
the child."

"Let me see if I have heard you aright, Upton," mur
mured Wickenshire. "You are entertaining us with this
splendid drama because you wish to be put in possession
of Lord Nightingale?"

"Indeed."

"And once you have him in your possession, you intend to take yourself off without harming anyone?"

"Just so. I will take this fellow with me, of course, to be certain you do not come dashing after me before my fellows and I have gotten to safety."

"But you will not kill Lord Peter—once you have gotten to safety?"

"No. But I will kill him, Wickenshire, if you do not give me that wretched parrot. I promise you that. I will kill him right here and now and my men will join us and I will have the bird regardless. You will only lose should you attempt to do anything but what I say."

At the other side of the room, beside the bird cage, the Duke of Sotherland's eyes had turned to ice. He mumbled low in his throat. Atop the cage, Lord Nightingale bobbed his head, spread his wings, settled again and seemed to mumble back. But no one noticed except Mary, whose fear-filled eyes widened and whose lips parted on an unspoken question. Sotherland wiggled an eyebrow at her as if in answer and then stuffed both his hands deep into his breeches pockets.

"Well, I expect you shall have Lord Nightingale then," sighed Wickenshire. "But how I am to truss him up, I have not the least idea. I have nothing here to truss him up with, Upton. Not a thing."

"One of the cords that ties those draperies back," Upton suggested.

"Do not you dare!" cried the dowager, turning to glare at Upton. "Of all things! My drapery cord around a parrot! And how is Nicky to do it? Tie the thing about poor Nightingale's wings? I should think not. He will die of fright at such cruel treatment. You do not wish to have a dead parrot, I think."

"No, my dear lady, he wishes to have a live parrot. One

that speaks," growled the Duke of Sotherland. "Delight, my dear, run out to the stables and ask one of the grooms for a sack, eh?"

"Oh, no!" Upton exclaimed. "No one leaves this room until Nightingale, this fellow and I have departed. Take the cord and tie his wings, Wickenshire. That spiteful old bird will not die from it. He is frightened of no one or nothing."

"Very well," Wickenshire muttered, and stepped toward the window. "Give me a moment."

Mary could not believe that Lord Wickenshire had given in so easily. This was not the Nicky she had known from her toddling days. Of course, he had always been sensible, and to do as this Lord Upton said seemed to be the most sensible thing. But it was not at all like Nicky to give up without making some effort.

But he does not wish for Peter to die, she thought. None of us wish for Peter to die. What can any of us do, even Nicky, but what we are told? She glanced again at the Duke of Sotherland who had made not the least move since she had seen him muttering to Nightingale. The old duke glared at Upton and the hatred that froze Sotherland's eyes ought to have burned Upton to the very soul, and would have done, had Upton thought to look in the duke's direction. And then Mary noticed that Lord Bradford's eyes burned with the same intensity as his father's. And when she turned to gaze at Peter, her heart came near to stopping. Never before had she seen such a cold, hard look upon Peter's face or such a deep, burning anger in his eyes, an anger and eyes that matched perfectly his brother's and his father's.

They are all at point nonplus, but they are none of them afraid, she thought. There is no fear in this room but Mama's and mine. Even Sera and Delight and Nicky's mama are not afraid. Well, then I shall not be afraid either. I shall not! There must be something— Her thoughts were interrupted by a gravelly cough from the duke, and her gaze flew back to him at once. His eyes caught hers and he coughed again as Nicky began to undo the drapery cord. And then his eyebrows both wiggled and his gaze went to Peter and back to her. He wishes me to do something, Mary thought. But what? What is it that I can do that he cannot?

And then it occurred to her. There was indeed something she could do that not one of the gentlemen nor any of the other ladies might. Something this cruel lord must accept as most natural and normal and quite believable, but something that might prove to distract Lord Upton enough so that one of the gentlemen could attempt to overcome him.

Mary lifted her chin, straightened in her chair and gave her skirts a bit of a shake. Then she stood and putting one hand to her mouth, sobbed loudly. "Oh, please do not harm my fiancé!" she cried, willing tears to her eyes. "Please do not! Peter! Peter!" and she rushed across the room like a woman madly distracted by fear and threw herself at Peter, causing him to reach out for her. She clung to his neck and kissed him wildly upon the lips, turning him, coming between Peter and Lord Upton's pistol.

"What the devil!" Upton exclaimed, and reached out to tear her from Peter's arms. And then there came the most terrifying screech and a petrifying pulsating sound and Upton shouted even louder—words that Mary could not make out—and Peter forced her to tumble beneath him to the floor. She could not see, but felt Peter kick out as he landed atop her. The pistol exploded, the pulsating grew louder and Upton screamed and screamed.

She heard boots dash from the room and knew that all the men had gone to keep Upton's ruffians from ascending the staircase. Above her, Peter shouted, "Stay down, Mary! Do not move!" And then he rolled off of her, gained his knees and crashed forward, senseless, to the floor. Beyond him, the horrifying screeches and the pounding and Upton's screams continued.

Mary sat up and gasped at the sight of Peter lying senseless on the floor. Blood like claret seeped up into the cloth of his coat. Beyond him Lord Upton rolled upon the carpeting, attempting to avoid Lord Nightingale as the parrot swooped down at him again and again, claws striking at the man, wings pounding about his head. Blood stained Upton's cheeks and chin and hands and the back of his neck, but it was not nearly as much blood as stained Peter's coat. Mary dove for the pistol that lay just beyond Peter's fingertips.

"It is no longer of use, Mary," Sera called over the horrifying screeches, hurrying toward them with a vase in her hands. "It has fired its only shot!"

"It is of use," Mary shouted back, and turning the pistol around, she scrambled across Peter, ducked beneath the frenzy of Lord Nightingale's attack and with a mighty swing, brought the butt of the pistol whacking down across a beleaguered Lord Upton's head. Upton ceased to move. Lord Nightingale swooped down at him thrice more and, meeting no resistance, fluttered down onto Peter's back and picked wearily at that gentleman's curls.

SEVENTEEN

"I would never have left you had I known that the pistol ball had hit Peter," Wickenshire said, his arms possessively around Serendipity and Delight. "We did none of us realize it at the time. All I could think was that Upton's ruffians must be kept from ascending those stairs."

"It matters not, Nicholas," Serendipity replied. "I truly think that Lord Nightingale would not have allowed that dreadful Henry Wiggins up from the floor again; Nightingale was that fierce. I have never seen him so before. So devastatingly savage, like a Scot protecting his homeland! I shall think about our sweet macaw in a very different way from now on, I will tell you that. And I will not worry at all about Delight's safety as long as I know that she has Lord Nightingale with her. Thank goodness that Mrs. Butterberry left word for Constable Leptforth to come. I will breathe a good deal easier to know that he has taken the lot of them away. Lord Peter is not seriously injured, do you think?"

"Sotherland says not, but Neil has gone for Dr. Parks regardless."

"Yes, and rightly so," declared Mary as she paced the room, her hair escaped from its pins and bouncing loosely down her back, her hands clasped behind her, her brow creased with worry. "How can his grace know how serious is Peter's wound? He is a duke, not a surgeon, not even so much as an apothecary."

"Bradford or your mama or mine will be down soon to tell us how he does, Mary," Wickenshire offered softly. "If you cannot trust in Sotherland to know how Peter goes on, most certainly you can trust in your mama. She has nursed six girls through myriad accidents, and not lost a one of you. Can you not just sit down and rest a bit?"

"No, I cannot, Nicky. I wish to be upstairs with him. You know that I do. It is most unfair that I cannot be with him now, when he requires me the most!"

"It is," nodded Serendipity. "But you cannot push your mama any farther, Mary. This one time, you must behave in what she deems to be a proper manner. If Peter is badly injured, she will send for you. She is not so cruel as to keep you from him should the injury prove most serious."

"Oh, why did that evil man come here and start such a ruckus?" Mary sighed, sinking down into the lyre-back chair. "Why must he attempt to steal Lord Nightingale? For what reason?"

"I cannot imagine," drawled Wickenshire, studying the macaw, who was perched contentedly upon the back of a chair nibbling at a cup of fruit and nuts that Jenkins had provided him. "Nor can I imagine what made old spit and feathers attack Upton the way he did. I never thought to see the day such a thing as that would happen. Never."

"The duke sent him to attack," Mary replied.

"Sotherland? How?"

"I do not know exactly. Somehow he *told* Lord Nightingale to do it. Did not you see him speak to the bird, Nicky, and the bird answer him back?"

"I did," announced Delight. "And then our duke wiggled his eyebrows right at you, Mary."

"Yes, he did. Wiggled and wiggled them until at last I

understood what he wished me to do. He wished me to distract Lord Upton. I should not have thought of it on my own—at least not as swiftly as I did when the duke kept signaling to me with those eyebrows of his. Then, of course, I realized that Lord Upton *must* be distracted, or none of you could chance attacking him. And I realized, too, that I was precisely the one who *could* distract him and quite without arousing his suspicions. Though, Lord Nightingale attacked so quickly once I began that I cannot think Lord Upton had time to be suspicious."

"Still," murmured Wickenshire. "How did Sotherland get him to do it? How did Nightingale know who *to* attack?"

"Because the duke told him, Nicholas," Serendipity said. "He whispered a word and Lord Nightingale took to the air, straight at that dreadful Henry Wiggins."

"M-Mary? Wh-what happened?" asked Lord Peter groggily.

"The gel is not here, Peter. I would have let her come. Brave gel! Pluck to the backbone! But her mama—women, you know, and propriety. At any rate, your Mary awaits word of you below. You were shot, my boy, and fainted."

"I what?"

"Fainted, you peabrain," muttered the duke, setting a dish of bloodied water aside. "What made you think that you could take a pistol ball to your shoulder and then just jump up and engage Upton in battle? It was the shock of the jumping up that brought you down, lad. Why did you not shout out that you had been hit? I would not have rushed off had you sung out. I would have stayed to finish Upton off myself."

"I did not know I was shot."

"Did not—of all the beetlebrains!"

"Father!"

"He does not mean it in a derogatory way, Edward," advised the dowager Lady Wickenshire, waving Lord Bradford back down into the chair that had been set for him at the foot of his brother's bed. "It is merely your father's way of expressing himself."

"I am accustomed to the way he speaks, my lady. I have heard it for all of my life."

"Then you ought to realize that peabrain and beetlebrain are terms of affection."

"They are?" Lord Bradford gazed up at the dowager with such a look on his face that she could not help but smile.

"It went straight through, Peter," the duke advised. "Thank gawd for that. I will have the packing now, my lady."

"And the bandages are ready," offered Mrs. Butterberry, carrying a tray covered with strips of linen into the room.

"Is Mary all right?" Peter asked. "She is not injured? She ought not to have put herself in such a position."

"Mary is fine. Everyone is fine except you," the dowager replied encouragingly.

"No, do not say that," declared Bradford, rising again from the chair and going to peer down at his brother. "Peter will think he was the only nodcock to have gotten hurt. I have got a devil of a knock in the jaw, Peter. Wickenshire's eye is rapidly swelling closed, and Father got knocked flat on his—"

"I did not!" protested the duke loudly. "I stumbled."

"If Wickenshire's dog had not come and grabbed that villain's leg, you would have been kicked in the ribs for that bit of a stumble, Father. And likely trampled to death, from the look in that ruffian's eye."

"Bah! The look in his eye! I am the one whose look can

stop a clock, and well you know it, Edward. And Mr. Blithe was merely repaying a debt of honor," the duke replied.

"You both sound very odd," observed Peter. "Is it because I have been shot? You do not need to be other than yourselves, you know, simply because I have been shot. I am not dying or anything."

"Well, of course you are not dying!" exclaimed the duke. "Great heavens! I should hate to be forced to face that gel of yours should I somehow allow you to die!"

"It is good of you, Father, to help see to my wound."

"Damnation, you are my son! Why would I not?"

"B-because you despise me and cannot bear to be near me."

"What?" gasped the dowager and Mrs. Butterberry in unison.

"Edward, help your brother to sit up a bit so that I can get this bandage wrapped properly," directed the duke gruffly. "Ladies, go away. We can get along without you now."

The dowager and Mrs. Butterberry looked at each other and nodded. "We shall be in the summer parlor when you have finished," the dowager said. "Do come down and have some tea, your grace, as soon as you have said what must be said."

"Said what must be said? What did she mean by that?" Bradford asked, sitting down on the bed beside Peter and helping him to sit up a bit more.

"Women. Think they know everything," muttered the duke, wrapping the linen strips tightly around his son's wound. "Think they know what a man intends before he even thinks to intend it. I do not despise you, Peter. And never was there a time that I did not wish to be near you. I cannot imagine what put such an idea into your head."

"You do not despise me?"

"No, he despises *me,*" offered Bradford.

"I do not despise either one of you! You are my sons. A man does not despise his own boys! I should like to beat Edward about the head with a stout stick, of course, but that is because he is thoroughly audacious and intends to marry a perfect Miss Nobody, not because I despise him."

"Eugenia is not a nobody! She is—"

"Yes, yes, she is the woman you love. And Miss Butterberry—a mere parson's daughter—is the woman you love, Peter. I am not mistaken in that? I thought it to be so the moment she came rushing in. Brave as she can stare, that one. And bright! Caught on at once as to what she must do to distract Upton. Of course I knew that she would. Nothing slow about that young woman."

"Yes sir."

"Indeed. Do I find that Edward's gel possesses half as much pluck and intelligence as your Miss Butterberry, I may be brought to think well of her, too."

"You may?" asked Bradford.

"I love Mary," mumbled Peter. "I love her with all my heart, Father."

"Of course you do."

"But what if I am as bad at love as Mama was and I cause Mary nothing but the same agony that Mama caused you?"

"Mama? Mama caused Papa agony?" Bradford stared at his brother in disbelief.

"Yes. It was Mama turned Papa's life upside down and her own as well. I have figured out that much. What happened, Papa?" Peter asked. "Between you and Mama? Why did she love you and you love her but all become anger and agony between you? I have always thought that you sent me away because I am the one most like her, because you could not bear to have me near you any more than you could bear to have her near you."

"What happened between your Mama and I—"

"I know it is not my business, Papa, but I love Mary so very much. I do not wish to make her life a Hades! I cannot marry her if I am so much like Mama that my love will destroy her! There must be an answer, something that I can change about myself. What was it happened between you and Mama? *Why* did you send us away?"

"I did not send your Mama or you away."

"You did not?" asked Peter and Bradford in unison.

"Damnation! Your mother insisted that she would go. Demanded to be free of the sight of me! I was so exhausted—I did not oppose her. And then—then—I could not bring myself to keep both of her sons from her when she did leave. Now, I think I ought to have done so. But I thought at the time that to have you with her, Peter, would make her more easy in her mind. You are not like her, my boy. Not at all. I wished to keep you near me with all my heart, but I could not be as cruel as that to my wife. I knew Tobias Quinn would look after you, Peter. And he did, did he not? Looked after you and your mother both. It was not Tobias' fault that your mama died, Peter," the duke added quietly. "It may have seemed so to you, but it was not."

"How do you know?" growled Bradford. "You did not care enough about Mama's death to even inform me of it. No, I had to discover it four years after it happened!"

"You never asked about her, Edward," sighed the duke.

"Why would I ask about her? Each time I did as a lad, you bellowed. Once you said if I mentioned her again you would have me roasted on the spit like a slab of venison. Of course I did not ask you about her!"

"I did the best I could," mumbled the duke, tying a final knot in Peter's bandage. "I could not bear to hear your mother's name, Edward. I attempted to write to you, Peter. To let you know that I—that I—but your Uncle Tobias sent me word that your mama burned the letters before you ever saw them."

"This Tobias Quinn is our uncle?" Edward asked, wide-eyed.

"Your mother's stepbrother, yes, and the only person to whom she would listen in her madness. Do not be afraid to love your Mary, Peter. Love her with all your heart as I am coming to believe Edward loves his Eugenia. What happened between your mother and I had naught to do with love. Passion brought us together. Madness drove us apart. Only your mother ever referred to any of it as love. Tobias warned me all those years ago that she was mad, but I would not listen, and I cannot count the lives my refusal to listen has ruined."

"It was you buried her then," Peter murmured wearily. "I wondered who paid such a price to have her buried like a queen."

Sotherland nodded. "She would not have me love her. She would not have me comfort her. She would not have me come near her but one time after you boys were conceived. All I could give your mother was a funeral. That one thing I could do without increasing her agony."

"You ought not be up and about yet, Peter," Mary protested, but only softly, clinging to his arm as he led her along the cobbled path through the rose garden at Wicken Hall. "It is merely three days since you were injured."

"Yes, and three days since I have been allowed to see you for more than a moment at a time. Too long. I cannot imagine how I ever thought to sail to India without you. I cannot imagine how I kept myself from you for two long years. What a dolt and a coward I was! It amazes me that you even care to hear my name."

"Oh, I care to hear your name, and I care to hold your hand, and to have you by my side now and forever. I love you, Peter Winthrop Finlay and you know that very well!"

"Yes, I do," he laughed, bringing them to a halt beneath the window of the summer parlor. He took both her hands into his own and gazed seriously down at her. "There are people gathering here, Mary, even as we speak, to celebrate my brother's wedding. Edward has found a young woman who loves him despite all his vagaries and all his faults. Even my father has been brought to concede that such love as Eugenia bears Edward is worth more than title or fortune."

"It is," Mary agreed, smiling up at him. "True love, Peter, love that trusts and accepts and abides, is worth more than all the titles and fortunes in the world."

"I know. And I know that your love is just such a love, though I cannot think why I deserve to have it."

"Sometimes I cannot think why you deserve to have it, either," Mary grinned, squeezing his hands gently. "Sometimes you are so very aggravating, and odd. Though, you cannot help being a bit odd, I think. Apparently, your entire family is odd. Are you going to ask me to marry you at last, Peter, or must I do the asking? For I shall have you to be my husband one way or the other."

"I will do the asking. I am not so odd as to leave that to you. I love you, m'dear, with all my heart and soul. I have always done, though I have not always known it. But I know it now. Will you marry me and share in my life forever?"

"Yes!" cried Mary happily. "Yes, yes, yes!"

* * *

"Finally they're kissing each other. Now?" asked Bradford, gazing down into the rose garden from the window of the summer parlor, his arm securely around Eugenia, and a roomful of family and guests crowding in behind them.

"Definitely now," laughed Wickenshire.

Bradford opened the window; Wickenshire set Lord Nightingale upon the sill.

"Heytheremister, I saw Hiram kissyersister," sang Nightingale gleefully. "Down in the shade oftheoold oooak tree."

"No, not that one, you old pirate," hissed Bradford. "Gentle thoughts and—"

"Gentlethoughts and tenderheart. Caaaaring. Kind andtruuue," crooned Nightingale, bobbing his head gleefully. "Thesebelove. Aye, these be love. I vowbyall thestarsabove. I did not know what truuue looove was. Until my hearrrtfound you. Yohoho Knollsmarmer!"

Peter and Mary separated and gazed upward, laughing.

"Will she have you then?" called Bradford down.

"And all my odd relatives with me," Peter called back, taking Mary into his arms and swinging her around. A cheer went up from all gathered at the window, including the Reverend Mr. Butterberry, Mrs. Butterberry and the Duke of Sotherland.

"Now," said Wickenshire, once Peter and Mary were back among them and all had settled down to a very fine tea, "you promised to tell us, your grace, about Lord Nightingale."

"Yo ho ho!" Nightingale cried at his name. "Knollsmarmer!"

"Well, he once belonged to a friend of mine. Mr. Michael Quinn, Tobias Quinn's brother. I do not know how you came by him or how this Upton fellow discovered Nightingale's secret, but I am beyond grateful that the old pirate has survived to this day and that the treasure has not been lost forever."

"Pirate treasure," murmured Delight, climbing up on the duke's lap and waiting for a story.

"Just so, m'dear. Let me see if Nightingale will sing his ditty. He is the only one alive now who knows the whole of it. Nightingale, come."

The macaw looked up from the top of his cage, bobbed his head and flew directly to the back of the duke's chair.

"He did that for me. I thought it a mischance," said Wickenshire, amazed.

"No, no, he understands come," the duke replied. "And he understands other things like 'villain' and 'strike,' though you must point out to him which is the villain before you tell him to strike. With Upton, all I needed to do was tell him 'hat,' because Upton was the only gentleman in the place still wearing one. The old bird knows what a hat is. Come now, Nightingale," he added, peering over his shoulder at the bird. "Sing your ditty for us. Knolls farmer did come upon them there."

"Knollsmarmer dit comepon them there," echoed Lord Nightingale, sidling back and forth across the chair back, his red head bobbing gleefully. "Wherewillows weep an witchescryaye. Anwatchedthemin the deadof niiight. Set featherserpen safely byaye. Knollsmarmer. Knollsmarmer. Yohoho! Knollsmarmer. 'Tisinthestones whatdostay dryaye. Knollsmarmer. Besidethestream thatrises highaye. Knollsmarmer. Yohoho! Knollsmarmer!"

"Excellent! You shall get a treat for that, my boy!" exclaimed the duke. "Wickenshire, have you a pine nut about?"

"I will give it to him," offered Delight, climbing from

Sotherland's lap to take the nut Wickenshire offered and then rushing back to offer it up to Lord Nightingale.

"Knolls farmer? Where willows weep and witches cry? Featherserpen?" Wickenshire gazed at Neil.

"Willowsweep," they said in unison.

"My farm at Willowsweep spreads over nine knolls," Wickenshire explained. "And Elaina Maria Chastain, for whom the house was built, was called the Witch of Willowsweep. And there is an old stone barn by a stream that floods every spring."

"It will be in the barn, Nicky," offered Neil. "In the loft. That's the only place high enough not to be flooded. But what the devil is a featherserpen?"

"A statue of an Aztec god called Quetzalcoatl. The Feathered Serpent," Sotherland explained. "Quinn was a sailor. Sailed with Cook on the *Endeavor* and again on the *Resolution*. Found that statue somewhere in the Caribbean, smuggled it home and stowed it away, then taught this pirate here to sing that ditty."

"Michael Quinn!" cried the dowager abruptly. "So that's where Albert got the parrot—from Michael Quinn!"

"Albert?" asked the duke.

"Yes, yes, my brother. Albert Spelling."

"By Jove, my lady, Albert Spelling was your brother?"

"And my father," offered Neil from where he stood, leaning against the mantelpiece.

"Albert did never say what happened to Mr. Quinn," the dowager continued. "They were fast friends one day and the next he never mentioned the man again."

"Michael was killed in a brawl on the docks," Sotherland replied. "Albert and I came near to dying beside him that night. So, Albert rescued the parrot! And he never mentioned a word to you about the treasure?"

"No. Though he said something about it to my brother

Ezra, because Ezra said once that there was something important about the word Knollsmarmer, but he did not remember what it was."

"We shall meet Michael Quinn's brother soon, eh, Peter?" Wickenshire asked. "And we will tell him his brother has left him a legacy. You do plan to invite Tobias Quinn to your wedding?"

Peter looked at Mary beside him and then nodded. "He will like to come and see me married, I think. And I will like to see him, now that I know I didn't kill him. Just think what he will say, Father, when he learns of all this."

"He will say that you ought to fetch the golden serpent as soon as you can, m'lad, because it will be yer wedding present from yer mama," declared a voice from the doorway.

Peter jumped up from his chair and spun around so fast that it made Mary giggle.

"Quinn! Mary, it is Quinn!"

"Yes, I know," smiled Mary. "We have all of us been keeping his arrival a secret for two whole days."

"Quinn!" Peter opened his arms and a veritable giant of a gentleman walked straight into them.

"You dunderhead," Quinn muttered. "I thought never to see ye again, lad. I thought my heart would break o'er it. An' then if Miss Butterberry's papa does not send word back with m'lads that ye will be in Wicken and marrying his daughter within a fortnight. How do ye do again, m'dear," Quinn added, stepping back and bowing before Mary. "I thank ye for taking this lad inta yer keeping. That I do."

"I am pleased to do it, Mr. Quinn. But Papa was mistaken. We cannot be married within a fortnight. The banns must be—"

"I have got a special license, Mary," Peter interrupted

shyly. "Your papa told me to fetch it in London. After all
that happened—but it does not matter. We need not make
use of it. You will wish to do all the things that young ladies
do for a wedding and—"

"Balderdash," Mary grinned. "There is nothing I wish
to do except marry you, Peter Winthrop Finlay. The sooner
the better."

"The house is already filling with wedding guests,
brother," Bradford said, his arms going snugly about
Eugenia. "I do not think they will balk at two marriages
for the price of one."

"No, and we would be honored to share the day with
you and Peter, Mary, if you would like it to be so," added
Eugenia.

"I should like it of all things," smiled Mary.

"Yo ho ho!" cried Lord Nightingale. "Knollsmarmer!"

"Knollsmarmer, indeed," muttered Sotherland. "You
have triumphed over a villain and saved Peter's life, and
now you and Quinn give him an ancient statue of gold for
his wedding present. The boy has not the right to be fratched
ever again, eh?"

"It is just like a faerie tale," Delight observed, "and Lord
Nightingale is the good faerie."

"Damnation," murmured Bradford, gazing toward the
doorway.

"What?" asked Eugenia. "Edward, you are scowling and
you ought not be. Oh, my goodness!"

Mr. Spelling's gaze traveled to the doorway as well, and
he straightened up and stood away from the mantelpiece
directly as every other gentleman in the room stood or
straightened depending upon their positions, except the
Duke of Sotherland, who with Delight firmly planted on
his lap, merely glanced over his shoulder, past Lord Nightingale's red and green feathers, expecting the arrival of an-

other wedding guest with whom he was unacquainted. And then that gentleman gasped aloud and his arms tightened around Delight.

"Lady Vermont and Miss Daily," announced Jenkins quietly, only the trembling of his hands and the commiseration in his eyes betraying that he was privy to the agony he had just introduced into the room.

"Alice?" gasped the Duke of Sotherland, setting Delight gently on the floor and rising to his feet, the most confused, yet longing look in his eyes. "Alice?"

Lady Vermont stood, flabbergasted, upon the threshold, glaring at the duke. Her granddaughter stood beside her, silent and elegant in a burgundy carriage dress. The young lady smiled at Bradford and Eugenia, and only then did her cool, blue gaze fall upon the gentleman setting Delight aside and rising from his chair, and her lovely lips rounded into a tiny *O*.

"Who is Alice?" Peter asked in a whisper, staring from his father to the ladies on the threshold. And then his own eyes widened and he drew Mary into his arms. He could not take his eyes from Miss Daily. "Who is she?" he asked again, a bit louder, not giving one thought to the impropriety of it.

"Alice is your long-lost cousin, Peter," Mary replied when no one else seemed eager to answer him.

"No, she is not!" declared Sotherland. "Who put such a Canterbury Tale as that about?"

"Alice and I did, Father," Bradford replied. "To protect her from—from the position in which you placed her! I intended this very afternoon to speak with you and Peter about it. To bring all out into the open. Welcome, Lady Vermont. Welcome, Alice. We did not expect you until tomorrow."

"The position in which *I* placed her?" cried the duke. "The position in which *I* placed her?"

Bradford and Peter both stared at their father as he took a step toward the two women at the threshold—a faltering step—like a man suddenly assaulted by the most unbearable pain.

"Who the devil is she?" mumbled Peter again.

"Alice is your sister, Peter!" bellowed the duke. "She is the daughter I have longed for eighteen years to hold in my arms. *My* daughter over whom that Vermont woman and I battled and battled until at last I was forced to see that I must surrender her for her grandmother's sanity just as I was forced to surrender you for your Mama's welfare!"

"I have a sister?" gasped Lord Peter, turning back to stare at Miss Daily. "*We* have a sister, Edward?"

"Oh my!" murmured Mrs. Butterberry, in a voice that sent her husband to digging through that lady's reticule for her smelling salts. "Oh, Henry! Oh my!"

"Yo ho ho!" squawked Lord Nightingale raucously and flew to the Duke of Sotherland's shoulder. "Yo ho ho! Knollsmarmer!"

BOOK YOUR PLACE ON OUR WEBSITE AND MAKE THE READING CONNECTION!

We've created a customized website just for our very special readers, where you can get the inside scoop on everything that's going on with Zebra, Pinnacle and Kensington books.

When you come online, you'll have the exciting opportunity to:

- View covers of upcoming books
- Read sample chapters
- Learn about our future publishing schedule (listed by publication month *and author*)
- Find out when your favorite authors will be visiting a city near you
- Search for and order backlist books from our online catalog
- Check out author bios and background information
- Send e-mail to your favorite authors
- Meet the Kensington staff online
- Join us in weekly chats with authors, readers and other guests
- Get writing guidelines
- AND MUCH MORE!

**Visit our website at
http://www.zebrabooks.com**

Dear Reader,

Well, there you have it—you now know what Knollsmarmer was all about. But is the treasure still at Willowsweep and will Peter find it? Has the Duke of Sotherland's heart truly softened? And what about Alice Daily—is she really the duke's long-lost daughter? Then there's Cousin Neil. Is he truly on the way to reform? The answers to these and many other questions are revealed to you in *Lord Nightingale's Christmas,* on sale just about now. (If, of course, you haven't finished this until the end of the month.) Please join Lord Nightingale and his extended family for a joyous, if somewhat chaotic, celebration of the Christmas season. He's already planning the most wonderful surprise.

My readers are important to me. I'm always interested in hearing what you think about my books. I try very hard to keep up with the mail and answer your letters promptly. You may e-mail me at regency@localaccess.net or write to me at 578 Camp Ney-A-Ti Road, Guntersville, Alabama 35976-8301.

Judith